THE LOST
FLYING BOAT

By the same author

Alan Sillitoe

THE LOST FLYING BOAT

LITTLE, BROWN AND COMPANY
BOSTON   TORONTO

LIBRARY OF CONGRESS CATALOG CARD NO. 84-80841

FIRST AMERICAN EDITION

BP

PRINTED IN THE UNITED STATES OF AMERICA

*This story is dedicated to David,
having been promised a long time ago*

PART I

1

❦

A listener from birth should not be surprised if his first occupation turns out to be that of wireless operator. So with me. I listened through earphones to messages which came invisibly from the sky, and was able to write, though not always understand, any language which used morse symbols.

I listened with the greatest intensity of which two ears are capable. Such willingness opened a way to the inner voice, and twenty-five years later all details of what happened to the flying boat *Aldebaran* and its crew of eight became clear, so it is perhaps as well that I waited before writing my account. By paying attention to the faithful voice I leave out nothing which insists on being told.

2

❦

The trio of Partagas cigars carried in the breast pocket of Captain Bennett's tunic were apt to crumble, so he coated each with cigarette paper as skilfully as if binding the broken limb of a pet monkey. He then puffed his whitened cigar into a simulation of alto-cumulus cloud above the blank spaces of the plotting chart, and gazed through the nebulosity in a way that showed he had his worries.

I had no qualms working for a man so preoccupied. It left me a great deal to myself while waiting for the rest of the crew to gather at the Driftwood Hotel, and that was what I liked. Going once a day to report my presence, I would find Bennett pencilling calculations concerning the range of the flying boat, the petrol its four engines would consume, and the distance to the Kerguelen Islands. At such times he would confide in me because he had no one else to talk to; though I think he wanted to listen to himself a shade more than he needed to hear what I had to say.

As he opened parallel rulers to draw the required track-line on the Admiralty Chart he expatiated on how essential maps and charts were for getting from place to place and for navigating over the water. 'We must always be aware in which direction we are going. I once knew someone who set out across the world with no more than a few sheets torn from an atlas.'

He looked at me with an enquiring smile, as if to get some reaction as to whether or not I fully understood. I gave no sign one way or the other. He walked to the large window, looked out for a while, and puffed as if to give the inhabitants of this obscure South African port the benefit of his cigar smoke as well. He turned and went on: 'Must have been an insensitive bod, to commit such desecration. I suppose he felt the need to bring a pretty diagram of his travels home for his children! They make people like that, these days.'

There was a bottle of whisky on the table, and he poured half a glass. 'Booze confuses, but in my case it reduces the speed of thought. I can then grasp what's in my mind. Otherwise my eyes slide across that vital small print of thought, and refuse to latch on.'

In the sitting room of his suite there were, besides the large rectangular table with a chair on each side, a sofa, a bureau, a separate wardrobe, and two huge armchairs. My cabin-like habitation on the floor above had a coathanger on the back of the door, a sink barely deep enough to get my hands in, and a cot. But it was all I needed.

'Maps and charts fix our position, and inform us where

10

we can and can't go, Mr Adcock. We little men on earth are constrained by space and topography, God dammit! All we can do is sign on the dotted line, and stand by whatever it is we've half-wittingly agreed to.'

Why he said this I don't know. I had never thought of doing other than carrying out what I was being paid for. The chart of the South Indian Ocean was scored with wriggling fathom-lines and cut by veins of isogonals. Between South Africa, where we were, and the Kerguelen Islands, where we hoped to go, were undersea canyons thousands of fathoms deep; and, mulling on such figures and profundities, I felt myself floating half-drowned through the blackest of killer-whale hideouts.

He showed me a smaller chart on which I was to inscribe the callsigns of radio stations. Wireless bearings obtained along our route would be useful to the navigator, he told me, especially if cloud reached so high that sights on heavenly bodies became impossible. 'When we cannot see, we often hear.'

'So I understand.'

He folded the callsign chart and gave it to me. 'That's why we're taking you – to be our listener. And wireless navigator, if necessary. It'll be a hard job finding what we want. In fact some might call it an expedition no sane person would approve of.'

I found his sense of humour reassuring, and said that, no matter what anyone thought, I was glad to be going. Much more was in my mind, but I felt this to be neither the time nor the place to say it.

'Don't think for a moment that there's anything shady in our venture,' he added. 'There isn't, believe you me, though while you're here, Mr Adcock, I might tell you that this little job is more than a godsend to me.'

We had not reached that level of familiarity when he might have called me 'Sparks', the generic name for all wireless operators, but on my asking why he considered the job to be such a godsend, he resumed: 'Because the time will never come again when it will be possible to do what we're going to do. You may not have noticed, but let me tell you that the shutters are coming down on any individual with enterprising spirit. We fought the war in the cause of freedom, but as soon as it was over there was no freedom to inherit. Freedom was dying while we fought. The war turned us into slaves, by making the bureaucrat supreme. The only so-called virtues left are idleness and cheating. Show initiative, and you're under suspicion. A spiderweb of red tape is woven around inventiveness. Fall into line, you get your reward – but not unless. A nation wins a war over the Nazis, but what does it signify if your own guts get kicked out in the process? All self-respect gone. Strangled by rules and regulations designed to keep bureaucrats at their posts and people in their place. I'll have none of it, Adcock, not while I have this scheme up my sleeve.'

Because he spoke calmly, his ideas seemed reasonable. I knew they were not, and in my unease hoped for an end so that I could go. He walked again to the window, closed it, and came back. 'The twentieth century has been poisoned by two bestial systems that have tainted everyone whether they embraced them or fought against them. For myself, I want to push this expedition through so that I can be independent of all systems. To become rich is the only defence against being without hope.'

Glancing over his shoulder at the blameless ocean of the chart, I did not know as much then as I do now. After a final puff he laid the whitened, still smouldering stub in the ashtray and began binding another, which I took as a sign that the conference was over. The last thing that occurred to me before going out was that the word PARTAGAS on the cigar box read SAGA TRAP backwards. I was going to mention this, but thought better of it.

3

〜〜

On my way downstairs I passed Shottermill, a big coarse-featured man of about sixty, with thin white hair so wispy he was almost bald. On the middle finger of a huge hand which gripped the banister was a ring crested with the coat of arms of some regiment or ship. When his pale blue eyes saw my glance he withdrew the hand and continued upstairs as if he didn't care to be seen by a younger man as needing the assistance of the banister. His stolid alertness was as if maintained by arrogance, and primed by scorn at any of the world's weaknesses which threatened to infect him. In the Air Force his sort had been the mainstay of the lower ranks, a warrant officer without humour and always aloof.

At first I thought he was just another layabout at the Driftwood Hotel, perhaps an escapee from Attlee's socialism who no longer cared to live with rationing and government controls, and to whom settling at a job in a cold climate seemed a lack of birthright after the war years, when any thought of tomorrow had been obliterated by the possibility that it might never come.

However I might dislike the expressions gathered into the orbit of his face, they were nevertheless of value to him and, his scowl implied, no bloody business of yours. What he had done before the war was impossible to say, but he was now a chandler contracted to provide stores for the flying boat. I suspect he also did smuggling and currency exchange, using his tourist agency as a cover. I sensed something of failure about him, but it was well held in, and perhaps came to me because there was sufficient failure in me at that time to make the connection. I had seen him only for a few seconds, but was young enough at twenty-six to indulge in snap judgements, and sufficiently dense to believe that each one must apply to other people. Now at the age of fifty I risk nothing and learn nothing. Youth only learns because only youth has to.

I was on my way out for a ten-minute walk before going to bed. Since arriving in Ansynk I'd had difficulty getting to sleep, and hoped the exercise and midnight air might lull me into oblivion. But coming back I succumbed to the idea of a last smoke in my room, and on the hotel stairs felt in my jacket for my cigarette case and lighter. On not finding them I thought that an efficient rob-job had been done. My pocket had been picked. But I had passed no one during the walk except a policeman, and he had been on the other side of the street.

I would always distrust others rather than blame myself, which was unreasonable, because though I had lost things I had never been robbed. I was wary of everyone, however, in a minor way, which perhaps explained my painstaking attitude to work, as in those long night watches in the Air Force when no planes risked getting themselves knocked about in monsoon clouds. I would contact other ground stations to test my signals, and sense their anger at being drawn out of slumber for a triviality. But if a kite had been in need of directional assistance, or had been forced to ditch, and air–sea rescue wanted its position, then my attention would have saved lives. Flying Control said no aircraft were about, but a civvy plane might have failed to notify them, which sometimes happened, so I would comb a few kilocycles either side of the frequency, with earphones dutifully clamped.

I remembered leaving the cigarette case and lighter in Bennett's room and, thought and action being for once the same thing, went to the door and knocked. Shottermill opened it. 'Who the hell's that?' the Skipper shouted.

'The wireless operator. I left my cigarettes and lighter.'

Shottermill looked as if he wanted to knock me down. His eyes showed that he was terrifically angry about something, but he was also the sort of man who, once he hesitated, was lost. I pushed by when Bennett called that I should come in and find the bloody things.

During the day his hotel suite was noisy because main-street traffic rattled under the windows. But much of the time he was out making arrangements for the trip – though I imagined something more important than such affairs had brought Shottermill to see him now.

Shottermill grinned as I looked around the room. 'Perhaps it's under the table.' He was trying to rile Bennett more than me, though I couldn't fathom the reason. 'I don't see why you want a wireless operator.'

The chart on the table curled at one corner, and I saw my belongings half obscured, though did not go to them. Bennett gripped the bridge of his nose as if trying to think his way out of a puzzle. Pressing at that spot brought back the pain of the bone being broken at boxing, which minimized his irritation. 'The supply ship will have a wireless operator, and I'll have one as well. I'm not crossing so much water without all the aids I can lay my hands on. There's no air–sea rescue if we get into trouble.'

'I just wondered what use he'd be.' Shottermill occupied an armchair, and pulled the whisky towards him but didn't pour. I amused myself by thinking that if I weren't too tired I would go outside and let down the tyres of his car. Bennett controlled his irritation: 'When I think of what you'll get out of the deal, he's cheap at the price. We all are, in fact.'

I was glad to hear it, and wondered how high Shottermill was in the scheme of the expedition, rightly supposing it was he who had sold Bennett the box of ancient and worm-eaten cigars.

'Fair enough, Captain,' he said. 'I only wanted to know.'

'We're here to talk about supplies.' Bennett nodded towards my lighter and told me to get it. 'All other arrangements were settled in London.'

Judging by Shottermill's frown and broad uplifted hand I was to hear nothing of any importance, though my suspi-

15

cions began from that moment, the worst being that Bennett did not have any. Whoever supposed that a wireless operator on such a trip was superfluous could not in his heart wish the expedition success. There were certain things he did not want me to hear, or messages to send, or vital contacts to make. Because as yet I knew almost nothing, these reflections fell into a vacuum, but I was to remember them.

I scooped up my stuff and went, hearing them arguing even from as far away as the stairs which led to the third floor – at which I gathered that someone had helped himself to Bennett's whisky without permission.

4

Of all the things dead and living, only God has no name, but the newly discovered is immediately delineated on becoming known. A name, a number, or a callsign identifies. A boat, plane or even a motor car is given a name because until then it doesn't properly belong. When possession is nine tenths of the law, a name puts a stamp of ownership on it. Possessions come by easily are named so that they are not blithely lost.

Everything has a name. From the door of my radio hut in Malaya I watched a C-47 Dakota come in to land. I had given bearings on the long haul from Burma, so took an interest in its safe arrival. Through Barr and Stroud binoculars I saw, as it turned into the dispersal point by the ramshackle control tower, stencilled letters on its fuselage which said *Sheffield Star.*

The aircraft had a name, and also a call sign, the letters

16

of which rarely made word-sense – though there were exceptions. To while away the time at the Driftwood Hotel I thumbed through the book of radio navigation aids and picked out three- and four-letter callsigns which made a word in themselves, hoping that a wireless operator sending morse from the coast station at Nordeich DAN did not sit in a lion's den. Neither could it be supposed that the operator at Cape Lookout NAN was a woman, or that some stray Scotsman was employed at Nagoya JOCK, or that the radio officer on the Estonian icebreaker ESAU despised his birthright. At Skagerrak SAM was not necessarily established as a prophet, though still sending morse when Oulu signed OFF. Maybe signals transmitted VIA Adelaide were relayed with VIM by Melbourne and picked up by a VIP at Perth. In France one could have FUN at Lorient, but find it cold enough to wear FUR at Rochefort, though it might be better to go to Madagascar and keep FIT at Tulear.

Perhaps a long association with the letters and rhythms of morse created a tandem proclivity to verbal dexterity. Perhaps not. But I remembered that anyone sending morse on our Malayan network whom we could not identify was called OOJERKERPIV, a nonsense word signifying (to us) 'unknown'. Some operator might be clacking two bits of wire together above the jungles of Indo-China, or doing the same from a mangrove swamp by the mouth of a Borneo river. Most attempts to make an OOJERKERPIV admit his identity failed because he had no business being on an official frequency. Occasionally the squelch of dots and dashes came from an aircraft too far away to make contact, so that on getting close he was no longer an OOJERKER-PIV but had a callsign and a right to be there.

No contact could be confirmed unless the formality of identification had taken place. Duty as well as courtesy meant that you obeyed the rules. An exchange of identity and signals strengths, of where coming and where going, and of latitude and longitude should the aircraft, for reasons known only unto God, suddenly plunge into the sea, were given with as much alacrity as those messages flashed between ships that pass in the middle of the ocean.

An OOJERKERPIV was not therefore regarded in friendly fashion. One wanted him to transfer his interfering pip-squeak morse elsewhere. But sitting in my hut beyond the runway, earphones on so that the rest of the world was shut out, I was one day called by an aircraft which identified itself by the actual name OOJERKERPIV. I could hardly believe it, but made contact nevertheless. On mentioning this to a fellow operator he said I should stop being a bloody liar, but when he saw details timed to the minute and neatly written in the logbook, each bearing sent to the plane underlined by the usual steel straightedge, he admitted I was right.

The full OOJERKERPIV came out as a kind of Hansardian shorthand by giving only the five letters OJKPV, which belonged to a Belgian aircraft taking people to Australia, and was indeed conceded to be a manifestation of at least one OOJERKERPIV that had plagued us for so long.

Through the same Barr and Stroud field glasses I saw the word ALDEBARAN painted on the side of the flying boat which was to take us to the Kerguelen Islands, its huge bulk with high wings set on flickering wavelets in the harbour. The word matched the boat, Aldebaran being a prime star of the navigators, meaning The Follower, which fitted because every member of the crew, even Bennett, would be one when the time came.

The name was everything, though we were not to know at the time just how totally this was so. The *Aldebaran* slurped at her moorings as we waited for the pinnace to take us aboard, not yet to begin our journey but to overlook the equipment and stow provisions in their places. The stilled propellers of her four engines faced us across the water, the stately prow rising in the wind-flayed bay. In a slow motion nodding to the rhythm of its sea-dance it seemed she assented to whatever we needed of her. According to the name, *Aldebaran* would go wherever coaxed, powered by any reasonable force.

The last three letters of the callsign PZX were most relevant to our navigator, for they denoted the points of the spherical triangle in the navigation training manuals, whose solution was necessary if the stars were to give our geographical position.

Thus in cabbalistic fashion I picked the letters of our callsign over and over, eager to find significance, until the meaning I imparted had more symbolic truth than I supposed.

5

As I lay on my charpoy after meeting Shottermill I heard the long-and-short blast of a middle-distance motor horn inadvertently signal the letter N, which told me the driver's name was Noah. Alphabetical dots and dashes had been pressed into my brain like voracious ticks never to be removed, and ever since that time I have picked stray messages from every noise. Three long retorts by the vehicle presumably avoided indicated O for Obadiah, while erratic bumps in the plumbing behind my bed suggested nothing more than the presence of an elusive OOJERKERPIV.

Sounds had no secrets from me. I was keen to the faintest sign while tuned to a wireless, but deaf to the rest of the world. Living indifferently, I listened in daylight to signals from half the earth that was dark, and then in the dark heard messages from the other half where it was light. My faculties functioned because the heavenly envelope stayed constant, the same constellations fixed in their places when

19

the clouds lifted, brought back by the revolutions of the earth.

In Malaya my direction-finding radio hut was far from the control tower, and several miles north of the camp. I would sit at my illuminated table with the doors wide open, one hand on the morse key and the other at the dials. If no aircraft were flying I might be reading a magazine, or sitting at ease with a mug of tea which caused sweat to saturate the waistband of my khaki drill trousers.

Or I would tilt the chair, earphones around my neck, and stare at the wall. Within moments I was beyond noise and seeing into space, at a point without coordinates of either sense or geography, so that I was out of myself and floating through vivid archipelagos of green, tucked into an elbow of the Heaviside Layer, feelings gone and never to return. Then, at the faintest initial squeak of my callsign's first letter, earphones were on and fingers at the key while the other hand did a square search for a pencil and smoothed the page of the logbook. In switching so quickly from one state to the other I felt controlled by forces other than those which were a fundamental part of me. The transfer from stark duty to transcendental wool-gathering and back again could happen several times in a night. The mechanism of coming and going was not deliberate, and not always desired, but seemed to take place as the spirit required, perhaps as an escape from the weight of listening and a craving to see how far into the other world I could go without being unable to come back.

When terrorists began murdering planters and anyone in British uniform, I closed the doors and used one light over the set so that any bandit in the trees four hundred yards away would have nothing on which to beam his gun. Sometimes I would turn all lights off, load my rifle, and set out against orders to patrol between the hut and the trees. When a man moved across my track I was unwilling to award him time or warning in a game of him and me. Without calling out I saw him edge towards the wall of

20

trees. He was full in my sights, and for a second, which was a long time, I wondered whether or not to fire. I tightened the sling against my shoulder to steady the aim, and squeezed the trigger. There was no question of not doing so. On hearing the noise, which must have carried for miles, a jeep load of soldiers came racing across the runway.

Earphones on, I said I'd heard nothing because of atmospherics. 'Listen,' I said, 'can you hear anything through that?' When daylight came there was no sign of a body, but there was blood on the grass.

The rifle was taken away so that the terrorists could not capture it after killing me. An army patrol would call every couple of hours to see that I was safe, but the possibility of being shot without a gun in my hands was a nightmare. A sergeant at the armoury liked his booze, and on passing him a bottle of Scotch he promised to see what could be done.

'Anything that will fire,' I said. 'Even a blunderbuss.'

'That's not very neat.' His gnarled fingers stroked the bottle. 'You want something neat, on your job, something very neat, Tosh.'

I still wasn't happy, but there was a chance that with a loaded revolver I would be in a better mood to recognize happiness if it came my way. The Smith and Wesson lay by the graduated scale of the goniometer. Both doors opened showed east and west. If Chang the Hatchet Man came from north or south I wouldn't hear. You can't have everything. Daylight made me safe. Visibility is thine, said the Lord. But night was on their side, and I itched at the dials, out of contact by earphones that locked my senses into the stratosphere. The signals officer said we could operate from the camp, safe within its perimeter. No, I said, I liked being on my own, and would let no one rob me of being afraid.

I shut a flap of each door so that it would be difficult to tell whether I was in or out, then plugged in the loud-speaker so that from a distance I would hear any morse calling me. A scarf of sweat criss-crossed my back. Sharp

21

patterns of equatorial stars decorated the outer envelope of the earth, but I needed only a hundred yards to be in elephant grass and beyond the glow I was assumed to inhabit.

The ground was my ally, and time on my side. The realization that they also can be deceived who have been in the country all their lives gave me confidence. I would not be picked off like a pig in a *kampong*, or cut to bits one night after I had nodded into an impossibly expensive dream.

With a bayonet in one hand and a revolver in the other, I crouched and waited. The cough of water buffalo, bull-frog noises scraping the sky, and the comforting thump of surf half a mile away were pushed into the background. But my crude ambush would deceive nobody. I went into a potent daydream of the night, under a half moon threatening to light up fronds of grass that rendered my body ambiguous in the scrubby landscape. Part of every hour I waited to kill whoever might be creeping up to kill me, my senses synchronized to the extent that they pushed out anxiety and brought happiness.

The centre of my solar system was the hut, and I shifted clockwise, taking bearings on its glimmer. I felt a tightness at my left leg after standing longer than the intended five minutes. Aches and pains were not my bane, but I had been as still as wood, and should have expected such a seizure. Jumping up and down to bring the limb back to life might have made me a target, so I resisted. The tightness increased as if a rope were applied above the ankle.

The pressure was uneven, and the few seconds while in the grip of the small and I hoped merely playful snake were longer by far than any spiritual trips I had taken in the empty watches of more peaceful nights. Stillness was life, and yet to breathe might mean death. I saw the shadow of the snake's head but, waiting for the sting, looked at the line of trees. Thought was my worst enemy, but all I wondered, over and over, was: if I touch it, will it turn into a stick? I didn't, nor counted the minutes, but as they passed I grew calm, until the snake unravelled and went on its way.

I was in no mind to linger anymore on midnight wanderings. Oil tins on a pile of stones acted as alarm bells. Between sticks dug in the ground I set a sharp wire to scrape any ankle. If I had read about such tricks, I had forgotten the books. My enjoyment was total, and I decided that to be mature one must be cunning and unafraid.

6

I was unable to make any decisions except the wrong ones, but since they seemed right I enjoyed making them. Life was good because it didn't matter what I did. Carry on sending. Everything would be all right as long as you couldn't care less. Fresh from the troopship, I put on my demob suit and after four years felt very much the jaunty ex-serviceman. I bought a large bunch of carnations and took the train to Mortlake. Anne was in her parlour and, though out of my element, I fell in love again. In three months we were married. I worked in a jeweller's shop and instead of life speeding up as I had expected, it got slower and one day stopped. I fell down behind the counter, and the tray of engagement rings I was showing to a girl and her young man sprayed over the floor. When I was strong enough to stand I walked out.

I said to Anne that the job had been a stopgap. She asked what my long-term plans were. I had nothing to say.

Such a question was unjust, and I could only hope that Fate would not let me down. Life did not seem real.

'It's more real than you think,' she said.

My feet refused to touch ground. 'I can't make plans.'

'Others do.'

Her information was superfluous. I knew they did. But where did that get me? And where were they? Whenever she was right she reduced me to silence. Mostly she was right, so mostly there was silence. For some reason this silence annoyed her more than if she had been wrong and we had gone on talking. Reality was when I twiddled the tuning knob of the radiogram and heard morse chirping from the speaker. Whatever was said spoke only to me: news agency reports, ships' telegrams, amateur chat, weather messages. The cryptic spheres washed me clean.

'You seem tense.'

I nodded, and switched off.

'Put on some Mantovani?' she asked.

The music soothed her as the morse had calmed me.

'I'm tired of loving someone who just isn't there,' she said.

'I am here.'

'You think so, but you're not. Not to me, anyway.'

I held my hand under her nose. 'This is me, isn't it?'

She laughed. 'I do love you, I suppose.'

I curled my hand into a fist. 'And I love your nice long ginger hair, and your beautiful neat cunt.'

'I hate it when you talk like that.'

'Sorry,' I said.

'You're filthy.'

'I can't help it.'

'You're still not demobbed, to say such things.'

'I won't say it again.' I was as contrite as could be.

She stood, and pushed my hand away. 'Why don't we go to the Feathers for a couple of hours?'

I belonged nowhere and to no one, so how could I claim to be in love? But I was. Being a girl of wit and perspicacity,

24

she sensed my trouble and decided there was no cure. She was wrong, but I couldn't blame her for not waiting.

She didn't want to believe in a remedy because her own circuit was already shorting. One evening I found the flat stripped to the floorboards. The fireplace shelf in the living room held me up. Staring into a dusty cupboard I didn't feel much of an ex-serviceman any more. I tried to dam the tears, but they found new routes down my cheeks. Four years in the mob, and I wasn't even back where I started. I needed to get on and out and through and up and across and in any direction possible as long as I didn't stay where I was. I had disappeared up my own arse and got lost.

I clung to the mantelshelf as if it were a plank of wood in the middle of the Atlantic, until I remembered the revolver in my attaché case. I spun a coin, saying heads me, tails her. Heads came three times, so I slammed in six and sucked the steel lollipop. I would have dipped it in jam, but she hadn't left any food.

I had been drawn into the lobster pot of marriage, totally unprepared for such an investment. No need to apologize, Anne said. But there was, I insisted, wishing there hadn't been. My face wore a twisted aspect as I looked in the mantelshelf mirror. After setting traps and perambulating the elephant grass to save my life, I had walked into one so obvious that I hadn't even noticed. The same loaded gun was ready to stop me protesting about fate now that I was in a far less dangerous predicament.

I took the gun from my mouth, feeling older than when the barrel had gone in – though not much. In the mirror, I preferred not to recognize myself. Love won hands down over war when it came to making people miserable. There was much to learn, but I wanted to hide so far inside myself that no one would find me and I would be safe for ever.

I walked out with a suitcase and went to a radio school on the south coast, paying tuition fees from my savings so as to get my service qualifications converted to a certificate which would allow me to work on a ship or in aviation.

Instead of being a shop assistant, I preferred listening to the traffic of the spheres. Marriage was for those whose emotional seesaw was properly centred. My spirit wanted to reach space where noises multiplied, in the hope that they would provide me with an answer as to why I was alive. I would stave off death by listening for the last message from ship or aircraft, or even while sending one of my own, and forget that I did not know what life was all about.

Anne, accurate in her knowledge, had seen no hope. I walked to one side of the pier and then the other, wearing two jerseys against the east wind. I would not try to make contact, even supposing I knew where she had gone, but hoped she considered me on the right side of forgiveness for whatever I might have done. For myself, I only forgive those I love, and she is still that person.

Separation gave me energy. I made acquaintances, but those at the wireless college who also came from the Air Force knew when to leave me alone. Perhaps a similar madness infected us all. If I went for long walks instead of passing an evening with them in a pub, no remark was made.

7

Some time during my marriage I bought a morse key and, when Anne complained of silence, would take it from the drawer and send insulting messages which she couldn't read, or repeat the SOS signal over and over after she had gone to bed. Another little mannerism which my dear wife pointed out, because she said it drove her mad, was my habit of whistling. I knew that I did it, because on catching myself I would break off in the mid flow of rhythmical notes which came out between a small gap in my upper front teeth. The sound, piercing though not loud, might have been a bird in its death agony under the paws of a cat, or the tentative beginnings of a kettle about to boil before emitting its usual scream. The sound could be picked up in a crowd by anyone with a sensitive ear, even from some distance away.

The habit was harmless, but I tried to cure myself because any messages sent not only made me vulnerable to the world but enraged my wife. So I stopped in mid whistle, and the noise would cease until, forgetting my resolution (there was no pleasure in such mindless whistling, after all) I would catch myself once more, while at a dance or tea party with Anne or, even worse, standing behind the counter of the shop being overheard by the boss from behind.

The habit ended with Anne leaving, or so I thought, but on finishing radio school, and after a spell at sea, and when getting another job seemed impossible, it came back. I walked into a pub in Albemarle Street and ordered a pint and a sandwich. Impatient at having to wait, the five letters of an aircraft callsign formed slowly on my lips, so that though not a wireless operator, Bennett, a mere stranger who stood nearby, was able to interpret the five letters of morse which I sent again and again.

It was a near miracle, considering the noise, but he had ears that could detect the breath of a dying man across a hundred miles of Antarctic peaks. He also put together the co-sign of my moustache, as well as the forward jutting chin and glinting grey eyes that denoted a man who would pick up any signals that were going. There is also something unmistakable about ex-airmen until they lose their youth, and maybe I reminded him of an aircrew member he once knew, perhaps one of those poor-show bods who had his guts splashed across the TR1154/55 above Bremen and yet was brought back to burial on English soil. There was no knowing. We had been born to give no sign, show no emotion, admit to no foreknowledge. Pragmatical we were, and phlegmatic we would stay, no matter how much the inner cauldron boiled.

He looked at me. 'RAF?'

'How did you know?'

'I'm asking.'

'Yes.'

Lunch came. 'I can't get the bloody mob out of my head.'

'Nor can a lot of us.' He smiled. 'What's more, we don't see why we should.'

'Funny,' I said.

'It was a good mob.'

'Still is.' I offered him a drink.

'No, you'll have what I'm having.' He called for double whiskies. Such stuff on top of a pint would clog my brain for the afternoon, but I was in no mind to refuse. 'What sort of wireless were you in?'

I put the beer aside for a chaser, and lifted the whisky. 'Mainly direction-finding.'

'The old huff-duff, eh?'

'The same.'

'Do any ops?'

'I was too late.' Lots of aircrew ended in the cookhouse, pushing food out to the queues. I was lucky to get on the radio at all.

'As long as you can handle the gear in a plane.'

'What sort of plane?'

'Flying boat. I need somebody for a couple of months. If you want a job.'

I looked interested. 'I might.'

'Did you do a gunnery course?'

'Only the basics. They didn't even want gunners. The war ended, remember?'

'Don't I know it?' He kept silent, and left me wondering whether he really had a proposition to make. Then he said:

'You'll get five hundred a month, plus expenses. And come out with another thousand in your pocket.'

I needed a job like I'd soon need a suit to walk about in. 'Sounds a fair screw.'

He slid down the other half of his whisky. 'It's more than eight-and-six a day!'

'But is it legal?'

He nodded.

Hard to believe, but I was in no state to argue.

'When can you start?'

I was off my food. 'I don't know. After you've told me what it's all about.'

'Now?'

'If you like.'

'I'm being set up in a charter business, and need a wireless operator to make up the crew. Do you have a civvy ticket?'

I did.

'All right. But no questions about legality. I don't like it.'

He was the skipper, so I soft-pedalled the interrogatives – and stopped whistling morse from that time on. He said that the original wireless operator, who had been a member of his old crew, had pulled out on hearing his wife was pregnant. He'd only got the phone call that morning, and was at his wits' end for a replacement.

'A Super Constellation leaves for Johannesburg in three days.' We were in his South Kensington flat to settle my travel details and sign articles that, I thought, may not be worth the paper they're written on.

8

On the quayside Bennett introduced me to Nash, his chief gunner. A squall hid the flying boat to which, day after day, a pinnace went out with supplies from Shottermill's warehouse. I wondered how we could need a gunner, but kept silent. To ask questions was to have curiosity prematurely crushed, and the hope taken out of expectation. In any case I could wait, no matter what risk such a course might put me or others in.

No landing ground is necessary for a flying boat, and because water covers two-thirds of the earth it has more advantages than any other machine: a combination of Icarus successful and the dolphin tamed. As the huge and handsome boat lifts, its hull bids farewell to the fishes at the same moment that its wings say good day to the birds. The craft meets both and spans two elements, an aerodynamic ark speeding through cloud and clear sky in turn. I had no wish to know what was carried, wanted only to make the flight and collect my bounty.

A policeman skiddled his stick along the corrugated wall of the shed. Bennett peered intently, as if to bring the flying boat back into clarity. 'Am I going to take that thing off again? I often wonder how much longer I can do it.'

Nash's laugh was the kind that passes between people who have known each other a long time. It was meant only for Bennett. 'They used to say you could do anything with the old flying boat, Skipper, except make it have a baby.'

'On this trip I'll need to make it have two – if we're to get back.'

Nash knelt to tie his shoelaces, then said: 'I remember a picture of the old Mayo-Composite before the war. I expect I saw it on a cigarette card. Maybe we should have dredged up one of those for the job.'

The *Aldebaran*, of pristine beauty and consummate power, shone almost silver under the sun which followed the squall. Bennett turned: 'I'm on the wong side of forty, and can't sweat like I used to. But I couldn't resist this little job. There'll be enough in the kitty for no more worries, so I shan't have to fly again. I'll be retired, and no one will ask questions. A bit of travel every year, a consultant for some firm or other to bring in a bit extra – that'll be my life. And if I can't stand it I'll come out here, or buy a few thousand acres in Rhodesia ' '

'You might as well,' Nash said. 'There's eff-all in Blighty, these days.'

9

Nash was a large man with dark hair swept back, thick lips and quick brown eyes. We smoked and talked in one of our narrow rooms after roaming the town at night for a place to eat. His father had been a market gardener in richest Lincolnshire, but Nash left school at fourteen and took any job he could find till voluntéering for aircrew in 1940. 'I wanted to get above it all!' he said. 'My feet had been too long on the ground, and I fancied a bit of flying, but I was sent to a station in Scotland to work in the stores. I lacked little, and thought I had a cushy billet for the duration, but two years later I was called to an aircrew selection board. There were so many changes of station to Birmingham I almost lost myself. Then I was sent to St John's Wood for physical tests. I got through those and went to ITW, a conveyor belt for training aircrew, and I was happy to be on it. We marched at 120 paces to the minute to get speed of reaction, and the infantry weren't fitter. There was classroom work on meteorology, navigation, engines – you name it, they taught it. I'd never worked so hard, going from one classroom to another, and then to do drill and PT in the hangar. Rain or shine, we never stopped.

'I went on a twenty-four-week air gunner's course, training on Bothas, Wimpies and Lancasters. I started ops in '43 as a rear gunner. I got the last of the central heating, and often froze so much I couldn't move anything but fingers and eyes. Which was all that was needed. I suppose I pissed up more Lancs than any other bod in the service. Apart from anything else I was physically too big for the job. I'm sure they picked big blokes on purpose to stick in those small turrets sometimes for eight hours at a stretch. I got a JU88 above Frankfurt, and damaged another over Holland – shoot first and die later, if you have to. Our luck was ladled out by the Big Dipper. We came home on a QDM from the wireless operator who had a piece of shrapnel in his eye. That was the trip we got the gongs for.

'Me and Bennett had done so many ops we could choose our time for a night off, and on one pass to London the rest of the crew went bang over Cologne, including the CO who'd given us the pass, because that night he was captain. We'd done our turn. Let somebody else sit on the flying bomb racks and flog Sodom and Gomorrah night after night just to get back home and have a fried egg for breakfast. Bennett wangled a conversion course to flying boats and took me as his tail gunner. I was game for a change. Over the Atlantic the stars were where they should be (when they were) and not burning to death on the ground.

'The Sunderlands carried a galley and a steward so that sausages as well as fried eggs could be had en route. A couple of JU88s once nosed too close, but after our gunners played the Browning version the skipper lost them in a cloud.'

Nash told the story of his life more than once, but I had the feeling that when the rest of our crew got here he would talk less. There seemed to be a gap in his story when he came to his time with Coastal Command. They 'killed' one U-boat, oil and dirty water telling of its demise. I knew from his wavering eyes, and disparagement about the mouth, that there was something of this incident that he wanted to tell but couldn't. I was fitted for the job of listening, and never poked my nose where it wasn't wanted. The trade selection tests hadn't been far out in deciding that Bennett be a pilot, Nash a gunner, and me a wireless operator.

'Though the Lord was a man of war, I was man enough to like peace when it came.' He poured out more of that vile and sickly Van der Hum wine. 'The first summer after demob was real life at last. A group of us would hire a boat in Boston and go out on the Wash trawling shrimps. We'd cook and eat them, and brew tea on a primus, and spend all day on the water, and come back with mussels by the pound, and I'd tip my share in the bath and throw them a handful of breadcrumbs. The good old days were here again, when you could expect to be alive a week, a month, even a year ahead.'

He couldn't sit more than half an hour without needing to piss. His restless eyes settled into a stare, and he stood up with an apology he never made until this malady struck. He had taken pills, powders and potions, but nothing stopped this clockwork aggravation of the bladder: 'A disease that no quack can cure, and which doesn't kill, is no disease at all. You've got no business having it. The symptoms may be imaginary, but the effect is uncomfortable. If you suffer, it's your own fault, so it's no use blaming the doctors, or getting God on the blower, like Job.'

By the samphire borders of the Wash, he stood on the edge of the boat and sent streams of amber piss into the water while his mates' backs were turned. A god to Nash would have been one who concocted a pill which allowed him a full night without getting up.

He would put money made out of the present trip into

resurrecting the building firm he had run with his brother. From jobbing work they had, despite chronic shortages (since everything went for council houses and repairing bomb damage), increased their range to bungalows, finding a way through labyrinthine red tape to obtain materials and acquire sites. Difficulties overcome not only brought higher profits, but laid down procedures along which one could afterwards run with the ease of a trolley on rails. A nod, a wink, a gift, a fiver (or more) at a tricky obstacle cleared the hairpin bends like magic.

For what the judge called 'a scandalous case of bribery and corruption' he was sent to jail for eighteen months. Given time to brood, he saw no sense in being penalized merely for using his enterprise in days of such gratuitously imposed austerity. He found ways around the rules. Show intelligence, and you get kicked in the guts. 'If it hadn't been for this flying boat job, I'd have gone down and never come up again. The skipper doesn't mind that I've been in prison. He stands by his old crew. And most of 'em do, which is something to be said for a doomed generation.'

This remark was the closest he got to self-pity, and I wheeled him out of it by saying I had never believed in such talk. 'Ours was doomed, though,' he said.'You missed it by a couple of years. Only ten per cent survived a tour of ops. Hundreds of bods fell out of the sky every night.'

I had often regretted not having been born earlier. When someone told me that a funny bomb had ended the war I called him a bloody liar. Adolescence was War, and suddenly both war and youth ended. Nash had come out with honour but an incontinent bladder.

He wiped tears from his left eye. 'Germany's pin-up boy sealed our doom. They killed whole fucking generations!'

'Each generation is made up of any number of individuals,' I said, 'and as one of them I didn't have, don't have and never shall have any intention of dooming myself.'

Then he said, and I was too drunk to ask why: 'When this flying boat takes off, you'll come as close to being doomed

34

as you'll ever want to be. If you team up with Bennett, you ask for all you get.'

I was always conscious, even at my most obtuse, of being wholesomely attached to life. At the same time I thought that the possibility of being doomed was not something over which I had any control. But we had talked so long that I had to give in and say I was ready for the straw.

'Sleep'll be the death of you,' he scoffed. 'Be the death of me, as well. Trouble with sleep is you might not wake up. Maybe that's why I get out of bed to piss six times a night. Shit-scared of going so far under I'll never get back. People spend a third of their lives asleep. Twenty odd years off three-score-and-ten. It's daylight robbery! You'll get all the sleep you like when you're dead, so why rush? If we could go through life without bed we'd live longer, and enjoy the final sleep better when it came. We'd kip so long there'd be no Heaven or Hell, or we'd be too tired to notice it. You only think such places exist if you have too much sleep when you're alive.'

We drank the last bottle. 'You've given it much thought.'

'That's because you think of rum things in that rear turret trying to stay awake and make sure the next second won't be your last. The navigator and pilot keep us on course, and your Sergeant Backtune wireless operator's tapping his feet to dance music from all over Europe, but your gunner has to keep himself warm and everybody else safe. Me and the skipper were one mind when it came to surviving. One whisper and the Lanc was in a corkscrew and I was belting the guns at a shadow that tried to follow us down. But sleep is public enemy number one, so you go off for your lethal dose of shut-eye, while I slope away for a leak!'

10

I had not expected so much delay in getting the flying boat ready. Waiting released gloomy premonitions, and the problem was whether I should leave to avoid disaster, which I felt was sure to come, or stay to see whether I was right or wrong about my premonitions. If I left I would never know, and feel a fool. If I stayed, I wouldn't live to tell myself I had made a mistake. Pride on the one hand, and curiosity on the other, had me locked.

The flying boat had been chosen from thousands of war-surplus planes, and I couldn't help wondering about its air-worthiness. I questioned the wisdom of placing myself at its disposal, an attachment which began after my inability to bed down into the married state. I had signed a contract as wireless officer for the Southern Ocean Survey Company on board the *Aldebaran*, and Nash told me during an interminable series of card games that we were to assess anchorage facilities in the Cape Town-Tasmania-Antarctic triangle, for a steamship company that would acquire and recondition a couple of redundant Liberty ships. They would go into the cruise market for naturalists, amateur geographers and middle-aged wayfarers with money, who had not travelled during the war and now wanted to take advantage of the reopening of facilities.

Nash saw that it would mean almost no change of name for the company when it became known as the Southern Ocean *Steamship* Company. There would be work for us all in such an enterprise, 'especially for you,' he said, 'as radio officer.' He reached across the table and nudged my chest, between one game of gin rummy and the next, though my own laugh was due to the unhappy coincidence of both acronyms.

I believed nothing of what he told me. A lifetime of listening had made me suspicious. A man couldn't survive seventy-six operations over Germany, as well as a stint with Coastal Command, and not have more cunning than was good for him. Nash knew something about the trip that I didn't know, and under his phlegmatic aspect was a caution hard to fathom. I had no evidence as to what it was, and my curiosity was so intense that I couldn't see a way to find out. To ask questions, however circumspectly, would lose me all standing among the crew. I had been left with nothing when Anne went out of my life except that kind of honour which, providing an all-round defence, led me to distrust everything but my own competence – such as it was.

I asked Nash when the flying boat would be leaving.

'In about a week.' He licked his finger before picking up a card. 'There'll be briefings first, though, and a few circuits around the harbour. Meanwhile, you won't be needing this.' He drew one of the gaudy banknotes to his side of the table, then handed me the pack because it was my turn to shuffle.

I walked to the window. The air in the room was thick with our smoking. Outside there was grit in the wind. Yesterday the houses along the street had been intact, now they were being brought down. How are the mighty fallen! Between gaps the deep blue sea had white tails curling on top. When waves hit the breakwater a geyser of smoke banged into the air and, even at this distance, looking between demolished houses, I could hear that searing rush as the liquid mass came down. Close to midday, half the block was gone. That's how they move in this country. A date-time is set for doing a job, and then it's done, without argument or delay.

I went back to the table. 'A poor lookout if it's dead calm on the day we're supposed to get airborne, with such a load to carry.'

'That's not your problem. Just deal the cards and pray for luck. You might win if you aren't careful.'

According to graphs on Bennett's table, the wind that prevailed on most days of the year, to any number of the Beaufort scale, when otherwise it was a calm of equal deadliness, was westerly. He'd fly the *Aldebaran* into the wind for lift, and we would have to rise before colliding with the escarpment on the other side of the harbour.

'They aren't used to such big flying boats out here,' Nash said. 'Only seaplanes. The skipper landed it almost empty, and a double run'll be needed to get off. If we have to taxi out to the open sea he'll have to wait for a calm day, and on such a day there'll be little wind for lift-off. He has his problems. You've just got to trust him – like I do.'

Now that the war was over, I didn't like to make anyone responsible for my life; yet Nash was right. On the other hand, neither he nor Bennett thought it necessary that I should be told the truth about the *Aldebaran*'s voyage. I wondered whether the navigator or flight engineer would reveal anything when they arrived, because they too had been part of the old crew. I was the only newcomer, and became more and more conscious of the fact. I had been chosen at random, or Fate had pinned a number on me which was impossible to pluck off.

If I took a train along the coast to Lessom Bay, and found work as an operator on some tramp steamer sailing to another part of the world, my last notion of honour would go. I would fall through the safety net of self-respect to the lowest state of all, that of breaking my word – the final dereliction of duty. I had been brought up to believe that once you lost that kind of honour you couldn't atone. I didn't think much of this precept, for there is such a thing as loyalty to life, which means taking reasonable precautions for survival.

'You should stop thinking thoughts,' said Nash, when I lost again. 'It's not good for you. It never did anybody any good.'

'It's worry,' I said, 'not thought, and it'll go when I'm flying.'

'That'll be too late. You'll have a rash by then. Get rid of it now. Take a tip from me. We can't afford to have anyone in the crew who thinks.'

'All right,' I said, 'you win.'

'See what I mean?'

'I do. So deal.'

Whatever the reason, for the rest of that day I won every game.

11

A man was playing a slot machine by the coat racks. Each spinning drum lit up red and yellow. He put money in and, after pausing to let a bout of coughing rack its way through him (he simply stood upright and looked straight ahead, telling the animal inside to do its worst but for God's sake to let rip and get it over with even if it intended killing him), pulled at the large handle as if knowing every move of the machinery inside. A juke-box in an adjoining alcove played the world favourite for that year: 'I'll Never Forget You . . .' A glass of beer was set on the table, and he reached for a drink when his cosseting of the gamble-box brought no results.

I finished a straw bottle of red before my spaghetti and cutlets, with juicy tomato on the summit, came to the table. The Italian proprietor, Mario Salvatore, who was from Turin, told me he had been a prisoner in South Africa during the war. His young wife looked around the curtain every few minutes, then brought my dessert of *meringue crème Chantilly* and a cup of black coffee. I left the dinosaur-trail of cream, and read a newspaper, little interested in reports of the Berlin Blockade and the same old ding-dong in Korea. The snowy ridge across my plate was more intriguing, and led me to speculate on the topography of the island that Bennett was taking us to. The future, holding no more anxieties now that I had eaten, existed only insofar as my wondering about it prevented me from feeling conspicuous at supper.

On my way to the restaurant I had turned away from the seafront and passed several eating places, unable to make up my mind which to enter. They were too crowded, or too empty, or too dingy. I got back to the quay, then walked along the street of storage sheds, as if my body had yet to work up an appetite. I continued along the shore of the bay, and morse-read the licence plates of passing cars, calculating how many dots and dashes were in letters and numbers and whether there were more dots than dashes, so as to define a car as a dash or dot vehicle. If a dot, the car would go to heaven; if a dash, the thing would go to hell. And if the cypher came out in equal numbers, then its pagan status would keep it from either place.

When there were neither houses nor pavement along the potholed road (and no more cars), I looked at the sunset reflection on the battle-plate grey of the harbour, and a glow of coalfire on the wall of mountain behind. The town was quiet with the peace that presages war and frightens children more than grown men, though they do not know what it means. I remembered being frightened as a child by the continual talk of war, until that fear was replaced by excitement at real war beginning.

The satisfactory eating place of half an hour before now had people waiting, so I circled the tree-lined square twice and walked into the Plaza Restaurant which was nearly empty. I hung up my raincoat and sat down. A few solitary eaters had their backs to me. I hated having to sit with others. Even when I had a table to myself I fancied people looking at what was being knifed-and-forked into my mouth.

40

The man at the slot machine played on. His teeth spiked a cheroot, and the only evidence of his agitation, or enjoyment, was when smoke swept back from the crown of his head as if the machine itself was on fire. He was determined, as coin after coin dropped into its demoniac conveyor system, on an all-or-nothing decision, being a man who, I thought, wanted chance firmly in his grip, so as to be protected from something even bigger which might callously injure him.

After a long draw-down of the handle, bundles of coins cascaded out of the tin pocket level with his groin, and both hands, in no kind of hurry – he had been expecting to win and knew clearly what to do – moved to extract his reward. Money continued teeming out and was heaped on the table until his glass of glowing lager became a regal beacon on the high ground of an island set to keep ships away from its dangerous coast.

Thin in face and body, he grinned, yellow teeth showing as he carried his winnings in troughed hands to his own table. He put on his ridiculously small nicky hat, perched as if to hold down the thatch of fair hair reaching almost to his collar. He sat, eyes glowing with exhaustion and triumph. After a quick reckoning, he laid part of his bonus aside, perhaps to put back into the machine, for he seemed nothing if not systematic. Noticing my interest, and realizing who I was, he said: 'Hello, Sparks. Let's have a bottle of steam to celebrate.'

He was Wilcox, our newly-arrived flight engineer. When he came out of Bennett's room that afternoon I knew who he was, and he knew who I was, but I did not feel like introducing myself, and neither did he seem eager, both of us perhaps preferring to let such a procedure occur in the normal course of events.

'Be glad to.' I got up to shake hands.

'Looks like I've broken the bank, eh?'

I went to his table, thinking it as good a time as any to get acquainted. Having watched him at his favourite pastime, I already knew something. His finely boned face took on a light shade of purple when he coughed, hands clenched and opened, as he fought to clear his throat without causing me to think that he put much effort into it. I considered him ill enough for bed, but he rallied and looked almost robust. He relit his cheroot, which calmed the coughing, and sat down.

'After I left the mob I couldn't settle at anything,' he said. 'I tried a few office jobs, but was as bored as hell. Then I worked in a garage, bodging cars together – some of which were nicked, I'd say. But one night I met some friends in a pub and they got me taken on by a firm which did jobs all over the country putting up scaffolding. I was never afraid of heights, or working long hours in wet and freezing weather, so with good wages we had a fine old time. Hell-raising wasn't the half of it – plenty of booze and women when we weren't working all hours God sent. Then I got married, and last winter I caught this bloody cough and had to knock off work.'

He gave a vivid illustration of what he meant, during which I thought he would end by coming to pieces, so that I considered keeping my head to one side in case I should catch whatever he had. 'I went down with a terrible dose of 'flu, and it hasn't left me yet.'

He hoped to have a few days' rest before we set out, to get rid of whatever it was. I agreed that he should. 'The climate's right, anyway.' He too was parted from his wife, but it was he who had walked out on her: 'We were passionately in love, but one morning she said that if I coughed once more she'd go mad. I knew then there was no hope for our marriage. She had lost confidence in me, and once that happens life gets intolerable. I couldn't see an end to my coughing, and didn't want to be responsible for getting her into an asylum. I have this thing about being sensible, and about confidence. If people don't have confidence in each other they've no right tormenting one another. The letter from the skipper saying he wanted me for this trip came just at the right time. In any case I was on sick pay, so I was glad it did.'

42

12

~~~

Why I should be followed around the streets of this obscure port of southern Africa I did not know, but one evening on my way to search out a place with a different menu I sensed a shadow some way behind. Though I heard nothing, the knowledge of being stalked was positive, as if my own shadow had pulled away in the shine of a street lamp and wanted to observe my intentions in an unfriendly manner.

To follow one man and not lose sight of him takes three men. If the man to be kept in view is on the move sixteen hours a day, then six men are needed to work two shifts of eight hours. If it is necessary to keep him under observation during the night as well, nine men would be employed. I liked the situation no more than when sitting on watch in Malaya with hut doors open and lights glaring from the double pack of accumulators, and thinking that a terrorist had me in his sights from the cover of the trees. As I turned a corner at my usual pace I wondered, not how to outwit my pursuer, but how I could discover his identity. Common sense suggested I swing from the next bend and walk back into him; but cunning advised me not to show that I was aware of his intentions.

Being a prey to speculation led me to query whether I was in fact being followed. Perhaps two weeks of boredom had deranged me. Idleness had been pleasant. The lodging, provision and lack of responsibility were so agreeable that I wanted to pass my life in this state, because nothing could make a wireless operator more content than a long break from tapping and log-filling. But the idleness went on too long and, like the painful stage of a disease, was beginning to eat into my soul. I was losing the ability to open and close my eyes at will. The calves of my legs ached, and my scalp itched as if, should I scratch, my hair would fall out in clutches. Too long from the disciplined stitch of morse code, the pit of my stomach started to solidify. Looking at my hand, I would see three fingers instead of four. The only cure was to be tucked into my operator's position with earphones and intercom-jacks pushed decisively into their respective sockets, and hands twitching at the coloured clickstops of the transmitter whose façade looks like a child's construction kit.

Being away from England, and pitched into a situation whose outcome was from any point of view uncertain, I felt myself to be at least two different people, both of whom it was difficult to hold together in one physical spot. Could not that person, therefore, who followed me and never varied the distance, be a third entity that had split off from the two of me already in existence?

I increased my pace from a surge of buoyancy rather than to outdistance my pursuer. If instead of one person tracking me there were in fact the necessary three – out of a conscientiousness to do the job properly – then the three parts of me within my controllable orbit had a chance of outwitting them.

Before deciding on the best means of doing this I wondered why anyone should so obviously track me, and hoped the reason would be revealed. Having discovered the fact early could only be explained by my lack of surprise at such a thing happening at all. Since meeting Bennett and reaching our rendezvous in Southern Africa, there had seemed something unreal about the purpose – if not the legality – of what he proposed to do. The only evidence for this uneasiness was that it poisoned my idleness.

The clatter of footsteps was my own. I would walk instead of march, do 90 and not 120 paces to the minute, preferring to show concern rather than anxiety. It was chilling to be followed. Being tracked can turn into a pursuit, and become a chase. Physically aware of the follower, you may be manoeuvred into a trap.

The streets darkened. I clenched my fists, and turned corners. The route must have shaped so many letter Ls they'd become like stairs on paper. I marched again, and at the left foot passing the right, as if on parade, the loud voice in me shouted: 'Halt!'

Both feet came noisily together. On a further command I did the 'about turn', drew back my left fist, and punched the body which came against me. He let out a cry, and fell into the road.

Having hit someone who as likely as not hadn't been following me at all, I thought it wise to run as far as my guilt would allow, especially since he might have been a policeman wanting only to check my passport. If he wasn't alone in his work, assistants would be coming up to help. Perhaps Shottermill, who would leave no trick unturned, still wanted the flying boat to set off without me. Or maybe he didn't want it to depart at all.

Acting without consideration never did any good, and now reason must be elevated to a par with valour, whereby it seemed tactically right to flee. I turned to do so and – no great feat to vanish into the darkness – heard my name called as clearly as if a coil of rope had hissed around my neck:

'Adcock!' A burly figure came towards me, brushing gravel from jacket and trousers. 'You bloody fool.' He didn't seem angry until: 'You're like a fucking wolf.' My blow had been a mere push, and he had only gone over on losing his balance at the drop of the kerb. He spoke in a North of England accent which I didn't trust an inch: 'It is Adcock, isn't it?'

'You were following me.'

His arm came close, and I dodged, but the gesture was to guide himself in the dark. 'How could I catch you up if I didn't follow?' His hand was for me to shake. 'But you walked as quick as if you'd just come off square-bashing. My name's Bull, flight-sergeant air-gunner, as I once was. Came in this evening to join the crew.' I shook the warm and meaty hand, which held on too long for my liking. 'Bennett gave me some of that lovely coloured money, more than a monthly wage packet back home. Then I met Wilcox coughing his guts up in the lobby of that Flotsam Hotel and asked where I could eat pork pies and black puddings. So he says I'd better follow Adcock the Sparks who is just going out, because he knows the best places to get scoff. I tried to, but you walked bloody fast.'

We went back towards the middle of town. I was unable to show instant comradeship for someone who had caused me to panic so ignominiously. 'Sorry about the thump.'

He laughed, and became more likeable. 'Wasn't much, was it? Like a kitten with mittens playing dobbie! I might have done the same in your place, only the poor sod I did it to wouldn't have got up in a hurry. Still, as long as you make up for your tap at me by finding some nice grub.'

'You won't get pork pies and pints.'

'Ah well!' He held my arm, as if he might lose me again.

'Wine gets you drunk quicker.'

'That's what I'll have, then, if you recommend it.'

I asked how many gunners we were taking on. There seemed no end to them.

'Two, besides me and Nash. I came down with my old oppoes Armatage and Appleyard. You'll be as safe as houses with us. We've shot coffins out of the sky many a time!'

All we needed was a navigator. As things stood, Bennett would fly the plane, Nash and the gunners guard it, Wilcox maintain it, and I would be all ears cocked against the world. But without a navigator on a long flight over the ocean we would not reach our destination. Though Bennett had a First Class Navigator's Licence, he couldn't fly the crate and do that job properly, because while the navigator took star-sights in the astro dome a good pilot had to keep the plane level and steady.

We faced each other, as well as chips and chops and chunks of bread and bottles of red plonk in between. It

46

suited him fine. He poured a tumbler and drank it like cold tea. He was thirty years old but seemed middle-aged. Civvy life had been so dull he had joined the Merchant Navy, doing any work he was put to: 'As well as being a gunner, I'm a rigger and a steward – a jack-knife of all trades, you might say. I happened to be at home to see my parents, because I'd just jumped ship. I thought I might settle down on shore for a while, but then Bennett's telegram came and I knew I couldn't let the skipper down. Well, could I? You know how it is. He's got us all now, every manjack of the old crew except the wireless-op, and you're standing in for him.'

He was open and friendly, and the more we drank the more I wondered whether he had in fact been following me. No matter what he said, mistrust came and went. At the third bottle he took off his jacket and rolled up his sleeves. I glanced at his decorated skin. 'That's how it is if you're a sailor,' he said. 'You aren't much of a man if you haven't got a bit of this stuff over your arms and tits.'

From the bulge of white muscles down to the backs of his wrists were red and blue daggers, hearts, reptiles, union jacks, buxom women and, on his chest, he said, a portrait of King George. My sight was glazed from too much wine, but I was sure that, even though I hadn't yet met Appleyard and Armatage, Bennett had gathered a very fine crew indeed – and, whatever I thought, I was certainly one of them.

'Oh yes,' Bull said, 'and another thing I forgot to tell you. The navigator came in as well. You're in for a treat when you see him.'

47

13

The water chopped itself about, objecting to the wind, but the flying boat was well-moored. When Bennett wasn't on board overlooking stowage, or in his room cooking up hypothetical navigation schemes, he was pacing the quay in strides too big for his frame, cigar going like a haystack, hands behind his back and glancing up every few yards, as if to a time mechanism, at the lift and fall of the *Aldebaran.*

His skin was the colour of milk from the tension of waiting. The bottle of whisky on his table was always half full, and of a different brand. For the captain of a flying boat his hands shook too much, but we all had aches and twitches of some sort that would not go away till flesh and blood felt relief at the great flying boat with stores and men on board lifting into the air, the rate of climb indicator, the rev counter and the altimeter doing their jobs, as lessening bumps under the hull told us we were almost airborne.

All we could do was play cards, walk the town, fall asleep in the local picture house, and get drunk. Six months will pass before we depart, I thought when I woke up the morning after my encounter with Bull, so that we'll have winter as one more enemy. None of the others seemed over-anxious, however, and Wilcox was positively glad of all the sleep he could get.

After a shower and breakfast I went out for my usual walk. I watched cranes at their demolition work with the fascination of the idle at the spectacle of the energetically employed. I did not know whether to go left and walk by the harbour, or stroll right and up the hill behind the town.

As I stood, work ceased for some kind of break. Blacks went to their dinner cans, and whites to a wooden hut, and I saw the wall that was left naked. Floors had been scraped away, and a purple mark remained as if it had been burned there. A groove was revealed, and with it a continuation that made a scar as if across a chin, and the blue wash of a wall crested an eye enclosed in tissues that gave the glazed, beacon-like stare of some prehistoric creature.

Illuminated by the sun, the composition was like an enlarged reproduction of the side of our navigator's face, turned from us when I met him in the breakfast room before coming out. The wound had been caused by a Very signal-rocket pistol. The stubby cartridge of brutal calibre had gored his cheek and burned there, a stray or accidental shot from the control tower window when he happened to have been strolling by. Plastic surgery had bettered the grisly enhancement, but not much. He later told me that he left the hospital after eighteen months because kindness was turning him clockwise into a lunatic. He hiked the by-ways for a year to get back health, and the only item of value in his rucksack was a bubble sextant which he would not relinquish. He did not know why, but while children ran from him he relished the extra weight. Sisyphus, he said, had nothing on me. At which Bull confessed that he'd had a dose of that, as well. Rose got a job, and went to live again with his mother, and stayed until receiving Bennett's telegram which called him, he said, back to duty.

As I stood across the road from the enormously enlarged picture of Rose's hideous blemish high up the wall, I wondered how long it would be before we took our departure. The livid vision made me active where I had been apathetic. I walked away as quickly as I could, unable to look a moment more than I had to. When I passed in the evening the whole building was level with the ground.

14

The seven of us waited in the hotel lounge, which was closed off for our use. A chart of the ocean, and a large-scale map of the islands, were pinned to the wall. As if to accustom us gradually to the scarred side of his face, the navigator kept it turned whenever possible. Because his name was Rose, I thought of him as 'Compass', though when none of the others took the sobriquet as in any way witty I let the name go. Smoke from his pipe drifted over a fleshy landscape of red and purple, to screen the distortion from anyone tempted to gaze at it. The pipe angled jauntily out of the disfigured side of his mouth, so that a languid puff slid up the lunar scars. If anything this made the effect worse, which may have been his idea, though I think he no longer cared for anyone's opinion. The glint in his eyes suggested that he was used to bearing the scar, and his nonchalant expression turned humorous when he considered what the world could do as far as he was concerned. But the lasting effect of the scar was to curb outright laughter from him. People in any case expected so little merriment because of his affliction that he eventually employed less than he had grown up with. The truth was that he had accustomed himself to his disfigurement, and it was up to us to get used to it.

He looked around. 'What a bloody shower!'

The others laughed, having known him well, but only in the wartime pre-scar days, so that to some extent he was also new to them. Perhaps we did look a shower, with our open-necked shirts and various kinds of jackets. I had a tie in my luggage, and supposed the others had.

'You may well turn out to be right,' Nash said.

'I sincerely hope not. You know how the skipper likes us to dress for dinner in mid-flight.'

I laughed with the others.

'We don't want any crisis during the trip.' In spite of twitting us, he had a gentle voice. He'd grown up in a small farming town on the northern edge of Salisbury Plain, and the pleasant burr to his speech remained. His father, a solicitor, had sent him to the local grammar school to which he had gone as a boy, and a distinction in mathematics for his Higher School Certificate had naturally led Rose to become a navigator on volunteering for aircrew.

He sat with the knick-knacks of his trade: a Dalton Computer, plotting instruments, star-finder, and a Bubble Sextant Mark IX. Maps and charts were spilling from a black bag by his polished shoes. Even Bennett hadn't such knife-edged creases in his trousers. He irons his laces at night, we used to say about such a type. Butter wouldn't melt in his turnups. You could smell his haircream a mile off. How wrong we were.

When the skipper came in, Rose, Nash and the others stood as at a pukka briefing, so I joined them. He looked at us one by one, then nodded. We sat down, and he talked for some time about the allocation of duties. We were informed that Rose, being the navigator and also capable of piloting the plane, was second in command. The flight engineer would, in spite of his cough, be able to control the aircraft and keep it on course during level flight, if necessary. He also knew some navigation. So did the wireless operator. It wasn't unusual for such a crew to learn something of each other's jobs, so we had the equivalent of three possible pilots and two good navigators, which was an advantage, considering what margins of error might develop on our lengthy flight.

The fact that there was one wireless operator gave me some satisfaction, because it meant that the ears of the craft and the transmitter were my own. There would be no one to interfere with me working the dials and clickstops. If I went down with illness or injury Bennett and Rose could do a slow morse speed of six words a minute and tap out an SOS,

51

but only providing the transmitter was on the right frequency.

Bennett pointed at the chart with a piece of stick. 'The first leg of the trip will be to the Kerguelen Islands, over two thousand nautical miles away. We reconnoitre the straits' – more indication with his baton – 'between one island and another, to find a certain cove' – a definite stab at that point – 'for anchorage. Using it as our base, we spend a few days exploring the west and north-west coast – a bit of surveying, you might say – and then set course for Freemantle, 2320 nautical miles further on. On our way to Kerguelen we overfly – or as near as dammit we do, won't we, Mr Rose? – two small inhabited islands, with no facilities, I'm afraid, of either petrol or beer. Also, there aren't any shipping lanes where we're going, which is why we have a navigator like Mr Rose to plot our way. Cruising speed will be something in the region of 120 knots, though the prevailing wind, if it prevails as it should, ought to give us a bit more ground speed, so we'll take about eighteen hours to reach our objective. The end of the second leg will get us to Freemantle, but after refuelling there may be no time to go ashore.'

Such distances deadened my head, imagination unable to register the sight of endless sea. While Rose played with the knobs on his Dalton Computer – 'You can do anything with it, except fry eggs' – we others were supposed to think up questions. Wilcox, still wearing his hat, stopped coughing long enough to comment: 'This place seems at the end of our range, Skipper, and the wind may not play ball with us. Is there a fill-up station on the way?'

Bennett smiled. 'I've stared at the chart till I'm blue in the face and still haven't conjured one up. Nevertheless, I shouldn't worry if I were you. We do have auxiliary tanks to give a range of two thousand five hundred miles, so we shouldn't be forced to ditch on the way. I wish you'd suck some Zubes for that cough, though. When the trip's over we'll send you to Switzerland.'

'It's only 'flu, Skipper.'

Nash folded an old *Daily Mail* into his jacket pocket. 'And where's the juice coming from for the flight to Freemantle?'

'A ship will meet us in a convenient stretch of calm water.' He waved his stick so that no one could be certain where it was, and I couldn't be sure that he wasn't being sarcastic. 'All hands will set to with gusto, and stock up the tanks.'

The notion that we would be a flying petrol tank for over two thousand miles gave me a strange feeling in the stomach. 'Do we have a dummy run to see if we can get off with such a load?'

'We've got the longest runway in the world, Adcock, a thousand miles, if the sea's calm enough. Let me worry about that. I've worked things out, never you fear.'

'It's safer to chug along with an extra ton or two of petrol than carry the same in depth-charges,' Rose said to me as he opened a stubby tin of Flowerdew's Cut Golden Bar and refilled his pipe. He smoked contentedly, but to puff such twist in the same room as Wilcox seemed inconsiderate, though I don't suppose he would have coughed much less without it. Bennett advised him to sit by the open window, but he didn't bother, saying his cough was sure to go as soon as the old kite got above the clouds.

Appleyard, one of the gunners, wanted to know how much airborne time we'd need before reaching Freemantle. He had a cousin there. Rose nodded, the scarred side of his face towards the skipper: 'Thirty-eight hours, give or take a day or two!'

Bennett came out of his reverie. 'How long we stay at Kerguelen depends on all of you. Intelligent co-operation is what I want, like in the good old days. We're a bit rusty, but we'll shine up. As captain of this enterprise – and God help me with such a shower – even I may have to lend a hand when it comes to picking up the goods at Kerguelen.'

'What goods?'

'That's between me and the company. Till we get on board, it's classified gen.'

53

I asked if there was a W/T met. station on the island.

'You'll be briefed on that later. But the short answer is no.'

'We'll hope for calm weather,' Rose said, 'and a good anchorage.'

'I'll pray fervently for both,' said Nash.

It all sounded, Appleyard observed, that a few prayers might not be out of order.

'Prayers never did an air gunner any harm,' Bennett said. 'As for myself, I muttered a quick one to the old God every time I had to get you lot off the ground. And gave special thanks when I got back.'

Armatage, another gunner, sat upright in the heavily upholstered chair. He had fair wavy hair and a handlebar moustache, as if he had always hoped to be taken from a distance for a pilot or navigator, which would at least have given a short burst of glory before whoever it was got close enough to see the badge on his battledress. He had worked in the office of an insurance company, but his spare time was given to running a youth club from which he led expeditions across Dartmoor at Easter 'when conditions can be fair to Arctic' and summer 'when it wasn't so good either.' Nash told me he had lost his job after something he'd done had got into the newspapers.

'Whoever thought up this stunt must have been round the bend,' he shouted. 'If I don't do a bunk it's only because I'm half way up the zig-zags already.' Then he laughed, a bray without humour, and lay back with irritation that would not let him say more.

Maybe he had spoken for more than himself, but before anyone could say so Bennett put in that if he lacked moral fibre he had better go now, and that if he didn't he had better shut up.

'He was often like that,' Rose said. 'Don't you remember?'

'Too bloody well,' said Nash.

'He was all right at the first upshot of flak, though.'

54

Armatage didn't answer.

'In view of the circumstances,' Bennett said, 'you can say goodbye to any celebratory booze-up, or aircrew hanky-panky the night before we go on board for take-off. Have your party, if you must, but make it at least twenty-four hours prior to getting your clearance chits signed from this hotel. In which case I might join you. You'll collect more than soldiers' pay when this operation is over, and you can go to pieces then if you care to. But for the trip, you'll be like teetotal parsons – if they ever existed – keeping an eye on each other to make sure there's no flouting that one. I want no hymn singing, though, on your part, nor any need for the riot act to be read on mine. We've got a tricky job, I don't mind telling you, and we want to come through success-fully. Once we're airborne we'll fall into our allotted places, even Mr Adcock, who hasn't flown with us before, so that after a few hours up top it'll seem as if we've never had a break from the last time we were together. Twenty hours is a long run, and I won't say that anybody caught slipping into the land of nod will be thrown overboard; but I will frown severely, and he might get his head knocked off. As for you gunners, you won't be playing poker in the galley, either. Nash will see to that. You'll keep your eyes peeled, and eat carrot-pudding in case any strange or otherwise unexplainable object comes into view. I want as sharp a lookout as for JU88s when flying up Happy Valley or across Biscay. Close to the Islands, the more you might have to do in the gunnery line, and when we land it'll be sleeves rolled up for everyone.'

The sooner we eight luminaries were into the wide blue yonder the better; then at least I would have no further illusions about being followed. I wondered whether I was the only one, and though we were as friendly as a crew should be there seemed no sane opening for me to broach the matter. If my fears reached Bennett he might throw me off the job as unsuitable, especially if the work we were about to undertake was as legitimate as he made out.

55

15

~~~

In a ship without guns there was a superfluity of gunners. The pilot, the navigator, the flight-engineer and the wireless operator had well-defined tasks, but so many gunners worried me – though no one else seemed perturbed. Perhaps they assumed that having filled such a role during the war, 'gunner' was now an identification tag, no more than a badge stitched under the lapel of jacket or wind-cheater.

All of us belonged to a crew in which no member could claim more importance than the next, but gunners were in the majority, which was valid only if they were to be employed as look-outs, or loaders, or stewards, or riggers, or bowmen, or whatever work Bennett was to find necessary. In which case it was easy to explain their presence.

The existence of each crew member had to be individually acknowledged. Bennett talked to Rose about routes and possible wind vectors, cloud ceilings and departure times, such a parley between pilot and navigator being long and involved. With the flight-engineer he broached engine performances and miles per gallon: how long the flying boat could stay in the air on a given quantity of fuel. Nash, as supercargo in charge of supplies and their loading, had to go over details of tool-stowage and survival rations, in case an accident should keep us on sub-Antarctic terrain, or if the flying boat alighted far from land and we had to wait for rescue by a passing ship. Distances were vast, and emptiness complete. Precautions had to be taken.

Away from air or sea lanes, the trip was exploratory, which was why we would collect a year's pay for a bare two months. The earth would turn sixty-one times on its axis and if, as the Bible says, life is seventy years long, what difference will it make whether the pole-axe falls at seventy years and four months or seventy years and two months? The contract was indeed generous, and whoever devised such terms put high value on sixty-one days, or 1,464 hours or 87,840 minutes. And which of the 5,270,400 seconds would justify the payment of what all of us took to be danger money? Sixty-one days sounded more sober as a period of employment, less perilous yet demanding a full sense of responsibility while living through the heaviest that were obviously yet to come.

And beyond the end of two full moons there was nothing. A medieval sailor thought he might fall off the world. So would I when our time ran out. Visibility had closed in regarding the future, allowing me to see no more than a day ahead in those two months which might contain the moment of my death. It was better to be blind and unfeeling than think too far in front, though after Bennett had said what he expected by way of duty I was able to see a picture of the flying boat lifting, and setting course towards Kerguelen.

'I tried to get eleven in the crew,' he said, 'but I was over-ruled in the matter and told to manage with eight. A hendecker – that is to say, eleven – would have given us an extra pilot, navigator, and wireless operator. To keep awake for twenty hours is asking a lot.'

Having done fourteen-hour watches, I told him I could cope, at which he said that no doubt all of us would do our duty. He sat so that he could stretch his legs and rest both feet on a corner of his desk. His worn face showed the battered spirit of a man at the end of a journey from which he had barely escaped with life and sanity, rather than the commander of an expedition about to depart and whose purpose none of us could understand. Perhaps the burden weighed so heavily on him because he was not so clear about it himself.

The deeply fixed lines down his face hadn't been so

obvious ten days ago. I waited, thinking he would never talk again, wondering whether I ought not to go out of the room. On the table was a fold-out stand of photographs, with a woman in the middle panel and a child on either side. She was dark-haired, with delicately lidded eyes and a sad smile, and a hand at her face as if to stop her long hair obscuring it. The children were ten or twelve years old, a boy and a girl on whom Bennett also gazed, though I don't think he saw them as clearly as he wanted to.

'I suppose now the gunners have arrived we'll be taking off, Skipper?'

He reached for a pencil, spoke after a while, turning the leaves of a springbound notebook. 'They're my old crew right enough, but I get to thinking they're here to make sure we don't go north instead of east. They had a stopover in London, which may have put a different picture into their minds.'

'Why should we want to go north instead of east?'

He gripped the notebook to prevent his hands trembling. 'We might. Then again, we might not. After Kerguelen, no radio stations en route. Nothing but empty sea. At Free-mantle the owners' representatives are waiting. We hand over the cargo we picked up. That's the picture. All arranged and agreed to, and the gunners are on board from take-off to see that we follow the plan and that none of it goes according to my wayward geographical proclivities. Our orders must coincide, Adcock.'

I lit a cigarette, wondering what the hell he meant. 'Don't you want the trip to go right?' – speaking not because I wanted to, or even out of any particular interest in his puzzling talk, but because my senses told me that it was expected. I was never one to recognize the crucial moment when it was obscured by a morass of deception. I should have demanded that he cut the crap and tell me what the stunt was all about.

But he floated back unchallenged into the great Bennett silence, leaving me to mull on the fact that he had only wished for a double crew on the flight deck so that we would then outnumber the gunners. With a single crew, working every minute and fighting to keep awake, the gunners would have no difficulty in keeping us under observation. 'Perhaps they were sent to protect us from something else,' I suggested.

He wanted to find out whether I was wholly on his side. If so, then it was five against three, supposing we could count on Nash; but if not, he would be lumbered with the problem of having only four of us to four of them.

'Both,' he answered. 'How far can you reach with the 1154 transmitter, Adcock?'

No distance could be guaranteed. Depended on your luck. One night I worked a Lancastrian from fifteen hundred miles away. His signals were faint but audible. I brought him right across the Dutch East Indies.

'And if we get up to eighteen thousand feet?'

Flukes were possible, sometimes prevalent, mostly out of the question. I didn't like giving figures. He craved them, however. 'Let's say, five hundred during the day, and twelve hundred at night. I'll do what I can.'

He wanted to buy something, and demanded that I sell, so I did in order to give him ease of mind. I could have been right, after all. But there seemed something lunatic about the conversation: he'd been familiar with my transmitter for ten years and knew exactly what it could and could not do. He threw the pad and pencil on the table and rubbed his hands. 'That's all I need. I don't want you to be God and promise me the earth. You'll have the usual three frequencies, unless I tell you otherwise.' I took out my notebook, though knowing them well. 'Listen on 500 as much as practicable, except when I put you on 6500 during the day and 3805 as soon as it gets dark. But as far as the gunners are concerned, you'll be on 500. They're very particular about safety. Some bloody clot said that the Sparks should always be listening out on 500. But there'll be no sending, Adcock. Keep your claws away from that tapper, unless and until I say so; but listen all the time and take down anything interesting. Swivel the knob every few minutes and let me know of anything else. Get what bearings you can with the loop aerial to help with the navigation. Leave the half-convergency business to Rose. He's used to that.'

I was uneasy about not being able to send. Every operator likes a bit of tap-chat with passing ships or planes, or with shore stations.

'I'll tell you when it's necessary. If you send, and somebody gets a bearing on us, it could put us in peril. You understand, Adcock?'

'Why is that?'

'Take my word for it. There may be some rum types roaming around the area we're going to. You never can tell. So no sending. We want to spend our hard earned money on Pleasure Island, not Devil's Island, don't we?'

I agreed that we did.

'You're our ears, our intelligence section. So listen, and keep your hands off that key. With you bloody operators it's like playing with yourself, but resist it. Everything you hear is important. Whatever little squeak comes into your ken, I want to know about it.'

The assignment was peculiar, yet such orders had more excitement than orthodox instructions. I was about to ask for how long they would apply, when he said: 'I assume that I have your absolute trust, Adcock?'

The question might have been tainted with insult to a certified and experienced wireless officer, young though I might be in comparison to the rest of the crew. If I had known myself to be untrustworthy, would I have given him an answer? Yet who could be certain until a crisis proved it one way or the other? I felt the same query going through him. He seemed burdened by such anxiety that, though it was automatic that he have my loyalty, it was far from guaranteed that he had my confidence. Yet anxiety seemed his normal condition, and because I did not want it to increase, I shook his hand when he stood up. The flesh was like that of a lizard, where it had previously been warm and moist. I supposed he had been through the same procedure with the others.

Shaking hands is often a competition to see who can crush most fingers. I've never liked the practice. There are those who assume that afterwards they won't see you again, and maim your fingers to give you something to remember them by. Others, who have already been caught out, slide their hand immediately away. Or they dread touching either man or woman, fearing strangers as much as they distrust themselves. There's no sincerity in it.

Hand-shaking is a language whose messages are peculiar to the moment, and Bennett indicated by his that he wanted to rely on me. Yet how could he expect such loyalty when he would not say why it was needed? If I knew what was in his mind I might have been sincere in my agreement to do more than the duty I was paid for. The text of my returned hand-shake must have been understood, however. He tapped the photo-triptych of his family, maybe by accident, so that I wondered if he had indicated it to the others on their separate briefings. I nodded, my hand on the doorknob.

'I'm going to need your loyalty above that of everyone else, Adcock. I hope you understand.'

There's a mock-solemn, patronizing quality about those who continually speak your name when talking to you. I don't like it. They look upon you as a child, and have an unjustified feeling of their own significance. Yet Bennett seemed less of the type. Whether his hands trembled from too much drink (the bottle was again half empty) or from sleeplessness, or from fear of something he would rather die than tell, I couldn't say. It seemed an act of mercy rather than friendship to affirm, before opening the door: 'I'll do all I can.'

Such candour, while helpful to him, got me nowhere. My curiosity was at its highest, but if I wanted to satisfy it I would have to wait till such time as I, and maybe the rest of us, became a victim to whatever was intent on destroying

61

him – because when, in an aircraft flying at eighteen thousand feet above the ocean, the captain discovers himself beset by enemies from within or without, then surely those foes – whoever and whatever they might be – become equally dedicated to the destruction of everyone else who has the misfortune to be on board with him. Bennett wanted to be the master of his own destiny, but I questioned the validity of this desire to involve me in any way.

A dream-serial played while I slept off the food and drink. A flying boat was hundreds of miles out, with but two of its four engines working. Instead of a normal aircraft interior there were the domestic furnishings of an ordinary house. There was no fuel left, and the flying boat came down on a rough sea and began to disintegrate. Waves spun and splashed with malevolence over the windscreen. When the perspex panels fell away I woke from the horrors.

Nash banged from next door: 'You all right, Sparks?'

16

❦

Rose sat in the smoking room, reading a copy of *Flight Magazine*, legs straight out as if 'don't disturb' was printed on the soles of both shoes. The high leather armchair in the shade of the aspidistra hid most of his body, and he was so engrossed in whatever piece of technical exposé had taken his fancy that I could hardly believe he was alive. He seemed in a state of repose that would be impossible to disturb, as if blessed with a power of automatic detachment that had been with him since childhood; and because the devastation of the scar was turned away from me, I saw him as if before his accident. Just as a person who has lost an arm eventually finds more strength than he originally had in the two together, so perhaps the livid corrugation of bone and flesh had in some compensatory way beautified the side I looked at and made it more perfect than if the other part had never been injured. Yet the boyishness that would stay even if he lived to be a hundred was only marred by a painful sensitivity which made his head too big for his body.

I had decided to tackle him about the real nature of our trip in the hope that his replies would at least indicate the direction in which any further questions ought to point. As chief mate, he was not exactly matey; but if he told me to vanish or get dive-bombed I would leave him alone.

A navigator, like others of the aerial fraternity, was jealous of his guild-secrets even when they were obsolescent, or sufficiently simplified that they could be passed on without revelation. I felt the same about my own trade. Questioned by an outsider, I would tell nothing because, unless to save life, my time would be wasted. Those who asked from friendliness might learn that I sat at a table sending and receiving messages in morse code; but that was all.

The roles of aircrew sometimes overlapped, but the fundamental part of each skill could not be passed on. If such details were handed over it was only to give the illusion that we were capable of sharing secrets, which built up our comradeship for the day when, as crew members, we would care for each other and the plane. If Rose was party to any secret with Bennett as to the true purpose of our expedition, would he be able to unshackle these principles sufficiently to tell me something?

There was no saying, but private communication between one crew member and the next would be impossible once we were airborne. To hugger-mugger in hole or corner would stink of conspiracy. Cool and intelligible words must go via the intercom, and any others must be kept healthily suppressed. Working as an eighth part of the common voice, a good crew has no use for secrecy.

I had very much wanted to believe in the neat package of a single task for one and all, as I looked at the flying boat the previous evening, seeing it as a refuge that I had spent a lifetime looking for, floating on the placid water like a white mansion under the moon, four engines in their sturdy cowlings, wings stretching as if they might grow to span the whole town, and the steeply sloping hull which, if it weren't for the wings, would be a galleon waiting for its pirate crew.

The flying boat showed only its registration sign, and I wondered what true colours it would be under when on the move, what flash should decorate its tailplane. Probably a constellation of blue stars on a white background, Ursa Major, or the buckle of Orion's Belt, or the seven visible stars of the Pleiades. Each crew member could no doubt stamp his individual badge on the *Aldebaran* according to how he defined the pattern of his own life.

The pennant would have been harmless, even humorous, because trust bound us together when we played cards and drank in the bar or lounge of the hotel, analysing endlessly some bombing operation over Europe during the war. In the space of a few days we had time to observe all mannerisms, assess each other's virtues, weigh up generosities and catch flickers of deviousness or diffidence with which we would have to live come what may. Our bodies and mortal souls depended on each man's inner emblem, and there was no way of knowing what they portended because all were buried under the common denominator of crew-like characteristics. We were to earn our money, and afterwards flee to the eight points of the compass. As long as we didn't talk about the purpose of the journey, we were content.

But there was little else that I wanted to discuss, and on wondering how I could open the matter with Rose I felt strongly that the journey had little interest for him. When he and the others had been told to bomb Hamburg or Frankfurt or Essen, they asked no questions. So it was now. At take-off they would get their fingers out and do their

64

stuff. Compared to the war it was a piece of cake. In view of which, it did not matter that, once airborne, there would be no possibility of private conversation. Being a prisoner of my own small private life, I was a perfect specimen for the job I had stumbled into by my senseless whistling of morse code in a London pub.

I sat opposite Rose. 'There's something I want to ask.'

He didn't look up. His arm squeaked along the leather from the pressure of turning the page. 'What about?'

'A simple question.'

He flipped another page, and cigarette ash fell onto the worn carpet. 'One of the cheapest planes you can buy today is an Auster. I flew one once. A strong wind almost pushed me backwards.'

I fetched an ashtray from the table laden with old magazines. 'What's that star called at the top left-hand corner of the Square of Pegasus?'

'Alpheratz. Why?'

'The word came to me in a dream. I knew it was the name of a star, but couldn't place it till I looked it up.'

He put the magazine on his knee. 'Why Alpheratz?'

'Because that's what all eight of us are: Alpha Rats – stuck in the front line, and numbered for this stunt of Bennett's that none of us knows anything about. What are we going to pick up at the Kerguelen Islands? I think you know.'

He hadn't navigated for two years but, after giving up his tramp around the country, had a desk job with Little Island Air Lines, until bankruptcy was fended off by amalgamation – and his own redundancy. A navigator has to work every day, otherwise he might lose his way through sight-reduction tables and relinquish that sixth sense by which, on long flights over the sea, he looks at the waves and knows his drift almost by instinct. Bennett must have pondered the issue, but he was God in his flying boat, and all was right in Heaven, so who could tell what he thought?

'There are nearly five thousand stars in the heavens,'

Rose said, 'which are visible to the naked eye, so why choose Alpheratz?'

'Because,' I said, 'Alpheratz chose me – and the rest of us.'

'Not a very bright star,' he observed. 'You're not a particularly bright Sparks, either, if you ask me.'

'Nash thought it bright enough. We laughed about it last night over a couple of bottles of Alphen Red. He said this trip was a matter of life and death eight times over, and that even if we did find the island, and I suppose we actually might, with a shit-hot navigator like you, the sea's likely to be so jumped-up there'll be no hope of landing without getting the whole rig smashed. And if we do land, we might never find whatever it is. And even if we do, who knows whether we'll be able to refuel, especially if, in the time it's taken to find what we're looking for, the weather worsens as it's likely to do in those latitudes. Because you know as well as I do, Rose, that forecasting is non-existent, as are navigational facilities, and the scarcity of radio stations is positively bloody horrifying. Now I don't mind all this. It's insane, I know, but I signed up for a taste of adventure so I'm prepared to have a go and do my bit at the wireless. But I would like to know what I'm risking my neck for.'

I tried to sound amiable, but he went nonchalantly back to his reading as if I were a rat that had eaten its way out of his Dalton computer with a bit of topographical map in its mouth. I stood so as to see the devastated side of his face, and made sure he knew it. If I had stayed immobile there would have been no bust up. Silence and stillness were good for both, the way things were going. But the contemptuous way he ignored me, and allowed his fingers to search blindly for the top right corner of the magazine before turning the page, enraged me. He was a better actor than a navigator, unless he really had forgotten my existence.

I snatched the magazine and threw it towards the door: 'Listen, Scarface, I asked a question. Either answer, or give a fair reason why you can't.'

The good part of his face turned white. I had gone too far, but because of his contempt he couldn't say so. He stood, and picked up the magazine: 'Last night I dreamed I was pissing blood, but it was sheer happiness compared to dealing with a bod like you. What we're going to Kerguelen for is no concern of yours. We're looking for harbours that future cruise ships will be able to anchor in with a fair degree of safety. That's all I know, and all I want to know. What do you imagine we're looking for, for Pete's sake? If we hadn't had to wait so long you wouldn't suspect anything. Look up your callsigns, get familiar with the frequencies, or calculate a few skip distances – or whatever you do these days. I suppose this South African wine's too potent for a head like yours. Can't take the stuff myself. As for my scar, I don't suppose I can object to you using it as an identifying mark, but be careful you don't attach a moral stigma to it. That would be unjust, and injustice is something that might make me lose my temper.'

I regretted letting go of mine. He lifted the magazine, then lowered it: 'You know how I got this scar? It was no accident. Somebody tried to kill me because he thought I'd betrayed him. I used to think more of the world than I do now.'

He held out his hand, and I was glad to accept that he knew nothing I didn't know. Too cowardly to tackle the pilot, I had gone for the navigator, and discovered he was better than I thought.

'I'm sorry, Rose.'

He was back behind his magazine.

But as I walked down the stairs I still wasn't satisfied. I never was, and never would be. Only the final death-shave, that I wouldn't wake up to know about, would cure me. Rose had brought up the concept of morality with regard to his disfigurement, and I wished he hadn't because from then on the word gripped me and wouldn't let go.

67

17

ȣɔɔɔ

With a dozen of beer on the table, and two of Voortrekker's Gin from which the corks were lost as soon as extracted, Nash opted for the Lancaster because of its range and bomb load. Except for the absence of a belly-gun, there wasn't much to gripe about by way of armament. A. V. Roe did a good job when they turned up with the Lanc, a kite that generally got through, and often came back. You had to say that for it.

Wilcox, in spite of his coughing, shouted him to a standstill. Too many had exploded in mid-air, or piled up on the runway after seven or eight poor buggers had slogged six hundred miles to get back. Inside the plane you sweated blood crawling over the bomb bays from one part to another. He filled his glass, foaming the table. His cough was no trouble while he drank a pint.

Discussing the best plane of the war was like talking about the merits of Milltown United as against those of Weathersfield Wednesday, but I placed my bet on the Spitfire. Without the Spit there'd have been no Lancaster. We would have been beaten into the ground. To see a Spit doing aerobatics was something never forgotten. The sight was like recalling a good dream.

'Good dreams are few and far between,' Appleyard said.

'Especially wet ones,' said Bull.

'The sky was its background,' I went on. 'Man and machine were wedded to each other, the highest achievement of technique and art! What more could you want?'

'Bloody hellfire!' Rose exclaimed.

'Schoolboy crap.' Nash went on to say that I should get some in. He was in Baghdad before I was in my Dad's bag. All the old laughter clattered out.

'Butcher Harris should be living at this hour,' Rose said.

Bennett looked from around the corner of the L-shaped room: 'He is, and not far from here, either.'

'Let's drink to him, then.' Nash held up his mug of gin: 'Here's to the best bloody leader anybody ever had.' There were grumbles from his gunners, who were too drunk to say anything sensible. Wilcox came out in favour of the Sunderland, which beat the U-boats. 'Britain would have starved to death without it.'

Bull called that he should tell that to the navy.

'Apart from which' – Wilcox's coughing sounded as if his chest was full of inmates trying to get out of a jail that had caught fire – 'the Sunderland was the most beautiful flying boat that ever was, and a treat to work on, as everybody knows. There was space, and two of each for the crew.'

'Sometimes,' said Nash.

'The lovely old bag was big enough to live in.' Wilcox said he would make a house out of one, fly to another place when he got browned-off, which would be pretty often, you can bet.

Appleyard staggered out to be sick, and by the time he came back the laughs had turned to jeers at Wilcox's idea. The black waiter brought a dozen more bottles. Armatage denied the supremacy of the Lancaster, and gave his vote to the Spitfire. There were tears on his cheeks – or was it because his spilt beer had ricocheted from the table? The good old Spitfire saved the best country in the world from the iron heel of Germany. It bloody had – say what you like. If they hadn't kicked the living shit out of the Messerschmitts at the Battle of Britain, where would we have been today, mate, eh?

Maybe the Spitfire wasn't the most renowned plane of the war, I said, and that if given time to consider the matter at leisure – as I had while staring at the beer label and sending its words out in morse – I would decide that the Sunderland qualified for that honour. This led us to compare the performance data of the Sunderland with the vital statistics of the Lancaster, and from that point, all things being equal, we went on to correlate the relative sizes of the three planes and, knowing that the Spitfire was the smallest, and the Sunderland the biggest, embarked on a passionate discussion as to how many Spitfires could be parked on the wings of a Sunderland.

Out came pencils and bits of paper. The number increased as more gin was swilled and beer put back. In our cooked brains even the exact wingspan of the Sunderland wasn't known, never mind the distance from leading edge to aileron. Yet it did not matter, because the Sunderland seemed to grow into the size of the earth itself, and what had peeled off from the original discussion as a technical dispute now became metaphysical. If you folded the wings of Spitfires and packed them close, they would make a platform for other folded Spitfires to be parked on top, and so on, and so on, thus building a tower of aircraft until you reached heaven or the structure capsized and sank without trace.

The sombre picture brought on silence, until in the extended right-turning part of the L-shaped room where Bennett and Rose were having their own pre-flight drink or two, I heard the Skipper say: 'How do we go, Navigator?'

'In a straight line, Captain' – walking between two carpets.

'There's no such thing. It's either a fixed Mercator course, or the shortest distance on a Lambert Conformal. A rhumb line isn't the shortest distance. A Great Circle is, but can't be a straight course, now can it, Mr Rose?'

'Don't mix me up, Skipper.'

Bennett opened his box of imperfect Partagas cigars and slowly covered a specimen with white cigarette paper. 'A straight line is the longest distance. A curved line means less miles, but who steers a curved line? And who goes the shortest way? The earth is a funny place when you want to get from point to point. Does your life from cradle to coffin go on a rhumb line or a great circle? Both have advantages.

A rhumb line uses more fuel, but a great circle gets you there sooner. A rhumb line is less trouble: you set course and arrive at a certain time, providing there's no wind, which there always is. On the other hand, a great circle needs more planning, as well as work to make sure you stick to it. It's six of one and half a dozen of the other, I'm afraid, because on either system you're at the mercy of malign tides and tricky winds, and the homely pull of the earth.'

'I'll make your course straight enough to do a great circle,' Rose slurred, 'which is the best of both systems. Or the best of this one, and that's a fact – if facts are needed.'

'They are,' Bennett said. 'Believe you me.'

'I'll work out the convergency angle, and calculate the different distances.'

'You've been to the right school. The only bogey will be the weather.' Leaning over the table to unroll his chart, Bennett splashed whisky across the southern half of Madagascar. 'Whether it's summertime or not in that land of glaciers and fjords, the weather is the thing. And the compass needle swings fifty degrees out of true.'

Rose turned his face away. 'The left hand as usual won't know what the right hand is doing.'

'Does it ever? It's immaterial.' Bennett poured whisky for his navigator, and more for himself. 'Only the planispherical stars will give anything like true direction, if they can be seen. And only the configurated scratchmarks of land the actual position, providing it can be found.'

'If only the earth wasn't round,' said Rose. 'How simple life would be! I'd never think about the end, if there was a danger of falling off the edge.'

'You're alive as long as you don't fear dying,' Bennett told him. 'Life is full when you aren't aware of spending your strength freely and yet are doing so. You get the best out of life when you act knowingly, and still don't know. Being close to revelation is never close enough, though all of us were near it when candle flames burned bright over a city in the process of devastation. In the total trips more than six hundred tons of bombs were unloaded, making nearly a hundred tons for each crew member. The Rubble Churners. The Fire Raisers. The Second Fronters. God's appointed Wrath.'

'There is no guilt where I come from,' said Rose. 'The Knights of the Apocalypse rode in squadrons of Lancasters to excoriate evildoers. I've seen too many perfect knights go down to feel pity for those on the ground.'

'A thousand Lincolns were being prepared,' Bennett said, 'to create a desert from a former empire and call it quits.'

'What the world's come to's no business of mine,' said Rose. 'The world made me what I am.'

'I rather think it was your parents,' said Bennett. 'When you begin to scratch, you itch. I'm drunk, Rose, and don't like it. The life force under the skin crawls and irritates. In the gap between moments you mindlessly scratch, and unwanted words are born. You resent the disturbance that has no name. Where it comes from you neither know nor care, but because you stare and don't shout doesn't mean its hooks aren't there. All in all, I'd like to stick a label on that door that opens onto the maelstrom. I hope the lock's secure.'

'So do I,' said Rose.

Wilcox built up the empties till his tower was a foot from the ceiling. His hand shook on lifting a full glass to drink, but when he set a bottle one stage higher his grip was steady and eye accurate, a liverish tongue pressed into acquiescence by his teeth to stop the coughs breaking.

The structure collapsed, and we each caught an armful without any bottle cracking, though it seemed strange that our laughter didn't shatter one or two. A clergyman and his wife, a red-faced farmer, and an old English colonel had already evacuated themselves from such aircrew behaviour. Nash remarked that it felt like the pre-ops mood in the worst days at the end of 1943, when kites were dropping out of the sky like coffins. You didn't even have the heart to go into the bog for a last wank before take-off, superstitious that it might be the last. This over-loud recollection drove the final spectator into the lobby.

Beyond the point of no return, the waiter came with a bucket to empty the ashtrays. He put six more bottles on the table. Bull said it was his turn to pay, and fell down unconscious, clutching the money. Nash thought we had better make our final choices, and I told him I now plonked for the Lancaster, but how final is final?

'More final than you think.' Wilcox looked as if he ought to know. 'The die is cast. I'll take the Sunny Sunderland.'

Which left Nash with the Spitfire. 'I'm the tallest, so get the smallest. Always the bloody same.'

We sat on the stairs singing: 'One step forward, two steps back', a bitter kind of boozy refrain, which set us grabbing ankles to stop further progress up or down. But we got to our doors and said goodnight. There's a purpose in hilarity. We were in it together, bespoke tragedians stitching our lives like figures dangling in a paperchain. But in that split second before oblivion I wondered what it was that we were in.

18

⚭

Because the oil supply to the port inner engine was giving trouble, it was not until two mornings later that we sat on either side of the motorboat to go on board for departure. Even so, we wouldn't be airborne for twenty-four hours, till a favourable weather front moved in to see us off.

I felt as pasty as the others looked, a mush-breakfast of coffee and buns like mortar in my stomach. Nash was so stricken by a fit of belching that at one splintering emission Appleyard commented that if he carried on like that he'd come apart at the seams.

Choppy water was like the shifting tiles of a grey roof. I had never been seasick, but felt there was no point in worrying about what might not come. I suppose we all thought the same. 'If it gets rough, hard-tack will be on the cards,' said Wilcox.

Bennett wore an overcoat, an airforce type cap and leather gloves. 'You'll organize the mess and serve proper meals, even if you've as many sealegs to get used to as a centipede.' Noticing that Bull shivered in the wind, he told him that without a jacket he was improperly dressed, a phrase we found quaint, under the circumstances. 'You didn't think you'd need one? On this trip you're not only paid to do as I tell you, but to think for yourself as well, when necessary. Anyone who can't work that kind of balancing trick won't be much good to himself or others.'

Bull did not need a sermon to point out his mistake. He winced at the stricture, and spat into the water. A red band beyond the harbour showed the sun, up but not apparent. An area of cloud fused into pink, then merged with a seam of muddy grey. We turned an arm of the inner mole, and were covered with spray as the boat winged from side to side. The horizon was cut from view by the white port-holed flank of the flying boat rising above the lap of water, and Wilcox interrupted his early morning cough to say that you couldn't go on board without feeling a lift at the bottom of the stomach. 'Every time, it's as if you've never been on before.'

Appleyard likened the experience to a woman he hadn't seen for a while. 'I might not be expecting to go to bed with her, but I'm happy to be close, all the same.'

Sun broke up the rolls of cloud, and Bull smiled at its warmth, out of the hump into which the skipper had put him. 'Dropped a clanger, didn't you?' Nash said in a low voice.

'I often do,' Bull answered. 'Law and Admin's a bit strong on this trip, though, ain't it?'

The boat went under the chill of the starboard wing. 'It's going to be a hard one,' Nash said, 'that's why.'

A gull swung by the float and looked in at the hatchway, as if knowing that our twenty-five tonner, on coming to life, would lift to heights it could never attain. Or was it scouting for choice leftovers? 'He's more like the bloody adjutant than the old skipper,' Bull grumbled. 'I only came for a good time.'

'You'll end up with a good dose, the way you've been going on.'

When he borrowed money from each of us we couldn't understand how he had spent up so quickly, till he said he'd been and found a nice black woman to pass the time with. We accused him of shooting a line, because you couldn't do such a thing in this country. But Nash, who knew better, called in disgust: 'He'd even shag an oak tree felled by lightning.'

Our pinnace nosed under the wing towards the tail, high out of the water. We were going a circle, as if Bennett wanted the man at the tiller to give us a last view until disembarking at Kerguelen. The bird caught the wind and came round again, button-eyes staring side-on at floats, hull, stern, wings and engines as if reconnoitring every plate and rivet on the mindless assumption that sooner or later an explanation would appear as to what connection the *Aldebaran* had to earth and sky, thus releasing the gull to fly away with curiosity satisfied. When the bird alighted on the cowling of the inner port engine, Bennett said: 'Get it, Nash. But don't sink the bloody ship!'

As we swung for the door Nash held a pistol at arm's length for a steady aim. The crack disturbed a feather of the gull's head, causing it to lift, roll along the wing then, apparently, recover and fly away. 'Just as well you missed.'

'Scared it, at least.'

'Can't have it shitting all over the paintwork,' Armatage

75

said. 'Shit from a white gull peels it off. Why is the shit of a white gull black?'

The boat bounced against the rubber tyres and Wilcox, with a final landbound fit of coughing, leapt in through the hatch. 'Because they eat black puddings,' Bull said.

'They don't have 'em in these parts,' said Appleyard.

'They do,' Bull grinned, 'and they're lovely.'

Bennett counted us in, the pinnace held firm by Appleyard's knots. Conscious that the holiday was at an end, I went over. We were on watch from now on. Duty was the word, and work our pastime. He called for all hands to get in the kit and last remaining stores. We were sweating. Armatage threw each piece into my arms, and I passed it to Bull. We were allowed one holdall or case, which Nash promised would go over the side if we developed a weight problem. Wilcox smiled when everything was stowed. During the work he hadn't coughed. Bennett climbed the ladder to the flight deck as if going up a monkey-climber in the back garden. There was a smell of petrol and stale food, of diesel oil and seaweed, which gave the kite a maritime personality – dead though it yet was.

Fore and aft, from floor to ceiling, the cavern of the boat's body caused me to wonder why I had waited so long to make its acquaintance. No aeroplane I had been in was so spacious. The cubic footage daunted me as far as getting to know each cranny, yet the size promised comfort and security. The unmistakable smell of a service aircraft, together with the rise and fall of the boat, brought a whiff of sickness as I went up the aluminium ladder. To the right, behind the cockpit, Rose lifted the lid of his navigator's table to discover a loose screw in one of the hinges, and asked Wilcox, at his knobs and levers panel, to lend a screwdriver.

In my section was the graduated receiver scale and homely façade of the robust Marconi TR-1154/55. I drew my fingers over the multi-coloured transmitter clickstops and pressed the encased bakelite morse key. There was space to stand up and swing my arms, and with little movement get a view of Appleyard going back to shore on the pinnace to fetch last minute necessities from Shottermill on the quay. The sun already warmed the flying boat, and a gentle rocking under foot made the craft less formidable.

The sickness passed. The outside was a picture to be looked at from this convenient vehicle making its way over the water surface of the earth. 'Plenty of room to work in, eh?' Nash spoke as if he had been responsible for the design. 'What do you think of the old cloud-lorry?'

'People must have felt good producing a plane like this.' I mentioned loyalty and co-operation, not to say patriotism, and even a kind of love necessary to get such a huge aerodynamic construction assembled from scratch. Almost like building a cathedral. The workers must have felt pride when they saw it newly finished.

He was laughing. 'Pride? Loyalty? Most of them wanted to earn as much as they could in the shortest possible time while doing as little work as possible as slowly as they could get away with – though I suppose it wasn't that slow if they got a bonus on top of their pay-packets.'

A flying boat is built by people who guide each strut, float, stringer, tailplane, aileron and leading edge into place, I said. The anatomical diagram is adhered to as a blueprint for every component from a tiny screw to the whole engine. After launching, the flying boat retains the touch of human hands. Even if few felt that they were creating a work of beauty, it justified what I was trying to say – which Nash admitted might be true enough.

Salt water cradled the hull, reflecting an underwing float beyond each outer engine. Extended wings mirrored a shimmering charmed image below, both entities joined by the umbilical surface where one ended and the other began. Though anything utilitarian need not be beautiful, beauty must have its use, and of all man-made artefacts I grew in the next few days to feel that the flying boat was one of his most graceful endeavours, a spiritual extension with a practical purpose.

The sea is its resting place, and when the hull pushes against water during take-off, driven by the engines' powerful thrust, or first glances the surface of the sea when coming down, designed to alight at a landing speed of less than a hundred miles an hour, it will gracefully meet its natural plain, but in an agitated sea the thin hull can be broken, and take the flying boat to disaster.

Where we were going, no marked area or man-designed breakwater would protect us. A cape might give shelter from prevailing winds and undue current, but guarantees of a safe anchorage were few. Our chart delineated the coastline but told little of the interior except that mountains and glaciers almost filled it. A flying boat was the only aircraft which could visit that tortuous terrain. To put a landplane down, Bennett explained, would be like trying to do so in upper Norway; but for a flying boat to alight in a fjord with two or three sharp bends was, for the sort of flying he knew about, a piece of cake.

I sat at my radio desk and took the List of Radio Signals out of my briefcase. There were no fixed stations where we were going, nothing but a few ships perhaps on the great circle route between South Africa and Australia. I stacked the Wireless Operator's Handbook, a copy of the Weather Message Decode Book, the standard Wireless Equipment on Aircraft, and a folded tracing of the Admiralty Chart.

Rose's larger collection of printed matter – Sight Reduction Tables, Sight Log Book, Star Almanac, Star Atlas, and the Antarctic Pilot which contained a description of the Kerguelen Islands – found a place in his desk, on top of which he spread the Mercator chart which he had patiently constructed at the Driftwood Hotel. Then came his Dalton computer, a bubble sextant, a marine sextant, a stop watch, a chronometer, and an astro compass for finding true north no matter what the magnetic variation, providing the sun was visible. The reliance placed on the heavenly bodies to guide us to our destination was almost total, and I could only hope that cloud cover would not fox us for the whole trip.

Wilcox in his office, facing the panel of knobs and levers, was simulating a pre-flight check – we would not take off till the morning – while Nash and his gunners were getting in the drogues and upping anchor before closing the hatch for our trip around the roadstead. Bennett started the port inner, and I fixed on my headset, hearing him over the intercom: 'Taxi-ing. Stand by.'

'OK this side,' Nash said.

'Try your wireless, Sparks, but disconnect the antennae.'

I listened out on 500 kc/s and, hearing nothing, tapped Ks for ten seconds. The morse thumped loudly through the phones, its rhythm tingling both eardrums while my feet kept time. The gear functioned, all knobs set, dials and needles back in action. I reconnected the aerial and listened to ships calling the local coast station.

The boat was turning, four engines going. Once we were in the air and hundreds of miles out over the ocean, who would we contact in an emergency? The wireless was, after engines and airframe, our lifeline. On medium wave, where there was reasonable hope that a ship would hear, the range by morse might be something like three hundred miles, assuming whoever was listening had a good receiver, and that the ether was free from interference. Short wave was a different matter. Provided the correct wavelength was chosen, my patter could be audible for up to several thousand miles, but might not be picked up if the operator wasn't specifically tuned in. No station, either near or distant, had been advised to listen for my signals, and without prearranged schedules worked on short wave anything was possible and little was feasible.

But I would listen, and beam my direction-finding loop on any ship's message in case it contained his latitude and longitude, which would help our navigation should sun or stars not shine. Such a bearing might be useful in assessing

79

our most probable position, but few ships would be in the area, and radio functioned best when close to shipping routes and coastal stations. I would also intercept met. information from any source concerning the South Indian Ocean. Even if for areas hundreds of miles away, they could be evaluated, providing we deduced the direction of the weather, though by heading towards a climatically unpredictable part of the world the results would be dubious.

As the flying boat turned, I left my radio to look out of a porthole. The water was calm. Then I saw that the gull Nash had shot at must have fallen wounded, and then died, for it floated like a scrap of grey cloth under the wingtip. I regretted that the bird had been so wantonly used for target practice.

19

Bennett's humour was always based on the scent of danger. The smile was youthful, even boyish, and his grey eyes lightened. His face, before he spoke, indicated a pleasant person, and the only time he seemed halfway human was when he was at one with his crew. But so far there was little of that informal wartime 'Hi-di-hi!' answered by a 'Ho-di-ho!' instead of a salute. Perhaps the crew hadn't been long enough reunited, nor yet faced danger. An easygoing relationship had to be earned.

He stood by the flight deck ladder and addressed us as if we were a bomber crew about to set off for Germany. The wall maps were lacking, but these our memories supplied. 'Some of you know more than others about this operation. A few may have put two and two together already – to make sixes and sevens. Well, you can forget all that, and listen to the pukka gen.

'We take off in the morning, and that's official. There'll be no last night ashore. I don't want to lose you, especially after what you're going to hear. Our reason for going to the Kerguelen Islands is to recover a ton of gold coins deposited by a German submarine at the end of the war. They thought it a good hiding place, until such time as they could recover it. A supply ship or raider must have refuelled the sub which, having concealed its load on the island, never got back to base, but was sunk by a flying boat. The captain of the submarine was the only survivor, and I took the map and notes concerning the gold after we picked him up from the sea. He died, and went overboard. You all know this except Adcock, though none of you realized what I took from the dying captain.

'Some of you have been worried about whether we can ship enough fuel to reach the islands. We can, so forget it. And as for getting back, a steamer called the *Difda*, of some six hundred tons, will supply us with enough fuel to fly out. You may ask: why doesn't the same steamer recover the gold instead of us? Speed, is the answer. And secrecy. We can be away quickly, and take the goods to market before any other interested party will even know it's gone. In a week's time your valuable services should no longer be required – and we are carrying supplies to last a fortnight.

'The Kerguelen Islands lie on the Antarctic Convergence, where the northward moving cold water sinks below the warmer, which means uncertainty of weather. But we're going at the best time of the year, and there are sheltered places where we can get down without trouble. The nearest fjord to the gold is sufficiently sheltered to hide the *Aldebaran* like a fly in a jar of blackcurrant jam. The snowline lies at about 1500 feet. In January there's fog on one or two days, and the air temperature is between forty and fifty – bloody cold at night, but we have plenty of equipment for that.'

He rolled white paper around one of his fragile cigars

more, I thought, to help put on the expression of boredom he by no means felt, and also in order to discourage questions. 'Getting there is the most difficult part, but Rose is familiar with the navigational problems, and Adcock will do his stuff with thermionic valves and bits of wire when it comes to making contact with the refuelling ship. The islands are uninhabited, though the French have talked of setting up a scientific station – a fair way from where we'll be dropping anchor. We've got to get the gold out now because it may be more difficult later.'

He went into his stateroom, and there was a lowered atmosphere among us. What had started as a job had become an adventure with too many imponderables. We were going to a place of which there were no adequate maps, and no radio aids, nor even, as far as we knew, any other human beings. The only ships would be whaling vessels, said Nash, which were as rare in any case as spots on a film star's face. If we alighted in that desolation of glaciers and could not get off again, food supplies would be of prime importance. I felt wary, and daunted. 'I'm getting cold feet,' said Armatage, as we moved back to the galley.

'You'll be lucky if that's all you get,' Appleyard said in his quiet manner.

'A touch of the old L of M F?' Nash said. 'It'll pass. It always did. And if it doesn't, what's death? Just another blackout after a party.' The primus stoves were lit, and Nash rolled up his sleeves to produce mugs of soup, followed by bacon, omelettes and potatoes that Appleyard had peeled. There was plenty of bread, and during the meal a pot of water was boiled for tea. Armatage scraped his leftovers into a bucket: 'I wonder what we've let ourselves in for?'

'Stop binding,' said Nash. 'You're getting on people's nerves.'

I felt that one or two of us would like to back out, though we succeeded in hiding our misgivings. Slip through the hatch and swim. Drown if you must, rather than go on.

Don't, I told myself. We are committed, cocooned in lassitude. I fought paralysis by disputing its effect, point by point as if I were a lawyer rather than a radio operator. But the pall would not go away. I chatted with Nash, however, in as cheerful a mood as I was ever in.

20

When going to see his mother, Bennett would nurse his cigar for twenty-five miles of the road. She was turning senile, and called him by his father's name. He stepped on that one: a monolithic skipper of the skies who believes in the future can't afford such memories when boning up for a long stint over the ocean. A two-and-a-half-thousand mile track from all shipping routes could, by an error of one degree on either side, miss the island entirely, in spite of its size, and cause the flying boat to crash through lack of fuel, or loom around the Antarctic for eternity like a ghostly ship of old.

'Unless we get good astro fixes,' he told Nash, who saw no reason not to pass on such details which gratuitously came his way, 'we're heading for a watery grave. A cold one. If we can't get angles on the stars, we'll have to fly low to calculate drift readings for dead reckoning. We'll get a little help from the radio. But nothing is as certain as the stars.'

He sweated at the risk, shaking more at such slender chances than he ever had flying through Trojan walls of flak towards Essen or Berlin. They'd ship enough fuel, but too much circling to find the bay and they might run out. Impossible to row those last few miles. He erased the figures and worked them through again. When did not success depend on navigation? Rose was the best, a shining asset to this shower of a crew. If God looks kindly down, we'll be rich. If he doesn't, it's Job's boils for the lot of us, and cold water for our coffin.

He felt the shock of the optimist who realizes that he has so far survived only by luck. But he did not then become pessimistic. The efficacy of calculations may not always reassure, but they held back mortal damage. Faith in mechanical reliability kept hope in an airtight capsule, like the vacuum of a barometer which enables the needle to show height above the earth when air acts on it. Years of operational flying shifted pessimism sufficiently for him to watch the smoke from his cigar roll over his coloured map of the southern hemisphere.

A Mercator sheet of the South West Approaches would have been overprinted with the purple and green and blue mesh of the Loran grid, which made pinpointing a piece of cake, so that the spot in the north Atlantic where the sub had gone down was fixed for ever to within a mile or two. We would be safer if we had at least Consol to help, Nash my boy, but only the busy parts of the world are covered. Down here you have to pray to the heavenly bodies.

We saw them struggling in the oil, Nash said, as we were about to set course for home: 'No hope, poor bastards.' If their gunners had been better we'd have been the ones to drink oily water. 'I feel like raking 'em, Skipper. They do it to our chaps.' Between thought and word was no space to Nash, but the route from word to deed followed zig-zags.

Bennett knew his chief gunner's malady: 'Have a piss, and forget it.' The turret full to starboard, Nash machined it back so that he could let Appleyard in. A steep bank to port rolled him over as Bennett, circling for another look, remembered his brother who died in India when his stringbag crashed. Too unorthodox for words: 'We zap the gollies up the Khyber Pass, and when you press the gunbutton your old orange-box goes backwards!' So he carried out the Prunish lark of picking up prisoners when you weren't even supposed to go down for your own pals. The skipper's intentions, said Nash, became your own.

They were on the skids, like landing in a channel of rocks, halfway into the wind, bumping before able to turn. One survivor was the captain, wounded and full of oil. The co-pilot flew while Bennett looked them over, and Nash stood guard. The captain's green face was only alive at the eyes. 'We should make him eat that Iron Cross, and see if he can shit it out.'

'I don't think he's in much of a state to do either.' Bennett pulled at a string around the man's neck. He cut off the celluloid packet and put it into his jacket, while Nash took a revolver and a bundle of wet cigars from the second survivor.

A pattern emerges after a number of considered decisions. Having carried out an action which is divorced from all sensible rules, a split appeared in Bennett's life, and he knew that it began while reading the U-boat commander's papers standing by the toilet of the flying boat. They gave details for latitude and longitude, bearings and distances. There were sketches of bays and hills. The positions were precise to a fraction of a second, and must have been worked out by theodolite. He had heard of the islands, a complication of bays, rocky peninsulas, fjords and glaciers.

The U-boat captain may have been on the active service side of middle age, but he died an old man. Without benefit of the Book, Nash delivered him and his companion to the deep. Back to the Waterland, said Rose. And Bennett's log did not record either the taking or the demise of their prisoners.

An inner voice insisted that he get as many of his old crew as possible to come on the expedition. The muster roll, more complete than expected, lacked only a wireless operator, and even he had been easy to find: 'I heard this chap whistling morse in a pub, and knew I'd got my man,' he said to Nash.

The voice talked against the power of rain, louder when his lips didn't move and the words turned inwards, and he heard the water no more. He was only really alone when he sensed his inner voice clearly. Even footsteps on the creaking floor as he walked from the chart-covered table to the door and back again did not break the sentences that came against him like files of soldiers storming a building. He had called the nucleus of his crew together because a scratch-gang of all-comers taken from any quarter would not have been reliable. He could not have created a team in the time available. On the other hand, the chances of success being about even, it would have been kinder to let any but members of his old crew take part. If without them there was no hope of success, to have them was halfway to murder. He was using them for his own ends, though by employing them he was putting more money in their way than they could earn anywhere in the same length of time. Those who invested the money would also benefit, and though Bennett knew he was not worthy of his crew's devotion, such people deserved it even less. He felt tainted by the issue.

Black market money floating about after the war was ready for investment in such projects. He had his proof, and they believed him. He went around clubs and hotels where food was served that he had not seen in a decade. Banquets with good wine and big cigars. He broached his scheme, promised evidence, and they listened. His eloquence turned into sharp business talk. Though he accepted their food and wine he wanted to wipe them from the face of the earth. His hesitation was their safety. Those who would have felt no such uncertainty were dead. Either that, or they would have been glad to see that the good life goes on, and take part in it.

When Harker-Rowe gave him the nod, he knew that his worries were about to begin. The gesture marked another stage in life. There were periods when he couldn't sleep. During the war sleep had been available the moment he returned from a raid. He almost fell into oblivion during tedious debriefings. Four hours of rest performed a miracle. Dreams, like the cities he had flown to, were wiped out and ploughed with salt. The day before was scorched from memory. Tomorrow never came. It was always today. Sleep was so close to the surface that he could stand up in his subconscious and not drown. But below that, the space was without limit. He called it sleep, which seemed, on waking, to be something you went into and came out of at the flick of a switch.

When there was a memory which sleep could not erase, the ease of sleep abandoned you. No way of winning it back. The innocent person slept like a baby – so it was said. Others did so who were unable to admit that they were anything but innocent. Lacking the moral sophistication to understand that they were not innocents made them more depraved than those who knew very well why they were guilty. The crime that had initiated the expedition was such that it could not be condoned. The action had come out of a centre whose evil he had never suspected. Erupting flames had been impossible to beat back, short of burning both hands to ash.

His hair had changed colour, but such iron-grey, when he visited business offices to arrange finance for his venture, had shown him as someone in whom they could have confidence. What he told them went across as honest and feasible. Once the gold was secure in the hold of the flying boat they knew it would not disappear into the bank vaults of Panama or Zurich. His half share would make him a rich man. Trust in him was firm, but even if it were not, his wife and children would guarantee a safe return. If the flying boat's engines failed on the way back, and Bennett's crew found the grave they dreaded, would Harker-Rowe and his consortium think he had followed some preconceived dead-reckoning plan and made a break with the known world? If he did not allow for the equally complete vanishing of his wife and children, might they not see his disappearance as merely an effective way of getting the final divorce from family life that every married man dreams about? It would be no more cruel than the way in which he had first come by his knowledge of the treasure, or than the steps he had taken to ensure that only he should know of it.

A conscience was not the worst problem. The crime might not have been as final and efficient as he had assumed. A supply ship must have refuelled the submarine close to the island before the trip back to Germany could be attempted. Though not knowing exactly what the submarine had carried, perhaps the ship's captain took the tale to the known world, so that the secret of the golden hoard was in someone's brain and yet to be acted on.

'What reasons do you have,' Harker-Rowe asked, 'for thinking the stuff's still there?'

Two men with bowler hats, rolled umbrellas, pink faces and impeccable accents were also at the meeting, go-betweens whose sense of humour was limited to the fact that they only laughed with Harker-Rowe. Because neither smoked, Bennett did not trust them. He said there had been one submarine. Not only had the captain of the U-boat and the other survivor separately informed him, but it was also written into the documents he produced. There could be no doubt. How do you know the gold was ever put there? Even Bennett laughed.

But he hated their guts. 'How do *you* know,' he smiled, 'that I'm not a confidence trickster of the most blue-eyed cunning? Not playing a hoax for money, you understand, because money would mean nothing to the kind of super con-trick which I'm trying to swing, which is to get my hands on the controls of a flying boat and hear the voices of my old crew over the intercom for the last time, because the doctor said I had cancer of the liver and only six months to live, and that before I die I want to go on the longest trip, from Cape Town to Singapore via the Kerguelen Islands and Freemantle, all at your expense, one last adventure before the disease gets such a grip that I can do nothing except drag myself into bed and die. I want to hear those four engines and see the endless sea from the flight deck at eighteen thousand feet. That's the reason I cooked up this cock-and-bull yarn, so that you would charitably – although unknowingly – supply the finance.'

He almost wished it were true. He would then have felt better when they stopped laughing. Humour had to be on their terms or not at all. Their pink skins gave an ugly tinge to such regular yet chinless features. 'Perhaps you'll now be good enough to sit down and tell me what you've heard,' Bennett said from his armchair. 'I want all the information, otherwise the expedition will be called off.'

'I don't sit,' Harker-Rowe smiled. 'Do too much of it in my life.' Neither did his bowler-hatted guards. One stood at the door and the other concealed himself by the window, observing the street so as not to be seen – as if, Bennett thought, he had been an instructor in street-fighting during the war.

'If you don't,' Bennett said, 'I'll pull out. The crew will understand.'

The pattern was too late to dismember. Harker-Rowe leaned by the shelf and, looking at himself in the mirror, ceased to smile. 'We've done our investigations. A minesweeper was bought from the Argentine navy three weeks ago, but you've a head start because it'll take at least a month to get seaworthy. Their first stop is Madagascar. We know about them, but they don't know about us. You can't help but get there first, with your flying boat.'

'Are you certain they aren't aware of us?'

'They knew there was a submarine, but assume it was destroyed with no survivors. They may wonder. I credit them with that. But they're quite happy to believe the best. Like everyone else. Though not us.'

'Madagascar's a good jumping-off place,' Bennett said. 'So why didn't we think of that?'

'We did,' Harker-Rowe said. 'But your story about an exploration company looks good, and it'll be easier for us to make arrangements for you in South Africa. You do your work, and we'll do ours.'

They showed an iron grip in protecting their investment, watching too closely for him to feel secure. Once the gold was on board, the danger would be mortal. Only in flying over the sea would he and his crew be safe. He would land where they would not be waiting for him. If he could get safely to the huge Pacific, the flying boat could land anywhere.

'One more thing,' Harker-Rowe said.

He reminded Bennett of a group captain who had come from the Air Ministry to go over the details of a spectacular raid, which would have been written up in the official history if it hadn't gone wrong.

'For a crew you'll need a navigator, an engineer, a wireless operator and your old gunner, Nash. That's five. But take the extra gunners. If there's trouble, you'll be glad of them.'

'It's flying that counts in this job. Nothing else.'

'We think you may want more safeguards,' the man by the window said.

Bennett hadn't come to be lectured by such a pinhead. 'I know what I need,' he said sharply. 'I'm the captain of this flying boat.'

'But I'm chartering, with a half share in the gold,' Harker-Rowe said. 'If it'll make you any happier, choose the gunners from your old crew. Appleyard, Bull and Armatage were in that list you showed.'

There was no way out. Bennett assumed they had already been approached, and suborned. They would watch our flight crew – and the gold once it was on board. He would take them. A certain amount of digging and carrying would be necessary when they reached the island.

'We knew you'd see reason,' Harker-Rowe said.

But did it make sense? He sweated too much to sleep, but losing such weight made him look fitter and more efficient. Having surrounded himself with so many uncertainties in order to find a way out of a labyrinth, he had reached the stage of wisdom which, such as it was, indicated that they only ceased to matter when you stopped thinking and started to act.

21

∽◦∾

We talked in the galley about being able to swim, and Rose with his scar in shadow said he'd never had the ability. At thirty, he was too old to learn.

'Too lazy to want to,' Wilcox put in.

Nash had done too much messing about in boats to think of swimming. 'I don't even like to walk more than I've got to. Walking makes my feet sore, and swimming would make my arms ache.'

'I tried it once,' Wilcox said, 'and started to sink before I could find out whether my arms ached or not. My father yanked me from a premature death by drowning. He was too scared to teach me again.'

Bull grinned at the memory of a few strokes with an inner-tube around his chest, but the valve opened and he saved his life by a panic-stricken dog-paddle to the bar of the swimming bath, a near-miss he had no wish to repeat. In spite of the dim light I saw his face turn pale. Appleyard confessed that his ambition was to be able to swim. He loved seeing people do the breast stroke, especially champions at the cinema.

'Like Esther Williams?' said Bull. 'I'd like to swim up her.'

'It looks so effortless.' Because Appleyard knew it wasn't, he got excited at the memory: 'To make your way through the water must give you a real sensation.' He was sure it did. Anyone who said otherwise should creep back into his hole and die like a liar. He had in fact been able to swim. 'You won't believe it.' He sounded as if he didn't know whether to laugh or cry. 'Perhaps it was only a few yards, so that with practice I'd get better at distance. And I would have. Once you swim you can go on for ever, providing the sea isn't rough or cold.'

'Belt up,' said Nash. 'You give me the horrors.'

He ignored the slur that he lacked taste. 'One day when I was sixteen I got cramp, and that put a stop to it. I'd heard about cramp, but never had it, and I wondered what the hell this wrenching pain was in my left leg.'

'It would have to be the left, wouldn't it?' Bull sneered.

'I was tied up in a knot. From being happy and lively I was in agony. Luckily a chap knew what was happening, and got me out. So I thought: swimming's not for me. If you turn to stone when you're walking, all you have to do is stop. You can't sink under the pavement. But if you get cramp swimming, you drown.'

'Fucked by the fickle finger of fate,' said Bull.

'Alliteration will do for you yet,' said Rose.

'Well, you *can* sink under the pavement if you get cramp while walking,' Wilcox said. 'If some idiot digs a hole and doesn't rail it off, you've had it.'

Nash looked at me. 'Can you swim, Sparks?'

There was an understandable need for us to be united by a common lack, but I did not want to erode our fellow feeling by saying that I could not swim when I could. Like coaxing a half-buried signal from monsoon atmospherics, I sensed that the common purpose among us was still frail. Each was here in the hope that the expedition would mend a broken dream, make it stronger in fact than it had originally been. To expect something better than before was, however, unrealistic. To pursue a dream is to go backwards. To go forward brings more reward than recapturing old dreams. But whatever state they were in, we were going forward nonetheless.

92

The life and death realization came too late. Having signed the contract, there was no backing out. But I wasn't staying on from a sense of honour. Nothing like that. Honour is only a cover for what can't be rationalized. Even if I hadn't signed a contract I would have gone if I had really wanted to. We no longer had any minds to make up, could only go to wherever we must, not because our souls or our honour said so, but because we had got into this situation with the single mindedness of a retreat into the Darwinian slime when life on land looked too bleak for comfort.

I told them that I had been able to swim for as long as I could remember. Rose said: 'I wouldn't bank on it saving you.'

'Them as dies will be the lucky ones!' Nash gloated.

To claim the skill of swimming in such a company of water-haters would be unfriendly. Perhaps the virtue of a flying boat crew consisted in choosing to scorn such life-saving abilities. A foolhardy courage would always be available when the tumultuous sea threatened to break up the boat. The blue of the glassy millpond would be no kinder. Salt liquid would swallow sooner or later. Only four Pegasus engines horsing through the sky held us from the eternal element of water. In any case, we could all swim.

When Rose parted the stem and bowl of his pipe, juice came out like a stream of cold tea. 'Swim or not, it's the machines that we rely on, plus the skipper's handling, my navigation, and your tip-tapping on the morse key.'

They laughed, satisfied that though I could swim I was no threat. All we had to do was keep our feet dry. I joined the hilarity. Apart from the millions of square miles that would churn beneath us, and five thousand horse power in the engines, together with the aerodynamic wings and sea-worthy hull, there was a force without a name which had a say in our safety. Perhaps Nash had similar thoughts: 'As long as the Gremlins leave us alone. Can't have them little buggers icing us up, or unsticking our ailerons, or unscrewing bits and pieces from the engines.'

'On one of our anti-sub patrols,' Wilcox said, 'I saw a Gremlin as large as life run onto the navigator's table, pick up his Dalton computer – Rose was asleep at the time – get out onto the wing, and drop it in the drink. Then he did the same with his sextant – bit of a struggle, that. I'll never forget the grin on its wicked little face. Stood by the starboard outer, doing a dance on his flippers before he let go. You should have seen Rose when he woke up and found his toys gone.'

The close night air was permeated with tobacco smoke and smells from the galley. 'I remember,' said Rose. 'You lot hid them. What a bunch of jokers!'

When more tea was made there was silence rather than talk. Armatage asked me to take a cup to the skipper. The boat rocked as I went up the steps. Bennett was looking at the flight engineer's panel. The shadowy light showed haggard features as he turned: 'There's no end to the homework.'

He had changed and shaved since the briefing. A dog-tag identity disc hung out from his shirt and clicked against the panel when he moved. That bit of brown bakelite with his name and service number looked ominous. Mine had gone missing – or I had handed it in. I saw a corpse in water, bloated by the power of the sun. The vision went. 'What if other people are trying to get at this gold, Skipper?'

The grey, granite-like structure of Bennett's cheeks and forehead tilted into surprise. Aircrew informality did not go as far as questioning operational orders, but I was curious about the danger that might be in store. It would have been unhelpful to ask at the briefing. No one could dispute that he was our captain. Each man to his work, to which all loyalty goes, but to be involved in a shady enterprise, and have even the geographical factors against you, did not make a good basis for employment. As individuals, we needed either the profit or the adventure – the more lucrative in the first case, and the more dangerous in the second, the better. Nor would a combination of both come amiss.

Those in for profit would not baulk at excitement, and whoever wanted adventure might well accept money to cushion their return to the humdrum. But it seemed to me that danger could only be exhilarating when right was on your side.

He put his tea down. 'As far as anybody can tell, no one else knows about the hoard.'

I was determined to say no more.

Do you want the job, or don't you?

I wanted it more than I'd ever wanted anything.

It's not too late to have you taken ashore.

I had spoken once too often.

We'll manage without you. Plenty of others to put in your place.

'Maybe it's already gone,' I said.

'Leave the thinking to me, Adcock. If there was a chance that the gold had gone do you think we'd go and look for the bloody stuff? Just sit at your box of tricks and tap out "Best Bent Wire" to the birds on your little toy morse key.'

I should have acted, but it was too late. One can't walk from a flying boat moored before take-off. The only way out was at the end of the trip, wherever and whenever that would be.

In the galley Nash and Appleyard were checking stores. Bull clutched a pack of playing cards to his chest and slept. The flying boat felt leaden, an ordinary squalid habitation that could not possibly fly; but Bennett and Rose were talking fuel figures with Wilcox, and our piratical galleon of the air was being primed for its task.

Armatage finished cleaning, and was reorganizing the containers of food. 'Skipper was right when he said we had plenty. Neither a ship nor a pub should run out of grub, as I've heard say. And that means a flying boat. Let me tell you, Sparks, there's nothing we ain't got on board.'

Instead of asking what he meant, I stacked each piece of washing-up for putting away, noting the different marks and decorative monograms of railway companies, hotels,

95

officers' messes and restaurants – all crockery in prime condition. The same with the cutlery. 'It's a wonder there was any left when the railways were nationalized.'

'Listen, Tosh, the government's a big firm.' He stowed things in the locker. 'And we know how to make ourselves comfortable. Nothing but the best, that's what I say.' He wiped the table and fastened it down, then laid towels across the stoves. 'If we're shipwrecked let's hope we get all this onto dry land. We might have to survive six months, never mind six days.'

Over the two bunks was a row of paperbacks and copies of *London Opinion*, and hardcovered library books with the coats of arms of various cities half torn away. I put one called *The Knapsack* into my pocket, in case sleep was hard to come by.

At my receiver I pressed the switch and stared at the glass through which the magic eye filled to the brim with green. How many times had that hypnotic light given me pleasure to watch? Operators were saying goodnight. A Lockheed Lodestar was calling Port Elizabeth. One half of the world in my left ear, and the other in my right, were joined by the brain; and this reading of rhythmical symbols oscillating into words at writing speed never ceased to strike me as magical.

I listened to messages from ship to shore, or from aircraft to earth, none of which concerned us. The transmitter of one ship, asking for a harbour pilot, sounded as if it had been recovered from the sea after accidentally falling overboard, its note farting across fifty kilocycles of frequency. Stations were going off the air as if a slow-moving tidal wave was sweeping the slate clean for take-off in the morning.

PART II

1

⤜✺⤛

Rose, having pre-computed the initial course to steer, acted as second pilot during the fraught minutes of take-off. A slight blue-black waterchop grated along the hull as he and Bennett checked the controls. Customs clearance had been given, and the harbour authorities were glad to see us go, because a flying boat was liable to drag its moorings and, being in a place where facilities for such craft hardly existed, could only be a danger to shipping – and itself.

Wilcox primed the engines, and when port and starboard outers were going, Nash and his bowmen-gunners slipped our moorings. Once clear, the inners were started, and hatches closed. I had already taken sycop gen of four-tenths cirro-stratus, visibility ten miles, pressure 29.8, temperature 71, and wind 280 degrees at 25 knots. A depression centred 300 miles southeast presaged a deterioration in the weather as the warm sector was crossed and the front approached.

The noise of four engines scoured our minds to emptiness on that nondescript dawn. We were on the move. No more doubts, and not much thought except for the job in hand. Harbour buildings, shabby like everything else from the glass windscreen of a flying boat, were a row of bad teeth lit by a spark of sun. There was a smell of fresh air and dust from the shore, and a saltier whiff from the sea. An amarillic band across the horizon was broken by a twig of steamer smoke.

We turned to starboard, well clear of shipping, taxied downwind and positioned ourselves between two buoys. The outers were run up, then the inners. Wings and fuselage vibrated, and I gripped the seat to stop my legs shaking like a pair of knick-knacks. All our problems were solved in that there was no turning back. Difficulties would arise, a disaster might occur, but the primary question was no longer valid.

A green flash from the roof of the harbour master's office was a dragon wink to warn us away. Engines roared a harmonious answer, and we moved forward. Bennett worked the control column: floats clear of water, stick back, a shade wing-down into wind to stay straight. A rock-bump denied we were up, and I wondered how long the run would be, as we dashed towards the town and high ground.

Ease stick back. The elements were taking over. Another feeling as if airborne. The skipper would worry, not us. But bump again as, in my own darkness, I held my breath, and at the roar of labouring motors prayed we'd get unstuck from the water and heave our tonnage into the air. Wilcox said that no flying boat had ever been so laden. Each power unit had to lift three tons of its own fuel, and race us to flying speed along the empty boulevard of water, a runway as hard as concrete should we come back down with too much of a bang. Seconds of time stretched as if made of all the rubber in Malaya.

I didn't know whether I heard or felt. The sensation, as of peril at the beginning of any enterprise, was indeterminate. I knew enough about flight to make me uneasy, but only the skipper had sufficient to engage the worry clutch, and the flight engineer to experience proper anxiety, and the navigator – later – the mathematical expertise to feel embarrassment. Perhaps only Nash accepted completely the fiduciary characteristics of the flying boat.

There was a gravelly scraping under the hull, as if a studiously fashioned fully fingered hand was feeling for the weak spot before punching a hole into which more water would flow than air. If I had kept a diary, the entry of January 1st 1950 would have told how a large war-surplus flying boat (the cheapest that ever was bought, said Rose) took off with eight crew and set course for Kerguelen, 2415 nautical miles to the southeast.

Instead of sea, the sky flooded in. A glimpse of brown and green land, then a few buildings. We banked before getting closer, and while I hoped God would keep that four-stroke cycle igniting, I tapped a message of departure to the coast station.

On an even keel the climb began, saying so-long to land and good day to the birds. Rose confirmed our course to steer of 145 degrees, which made us henceforth playthings of drift and track, vectors that boxed us in and styled us airborne. Morse warbled among the atmospherics. One operator pounded his key as if using a transmitter from the stone age. Another sounded like Donald Duck trying to tell us the long and the short of it.

Bennett's reactions were needle-quick: sight keen, hearing sharp and muscles in trim. Such flying called for the same skill and co-ordination as steering a large sailing boat single handed. Any deterioration of well-being, even with the best pilot in the game, was dangerous. One false move and the trip would be over.

Set against the immensity of the sea, the flying boat was frail indeed, but we had settled into our large and wieldy home by the time it gained that peerless sky waiting for us two miles up, the endlessly wrinkled sea scored at one corner by a coal-burning ship. I knew where we were heading, but what about that old steamer? He saw us, and we him but, caught in our own sounds, neither could hear the noise of different engines. Such detachment drove me to the rear turret where I took a back bearing for Rose with the hand compass which confirmed our track.

Land melted into the haze and, fly as long as we could on the fuel we had, I wondered if after twenty hours we'd find a place by which to put down. Perhaps soil or trees were gone for ever. On my first troopship-crossing of the Arabian Sea I had feared that land would not be found even with the most refined navigation. The world would end as at the beginning, leaving us no choice but to alight on water.

I glanced at Rose as he laid his ruler straight, turned the Douglas protractor, twiddled the knob of his computer, and worked a pencil deftly over the chart. He sat as cut off at his table as if a door were closed on him. He reckoned his tracks and course in deadly earnest, assembling the many factors by which to decide our most probable position, and the prudent limit of the flying boat's endurance.

2

The plane entered cloud but hardly ever stayed there. Yet it always seemed so. Beads of moisture hung on the perspex. The engines took on a harsher and more vulnerable tone than in clear sky, though this, like a tinnier vibration detected in the airframe, was an illusion. Bennett nursed the kite on its gradual ascent, and my unexplained fear was emphasized by the effect of being in cloud and climbing at the same time.

Ripples of indistinguishable morse came from God knew where, as if even at this late stage someone was making, though without much hope, an attempt to call us back. The plane shuddered, but ploughed beyond the speed of stalling or hesitation, and we sat at our duties as if we had never left the earth.

The more we stayed in cloud the more null my senses became, till I seemed to be alive after death, not able to see or be seen. The cloud cotton-woolled us out of existence. Solitude and lack of visibility caused the engines to go silent as I turned the frequency needle of the Marconi more for something to do than in the hope of receiving any vital data, which made it seem as if the world had abandoned us rather than that we had waywardly departed from it.

After six miles without visibility my bones ached for the emptiness of blue. Nash called from the mid-upper that we would go blind unless somebody turned the sky back on. In such latitudes there was no chance of a collision at least.

Daylight dazzled the fuselage. Bennett whistled to himself, glad to have made a start. Cloud tops were the surface of another earth whose white soil we had sprung from fully formed, a landscape of spun glass, knobbly obelisks, mushroom columns, wispy stalagmites and, further away, caves suggesting mysterious hide-outs on some polar shore. We gained height till the milky landscape below was like a world in the process of being formed, lit by the sun's flood but now tinged with grey. There was nothing between us and the universe as, after a hundred miles of gradual climbing to go easy on the fuel, Bennett levelled off and kept us on course for Kerguelen.

Anyone able to stand on an anvil of cloud would see our flying boat going gracefully through the blue at two miles a minute, with its turrets and aerials, tailplane and vast four-engined wingspan. I would have wanted to wave, much as I had lifted my arms as a boy to trains that went by, craving to be one of its passengers.

Cloud tops we flew between were like plumes of the Prince of Wales' feathers. Earphone wire trailing, I tried to rid myself of a feeling of isolation, almost afraid to look out at the wings in case I witnessed them being rent from the fuselage. I wanted to live for ever, whereas on the ground I had not much cared whether I lived at all. Every moment that I was not at my wireless filled me with anxiety, unless I consciously marvelled at how four great engines propelled us along as easily as a bus on a country road. I was only alive when listening to morse while being carried through the sky, ten thousand feet above the sea.

Bennett stood behind me. The bounce of wireless signals was our lifeline. Whoever heard could write the call sign in their log, and if we vanished into the water of the South Indian Ocean, at least there would be the record of a last message, even if only a call tapped out to reassure the crew that we still had some connection with the earth.

Sweat fell from my cheeks. We were an hour on our way, with nineteen to go. A coast station tried to get me with a QRZ, so I asked Rose for our position and established contact by the return compliments of a QTH. Bennett smiled at seeing me busy. He had amended the position report, and what I sent, while the correct distance, put us on course for Madagascar.

He descended to the galley, satisfied at our attempt to obfuscate. The legal situation intrigued me. We were crossgraining all the laws. The sending of false signals was strictly forbidden, and I had committed the first criminal act of my life.

In the kernel of such detachment, highlighting my lack of connection to whatever in the world had any meaning, I felt allied to something that was not *good*, almost to a sense of evil. I put my fingers on the morse key and thudded out the call sign of the flying boat so as to imprint our identifying letters on an unlistening void.

3

Bennett called for less chat on the intercom. As he got older he wanted more perfection from himself, and consequently only spoke to others when he could be sure of being obeyed. He wished for perfection from them too, so that what he demanded contributed to the standards he had set himself, and thus enhanced his perfection. But if he wanted obedience he had to be reasonable. He had to be right, and because it was getting harder to match the two demands, he gave the impression of being taciturn.

The price of such individualism was often at the expense of others' conformity. No one knew it more. But he expected it nonetheless, not only because there was so little about but also because it was part of his nature to strive after perfection. He wanted it from others as well as from himself, as a defensive bastion against all comers. The cost to himself was nil because his value increased the more he acquired it. And as for the cost to others – it was no concern of his.

He faced the clear blue, getting bumped by upcurrents from cloud tops a few feet below. The boat trundled at 110, plus the push of an almost following wind. The more such windy knots the merrier, caught in the Roaring great-circle Forties, but any speed would have been too slow.

The furrows in his brow seemed to go into his soul, and cut it into fragments, which was better than merely cleaving it in two, because while many parts were manageable, two would be stalemate. Diplomacy could be brought to bear on many parts, while with two it was a fight to stop them destroying one another. All the same, he did not know which system he was most in the grip of, or in need of, nor even in the end which he preferred. He had long been a battle-ground, but the fight for stability always resulted in a strong and perfect balance in himself which he presented to the world.

The inner fight to stay firm did not allow for speculation. He was happy with the bargain. He had to be. Pragmatism was the way to survival. There was no point in allowing self-knowledge to destroy you. To keep a balance between knowing yourself and survival might be feasible during a holiday in the English countryside, but on this trip the difficulties could break you if steps weren't taken to defeat them.

Sitting for hours at the controls, mulling on chances and pitfalls, it wasn't easy to stop chaos coming with malicious intent from beyond the horizon. The furrows on his forehead had similarly sharpened as a schoolboy when he crept upstairs to his mother's bedroom. She had gone, so he opened her Bible as if committing a sin. Thin paper flipped like a cloud of butterflies crossing a turbulent river. He had forgotten the name of that great river. The butterflies had a name from cigarette cards. He read some verses about Isaac and Abraham. They smelled of face powder from the dressing table. The book made him want to die. When he grew tired of opening and closing, he tore out the page and swallowed the pieces as he stood at the window.

No one walked on the garden path. Beyond rows of lettuces were redcurrant bushes. He could taste their fruit by looking at them. Dahlias and chrysanthemums coloured the fence. Instead of going to school he wanted to spread his arms and fly from the window, reach the bushes before it got dark, when they would leap even redder with their flame.

The clear and aching light of long summer evenings needed all day before stars came out. His father was up there, his mother told him, but he was under redcurrant bushes where she had buried him. If he flew, he would fall.

You couldn't fly without falling. Not even time to scream, your eyes would drop out before you could see the earth that hit you. You would be too dead to feel it, just as his father was too dead to know anything, whether he was in the sky or under the bushes, because how could he be in two places at once? Maybe he would die from the bits of paper. Either that, or they would make him better.

Captain Bennett smiled at the enormous hemisphere of the heavens.

4

Rose came on the intercom with a course correction for the thirty degree latitude south and forty degree longitude east position. He had released a smoke float to get drift. I swept the ether with a fine tooth comb, going up to eighteen megacycles, then dropping back to search on medium wave. I was tempted to click my callsign to the few audible ships, but radio silence was the order of the day. Everything went in the logbook nevertheless, in case it was useful later. Liking to keep busy during bumps through cloud, I took a gonio reading on a coast station for Rose.

'It's not much good,' he said, 'but they might help one of these days, though I hope I won't be reduced to such ham-handed navigation. Be the end of us all, if so.'

'Levity is coming back,' said Nash. 'He's a young soldier, Nav, so don't discourage him.'

'Bound to, once we're airborne,' said Wilcox. 'We get light-headed, don't we, chaps?'

Two hours out, and I could relax my tight-fisted contact with the ether. 'Permission granted,' Bennett called.

'Got dots and dashes before the eyes?' said Appleyard as I walked over a heap of parachutes to get to the Elsan. The plane grumbled. 'What do we need those for?' I asked Armatage, as I buttoned my flies. It was like being in the cellar of a laundry, except for the smell of last night's cooking instead of today's washing.

'You'll see that hanging up soon enough,' he said.

'Do sailors like us need parachutes?'

Armatage hung them in some sort of order. 'You never know. But I expect the only time we'll bale out is when the dinghy starts to split after we're in the drink – if we're lucky enough to get that far on our way to salvation. Or bailed out of some foreign copshop. But while we're in this flying bailiwick we're more than safe, Tosh.' He tapped one of several packing cases with his boot: 'It'll be the others we meet who'll need bailing out, or to bale out, believe you me.'

The wood smelt fresh. 'What's in them?'

'You'll see when we open up.'

'And when will that great day be?'

'When, mate? When? When Bennett gives the verbal nod over the speak-tube, just beyond the third-way mark. That's when we'll do it. I'm a dab hand with a jemmy.' Fingers at his left cheek rubbed the smile away. 'This toothache's giving me a bit of stick.'

I was ready to laugh at such a common malady, but it was clearly no joke. 'You could have had it pulled before we left.'

'I didn't know, did I? Anyway, it comes and goes.'

'On Antarctic expeditions some blokes have all their teeth taken out, good or not, and steel ones put in. Saves 'em suffering if they're two years in the wild.'

His grey eyes turned watery. 'If I'd told the skipper, he'd have left me behind rather than put the trip off for a day.

108

That's the skipper all over. One of the best – but no sentiment. Iron Jack, some of us used to call him. I heard that swine Shottermill talking about having too many in the crew and wondering whether they shouldn't ditch a couple of bods. I can't think he was genuine, because if the Antarctic ice sticks hard on this white elephant we'll all be out on the wings melting it off with blow-lamps.' He smiled when the pain went. 'And if there's a bit of a scrap over who gets the damaged goods, there won't be too many of us on board to handle it.'

'Are we expecting opposition?'

He sat down and nursed his face at another wicked twinge. 'Who can tell?'

I felt sorry for him. 'It can't last forever.'

'Maybe. But we've got to be prepared.' We were part of a machine, each at his job to keep the props moving. I sat in my wireless section and spun the needle over coloured markings. In an emergency, one man with ordinary toothache would put us off schedule. He would be as bad as a stretcher case. But I felt as if I'd had a few whiskies, and couldn't care less.

An Italian opera from Cape Town or Johannesburg had a hard ride with such bounce and crackle waiting in ambush along the route. I adjusted the wavelength, and poured music for enjoyment through the intercom, vibrating what phones were plugged in.

'We'll make you the ENSA wallah,' Bennett said, 'if you aren't careful.'

Nash wanted the Warsaw Concerto. 'It always gives me a lump in my throat. One of my best oppoes was a Polish gunner, alas no longer with us.'

I put up the volume.

'A piece of Beethoven,' Rose said. 'Much better than your bent bearings. What about *Fidelio*?'

'Fidelio's a dog,' said Appleyard. 'In quarantine.'

'You mean Fido,' Bull barked convincingly. 'That's a fucking dog, not Fidelio. Get back into your kennel.'

109

Wilcox asked for Mantovani.

'You can't have him,' Appleyard called.

'It might stop him coughing,' said Nash.

'Or play Victor Sylvester,' said Armatage.

'No dancing,' said Nash, 'or you'll be on a fizzer.'

'You'll bugger up Mr Rose's sunsights,' said Bull.

'Cut the language,' said Appleyard, 'or you'll get no tea.'

One of the gunners booed, Armatage I think. There was rediffusion of flying boat favourites till the music crumpled against a mountain range of static and disappeared.

'Back to business, Mr Adcock.'

I switched to ships and coast stations. My fingers itched to tap a greeting, but I roamed up and down the wavelength, never long enough on any to get a whole message. What did I expect? No weather report could come from where we were going. If a rolling stone gathered no moss, whose loss is that? It was the pattern of my life, and after so long I thought that nothing could break it.

We were the filling in a cloud sandwich, two thousand feet of sky through which we droned, a movable feast activated by so many currents of air that the plane had to be ridden rather than driven. A topography of ridges and cauliflower hillocks passed us by. Rose jerked his elbows back and forth. 'A cold front's coming from the southeast.'

'How do you know?'

'If I knew, I wouldn't know. Take it from me. There'll be a bit of turbulence before we hit the drink.'

He paced irascibly against the bumps and lurches. 'Calm down.' I made myself heard as he came close. A hand covered the scar-side of his face, while the exposed half was pale and leaden. He shivered with cold. I wondered how we would manage if our navigator passed out.

'Maybe something I ate,' he said. 'It's not unusual for me to feel air sick. Every other trip, and I spend half my time staring the bog out.'

I found a canister of water and filled a mug, spilling

some before getting it back to him. Bennett was dodging the black three-dimensional coastline of cumulus, trying to rise to where the kite might be steady enough for Rose to obtain his sunsight. We went onto oxygen at twelve thousand feet, though I delayed as long as I could, hating that rubbery medicated tang that crept into the throat. 'It's like the whiff that comes out of a Selection Box of french letters,' said Bull. A disembodied croak over the intercom agreed, adding that his popsy had given him such a gift at Christmas.

'Shut up,' Bennett said.

I hung on, oxygen tacking and veering through my veins. My ears were buzzing, and a bodily nervousness – while at my wireless table – presaged a heavenward lift where all might be well. The impression lasted a few minutes, time for the system to get used to alien air taking hold. For whoever had work, reality reasserted its grip. A ship sent a routine message, faint but readable, which I logged, returning to the illusion that my work and I were inseparable. On this trip we had to be.

Another ship's operator, having difficulty reaching a coast station, was sending so slowly that I'd have had time to part my hair between each letter.

5

Height was the best aerial, but there was a limit to how far it could be extended. Infinity was not enough, though the higher we climbed the more I could hear. To bring in Madagascar and Mozambique gave a sense of power. I

111

heard Tasmania and Nairobi with pleasure. Rhodesia and the Seychelles were registered with childish pride – yet the world was no bigger than the space between my enphoned ears since, in spite of what I wanted to believe, each place came in of its own accord.

I heard them all, dots-and-dashes denoting each locality, showing picture-book scenes where I would rather be than in the bucking slum-galleon of a flying boat going to a place that lacked the morse symbols which my imagination could embellish with reality. Without those electrical impulses (affected, as the handbook might say, by keying across a resistance in the high-tension negative supply), a place had no identity. Robbed of a name, it was erased from latitude and longitude, and so was denied existence.

And yet where we were going was on all maps and charts, and perhaps even shown on those small globes used as pencil sharpeners. Its natural harbours had been known for two hundred years by whalers and seal hunters. Explorers had laid up in them to fair-copy their surveys, piratical merchants had hidden to count the score of their plunder, and the Germans had used the area as a base from which to prey on shipping. But without a wireless station the region lacked a soul. No sound meant no life. No aerial system on high ground conveyed intelligence to other places. We were heading for white space because my earphones could not bring in the necessary signals to convince me it was solid property.

Rose's table took most of the sun as we ascended from the gloom, but a narrow shaft illuminated my log book. Cloud below was flat like the sea, fixed ribs crossing our track. The plane was steady, and Rose got into the 'dome with an Astro-Compass to check the course, while I stood below with his watch and wondered whether, should it become necessary, I could navigate our boat on its trans-ocean flight. Apart from radio bearings, it was not beyond my competence to lay out a course if provided with the wind

112

vector. There was no mystery in sextant and timepiece as long as sun or stars were visible, and a book of Sight Reduction Tables available to work out a position line. You always learned something of the next man's job, occasionally without him knowing, and hardly aware of it yourself.

But the proper exercise of navigation demands arcane knowledge during a long flight over water, as well as subtle judgement when putting together the factors of dead-reckoning, astro navigation and wireless bearings. Therefore I couldn't do it, no more than anyone on board could do my work, though they tended to regard the wireless operator as having the easiest task on the flight deck. His technical knowledge was thought to go little beyond rectifying a few obvious faults, and using Morse Code could not be compared to the arduous work of flying or navigation – both of which are as much an art as a craft.

With senses of a more primitive order, the wireless operator needs experience and patience when pulling in any data for the well-being of the aircraft. He interprets symbols coming into the earphones, and uses the international 'Q' code as an operator's Esperanto. To take morse at speed calls for the sense of rhythm possessed by a poet – or an African in the bush manipulating his tom-toms, as Rose scathingly said. The wireless operator's brain receives a series of beats which galvanize him into writing words originating from someone else. Others will in turn take down words or initials tapped out by him, both senders and receivers being mediums to transcribe electrical patterns from the sky.

At either end of the contact there is a human touch. If you miss a letter, you either let it go, thereby losing all trace, or you make the correction and then try to catch up with the speeding text, with the risk of missing some which is still to come. If the message isn't intended for you, yet is essential for your wellbeing, and you can't get in touch with the other operator to ask for a repeat, you are in trouble.

Each operator is distinguishable by idiosyncratic sending.

113

Those whose rhythm is of a pleasing regularity are artists at the job, possessing stamina and an infallible sense of style, their evenly spaced strings of dots and dashes being a delight to transcribe. But most operators have mannerisms which make their sound patterns as unique as fingerprints. One can detect a change in operator, can tell when an inexperienced sender is tired, or lazy, or permanently irascible, or inwardly disturbed.

If half a dozen stations are hammering for attention you note their call signs and then, in an orderly manner, bring them in one by one to transact business. When a dead-keen coast station thumps out automatic five-kilowatt morse on eight megacycles, symbols come into each ear like needles intent on pricking your brain in the middle. Your vital interest may be to listen instead to the mewings of an underpowered pip-squeak tramp steamer. His feeble transmitter, so far away, may not realize the strength of the opposition that besets you while trying to read him, for the interference is in your area, and not his. What is preventing you from listening may sound no louder to him than the strength at which you hear him. In any case, the ship's transmitter, being right next to him, drowns all but his own morse.

The onus is on you to assist the weak. Moral considerations overcome any difficulty in the execution of your task. Human feeling encourages you to hear that small voice behind the great bellow, and struggle to bring forth meaning in case the lives of the sender's crew depend on it. The most important article of faith, hidden yet not hidden, without which you would only do your job and not your duty, is that which elevates your purpose and takes your craft close to art.

Your integrity can survive only by the proper rendering of the message onto paper, so you nurture those disjointed sounds, sweat at the finger ends, and tremble, and squint in order to cool yourself – and you may still, for all your effort, lose the thread. You hope for contact to be properly established, and do not give in to the evil of despair, which is too easy to accept and always to be turned from. A lost soul is revived with the belief that it is not finally lost and, rekindling your attempt to hear it again, you force your ears to conquer the bleak static of the ether and double the sharpness of your senses in order to encourage those in peril.

I listened for any such ship within the radius of my receiving aerials. A wireless operator in an aircraft is the lookout man in the crow's nest, the first to hear any manned object in the circumference of sounds. There was self-interest in my endeavours, for whatever I heard proved that we ourselves were not lost, whether the signals were to be of assistance to us, or a threat. Unable to accept that we were totally alone was an imperfection of spirit which should have made me ashamed – but did not. The individual cannot be supreme in an empty world.

Two hours out, I heard a ship send a weather report to a South African coast station. His QTH was a couple of hundred miles north of our onward route, so I noted it as being of some use. The force five wind was westerly, weather mainly fair, visibility moderate or good. I got a bearing on ship and coast station and, allowing for half-convergency, handed the slip of paper to Rose.

When I showed the report to Bennett he jumped as if bitten by a tiger-ant and called Wilcox to sit at the controls. Was there anything about where the ship was coming from or going to? He was disappointed at my answers. 'Glue yourself to those valves,' he said, 'and keep listening to that ship. But don't for God's sake send a single squeak on your key. Understand?'

I did. He went down to talk to Nash and his gunners. But if, on this enormous ocean where ships were scarce, aircraft rare, and a flying boat perhaps unique, I heard a vessel in distress, would I keep radio silence as commanded, even

115

though such a policy was vital for our safety? Or would I inform them with alacrity that they were not alone, and relay a message to other ships which might be able to help them?

Bennett's pressure to push on, come what may, in silence and as if invisible, need not clash with the distress of a cottonboat or sugar-carrier. I lived in hope of lesser moral choices, but knew which one I would make if the moment came.

6

Armatage flicked his moustache, and looked as if he had woken up into the Stone Age. He wanted only to get back to sleep, but said: 'I heard scratching underfoot. From when I closed my eyes to opening them again.'

'Scratching?'

'Have you ever heard of rats in a flying boat?'

'You must be dreaming.'

He got out of the bunk and stretched. 'Claws were going, ten to the dozen.'

'Can't hear 'em now.'

'You wouldn't, would you?'

I laughed at his irony. 'I would if they made a noise. I can usually hear things like that.'

He rubbed his face. 'I suppose it was a dream, though I never dream, so it's hard to believe. Why should I, on a flying boat? Makes no sense. Scratching, as plain as anything. I thought claws were going to come through that door.'

116

I jumped away.

'See? Gets you, don't it?'

'When they stop scratching,' I teased, 'let me know. It'll mean they've left. We'll be in trouble.'

His face was covered in sweat, as if he had been under a shower – and we were freezing at ten thousand feet. 'Do you want a drink, Sparks?'

I thought he was joking. 'I'm not thirsty.'

'I never said you was. I mean a tot of old grouser to steam its way up and down the tripes.'

He winked.

'There's not supposed to be any on board,' I said.

'That's all right for such as the skipper. For us it's King's Regulations and Station Routine Orders. He'll have us on bloody square-bashing next. But he's got something else to warm him up, though I'm not sure what it is. But it warms him, all right. You can see the hot spot burning his brain. If I had a tenth of it I wouldn't need a secret bin of firewater to wash my throat in. And besides, he ain't got toothache.'

'You'll get thrown overboard if he finds out.' His sweat stank of alcohol, but I didn't care how much booze he put into himself as long as it was after we had reached land and the job was finished.

'I've got my flask,' he said, 'and I can refill it any time. You've never known a gunner to be without his flask, have you? Even on ops I took one, though I'd have been on the carpet if I'd been caught. Being half-cut on the way back from Nuremberg sharpened my sight. Saved my life a few times, such as it was. This is the last op I'm doing, though, and it feels the longest already.'

'We've only been out three hours. Still, if you kip down for another half hour maybe you'll wake up feeling better.'

'I can't sleep,' he grumbled. 'There's rats in the hull, scores of the bleeders squeaking and scratching.'

I lost patience. 'You're round the bend, if you ask me, and halfway up the zig-zags.'

'I wish I was.' He pulled at my lapel, but I shoved him off. 'And not only rats. I heard voices.'

'Voices? You're getting my bloody goat.'

He came close again. 'In Bennett's wardroom somebody laughed and it wasn't Bennett. They were talking, all gruff and matey. Wilcox was at the controls, you was at your gear listening to Geraldo, Rose was at his table doing noughts and crosses, Appleyard was in the mid-upper, Nash was in the tail, and Bull was sleeping on the parachutes. That left me on my tod – hearing voices.'

It was the wind, the shaking, the drone of engines as we changed height. The effect was to make you hear things.

'Oh,' he said, 'it was that, was it? Do you think I don't know? I've logged more flying time than you've spent listening for the first cuckoo in spring.'

He took another swig from the flask and, wanting a drink as much as anyone, I thought him more funny than dangerous. But I was angry at knowing there was liquor on board, and wondered who else was getting at it. 'Does Bennett know the mess is no longer dry?'

He ignored my question. 'I'm bloody freezing.'

I envied him having no work, unlucky as he was in being crippled with either drink or toothache. His expression of malice diverted me from worrying overmuch at his boozing. The only fit response was to do the impossible, and laugh. I pulled a blanket from the rack and let it fall.

He belched his thanks. 'You're a babe unborn, Sparks.'

The floor of the plane dropped under our feet and, while I held on, Armatage crumpled into the bunk and was straightaway unconscious. I had no further weather reports to listen for, so had time to watch the others opening a packing case with crowbars. Bull fixed the claw under a batten, strained like a sailor at the capstan, shirt off, arms chevroned by elaborate tattoos, lips clamped as if knowing that the noise of the engines would drown any shanty. Nash and Appleyard held the crate from sliding.

'Do you need help?'

'We'll manage.'

I stood by, but kept clear. The cases were labelled 'Engine Spares'. An outboard motor for the dinghies? Tents and equipment? Shining nails gave without trouble. A smell of oil and paraffin floated up as side planks splintered away, leaving plywood and thick card to pull free. 'We should get Armatage on this stunt,' Bull said. 'A bit of hard labour would do him good.'

Appleyard took the crowbar. 'He's as pissed as a falling flare.'

'He's down with the toothache.' Nash steadied the crate. 'Leave him for a while.' They rested when the work was all but done. 'We'll give him an hour to spruce up.' He turned to Appleyard, who was rolling down his sleeves. 'Why don't you boil some water for coffee? Make a start on cobbling a meal together. You'll find tins of M and V, a bag of spuds, a wheel of rat-trap, and some fresh bread.'

Bull agreed. 'Flying makes me ravenous. I once ate a whole packet of cream crackers over Berlin.'

'Me,' Nash said, 'I smoked fifty Players.'

'I said my prayers,' Appleyard called before he went, 'and bit my nails. Bull got drunk. He ought to pull his finger out and sweat like the rest of us.'

Beneath the cardboard, sacking was darkened by grease stains. Nash braced himself to pull one container free. 'They're our stingers. Or will be when they're assembled. We'll sweat like pigs to get 'em up in time.' He cut into the coils of string with a black clasp knife. 'Treat 'em nicely,' he said to Bull. 'When the job's over we'll pack 'em up and sell 'em back. They cost a few hundred each. We can unload them on China for a lot more if we fly our kite up the Yangtse. Might as well make all we can out of the trip.'

'I wouldn't care if we chucked 'em in the drink.' Bull cut the string into small lengths, then peeled away the sacking till bits and pieces of a Browning .303 machine gun gleamed on the floor.

Nash stroked the barrel. 'We've a few hours to work like grease-monkeys and put four of these beauties in the tail.' After a rapid check on the various parts he laughed at my surprise. 'You didn't have a clue, eh? If anyone comes up the fjord and tries to stop us, we'll rake 'em.'

In the guise of a mechanical skeleton, the gun looked ominous. 'Maybe they'll have a similar shock for us.'

'Maybe,' he said. 'But listen, Adcock, the world's full of bloody *maybes*. You can't live on 'em, I'll tell you that. And in my experience one *maybe* is as good as another. All you've got to do is get yourself ready to meet one *maybe*. And if any turn up that you don't expect, you'll just bloody well defeat it, if you've prepared properly for the first *maybe*. That's the only system I know, and it hasn't failed me yet. Now we're out of territorial waters we'll gun the old flying boat up like it was always meant to be, and once they're mounted there'll be no trouble we can't get out of.'

The more the flying boat went on, the more I was disturbed, a condition strange and painful because I had been trained to create order from a multiplicity of signals. Confusion in myself was unfamiliar and therefore insoluble. The only way of staying calm was to close down the wireless, hold back from the one thing that might help me to bear it – which would be as impossible as pulling open a door and letting myself fall into the icy air. I envied Armatage his drunken sleep.

The headset back on, I immersed myself in an endless waterfall of static. Vital gen known to everyone in the plane would not be imparted to me. Latched to the outer atmosphere, I was certain to stay innocent. It was not a matter of knowing nothing, but of believing that what I did know was not worth knowing, and of assuming that what I didn't know was the only thing worth knowing. The balance was crucial, yet as gentle as the motions of the flying boat

120

following that invisible line of the Antarctic Convergence, where warm and cold water mixed to give high winds and thick cloud above the troubled surface.

7

A landslide of static was swept aside by a continuous signal. As my tuning needle went over it became an attenuating whistle, like a bomb falling into infinity and unable to explode. By the time I thought to take a bearing it had disappeared. It should not have been there. Someone had inadvertently leaned on his key, or was tuning his transmitter. If the latter, who did he expect to contact? To judge by the intensity of that accidental signal, if that's what it was, and allowing for skip distance and freak reception, he could be up to a thousand miles away, in which case he was likely to be on or over the sea in the direction of Kerguelen. Perhaps he was interested in our whereabouts.

Such deductions might sound like so much magic. Intuition was not evidence. Assumptions were not facts. Feelings could not rate as intelligence by which to assess danger. In the imagined conversation, Bennett told me to pull my finger out and find clues he could work on. My job was to inform him, not worry him.

The green eye glowed. Atmospherics dominated. The universe of noise was like a house of many mansions latched on each ear, doors and windows firmly bolted against lunatics scratching inside. Maybe, like Armatage, I was hearing things. A long bomb-like whistle had no symbol for the logbook.

The knowledge of the Browning machine guns made

121

every sound seem like a threat, and kept me extraordinarily alert. I had to do my job well, though sworn loyalty to Bennett hardly meant helping to find bullion which did not belong to him. Yet if I didn't chip in to the best of my ability the sudden onset of peril from any direction would be as much a threat to myself as it was to the others. Having signed my way into the trap, I must learn to live in it.

The flying boat moved on. Rose passed a new course of 138 degrees when we reached, by astronomical computation, 45 north and 40 south. The local time was 11.52, three hours and forty-seven minutes after setting out. A rippling stream of high speed telegraphy tinkled between Singapore and Home Base. My crow's nest could monitor half the world, but I only needed to beware of ships steaming in the area we were heading for. The first headland was over 1700 nautical miles away, though it wasn't too far if I kept my fingers at the corrugated tuning wheel as pertinaciously as a safe-thief trying to unravel the combination of a lock.

The second leg of the trip meant we were making progress, said Nash. 'The Alpha Rats are on their way.'

'Skimming along at 120 knots,' said Rose.

'How much is that in Dolly Mixtures?' asked Appleyard.

'Damn near a hundred-and-roaring-forty, if you're talking about statute miles,' said Bennett. 'The speedier this old bird shivers along, the better for my blood pressure.'

'Do you measure that in millibars?' Wilcox wanted to know.

'Mars Bars,' said Appleyard.

'Don't mind if I do,' said Armatage.

'If you aren't careful,' said Rose, 'I'll sing "The Navigator's Lament".'

'I put men on a charge for less,' Bennett said, 'when I was Orderly Officer.'

Rose took another look at the sun, and Nash hoped he wouldn't drop his Mark IXA Celestial. My eavesdroppings were brief. I roamed to either side of three chosen frequencies, and static sounded as if the world was wrapped in a scarf of water, heightened crackles like rocks or fallen trees in the way of the liquid's headlong route. I caught news-agency morse from Tass in Moscow, crackpot claims about life in Stalin's paradise. Silence on my own frequency was more golden. 'The less heard, the better, Sparks,' Bennett said. 'We want to be the only ones in a thousand-mile radius when we get there.'

'As long as we have no trouble from the Gremlins, Skipper,' said Wilcox.

I cursed the jungle of static. 'Or the Marcolins. They eat the filaments out of the valves, and chew at the connections, and gnaw the impedences.'

'I'll sing "The Navigator's Lament",' said Rose.

Bennett at the controls lit a cigar. 'Let rip, if you like. We can be happy till it's time to dig up the doings, pull out the plum, refuel our tanks, and fly away like good little blackbirds. God is with us, don't forget. He'd better be.' His laugh swamped all rejoinders.

Rose was so busy that his Dalton computer was in danger of seizing up – he said. But maybe he could spare a moment. Appleyard was duty cook: 'Like me: both burners going, and a stack of plates to fill.'

'Gangway!' Nash called. 'I hear a throat being cleared.'

Rose tapped his tuning fork against the Bygrave slide-rule.

'Stap me if I too didn't hear the dull click,' said Wilcox. 'He can use the tattooed gunners for a chorus.'

'Shut your soupbox,' Nash growled. 'If you put him off you'll be confined to the port float on bread and seaweed. Jankers has nothing on that.'

'Navigators never lament. If they can't get a fix they break down and cry.'

'You remember "O My Darling Clementine"?' said Rose. 'Well, my song sings to that banshee wail. I didn't write the music.'

Armatage came up from the depths of his boozy snooze. 'You bloody wronged it, if I remember.'

'It was the highlight of the old squadron concert party. The comb-and-paper melted in my mouth at the thought of how many of us would be gone by the morrow.' When he could get space on the intercom he put out his melody, in which the others joined without waiting for the chorus:

> Taking bearings on a lightship,
> Don't know where the hell we are –
> Flying round in oblate spheroids
> Will not get us very far.
>
> O my darling, O my darling
> O my darling Clementine
> Book of Tables full of misprints,
> O my darling Haversine.
>
> Take a sight on old Capella
> From the leaky astrodome
> Got two bubbles for my trouble
> Will this sextant get us home?
>
> Don't known how far is Polaris
> Lost my pencil and my rule
> When I get back (if we get back)
> You can send me back to school.
>
> Deviation, variation
> QDMs and QTEs
> If you've got 'em, I can't plot 'em
> Can't you see, I'm on my knees?
>
> Lost my stopwatch, broke my sextant
> Torn my logbook, burnt my map.
> I've gone blind and lost my fingers:
> Skipper, can I take a nap?
>
> God will help us, God will help us
> God will help us, don't you know?
> For we're lost and gone forever
> To the land of ice and snow . . .

Bennett broke in: 'Cut it out. Nash, get those guns into position.' A lace-curtain network of high frequency stations came to pieces before an onslaught of atmospherics. Blinded by so much din, I put down the volume, detached the headphones and stood by Wilcox to look into the dazzle of oncoming sky that was like drink to my spirit. Space we needed, space we got. Four engines propelling the weight of our flying boat, we rode the air smoothly, however the boiling sea behaved two miles below. I had known no other life. The rest was a dream. Nothing and no existence prospered beyond our fuselage.

Wilcox held the controls so that Bennett could go to a meal in his room. By rights on a long journey over the sea there should have been a double crew. A nineteen-hour stretch or more at the wheel, wireless rig, navigation table, or engineer's panel was too long a time for comfort or safety. But a double crew, as well as entailing double cost, would also mean double weight, and almost equal that which we expected to load on board.

Below, on another floor level, Nash manoeuvred a Browning towards the front turret. We would defend ourselves from all directions. Elaborate rearmament was not carried out unless to stop others taking the gold. 'We should run up the skull-and-crossbones.'

Wilcox coughed his cough to the end. 'If we get into a jolly-roger scrap, we'll blow 'em out of sea or sky. We haven't come this far to take chances. Anybody tries to stop us, and they'll walk the plank.'

I was a prisoner of their harebrained scheme, and had too much pride to express regret at the speed of my conversion to the general cause.

8

〜〜〜

The skipper wanted to see me, Appleyard said, so I climbed the ladder and found him at a table laid not with odd knives and forks but a silver set resting across the remains of his meal on a large dinner plate – a pitcher of water and half filled glass by his elbow.

'Hearing any funny noises on your box of tricks, Sparks?'

'Not so far.'

Plywood walls made his compartment seem solid and soundproof. A plantpot adorned a metal shelf under the porthole, and a small plan chest against a partition had the bottom two drawers half open. He told me to sit down. 'The time to glue yourself to the radio is when we're five or six hundred miles away. In the meantime, take a rest if you feel like it. I want you as sharp as a needle for the few hours before landfall.'

The bunk opposite had its bedding neatly stacked, and above was a framed photograph of a Lancaster bomber, Bennett prominent among the crew lined up on the ground. 'What exactly should I listen for?'

Appleyard put down a dish of pineapple and went out. 'The faintest bleat or crackle.'

'I hear all sorts of noises. None make sense.'

'When they do, tell me.'

A chart on the plan chest was held down by a sliderule, which suggested he kept a constant check on Rose's navigation. 'If two ships are in contact they might use duplex, so I'd hear only one.'

He picked at the fruit. 'The boats I'm thinking about have simple rigs.'

126

'I'll keep tabs on the calling frequency, log everything, and let you see it by the half hour.'

'Be sure to miss nothing. And I want to say this, Sparks: piloting the plane is a normal job. I've got the controls in my hands, and can see the engines going full spin out of the windows. As for navigation, Rose is second to none. And Wilcox has the panel to tell how the engines are functioning, and what fuel's still floating around. But you've not only to listen: you must also hear. Everything. I can't tell you what to listen for. You have to decide that for yourself. You'll know what to tell me when you hear it. The least thing will make the difference between us getting home dry, or ending up in the drink.'

Appleyard came in for his plate and dish. 'Bring a cup of coffee for the radio officer.' Bennett looked at me: 'I suppose you've seen the measures we're taking for self-defence?'

'As if we're going to war.'

'The last of a tour of ops.'

'I can't get a straight answer from anybody.'

He rolled several white papers around a cigar. 'Straight answers stop you thinking. Another thing to remember, Adcock, is that busy people don't like to talk much. You've got eyes, and you're supposed to use them. But look not too long in the face of fire. I'm in command of this ship, and I'll bring her through. That's what I'm here for.'

My guts went cold, no embers apparent. He was testing my fitness for some devastating encounter which he clearly expected. I wanted to be trusted. He could rely on me, in spite of my aversion, not from loyalty but because I felt a stronger urge than his to get into the unknown. I was afraid and exhilarated, and wouldn't have traded such mixed feelings for anything. I was more willing than he was because, not sharing his obsession, I felt the kind of gung-ho keenness that he had probably forgotten about.

He was alone, and lonely, but instead of being sorry I knew I had to be on my guard. He lit his cigar. 'This ship will be my last. No more flying. My life's been a long chase after freedom. I don't suppose that means much to you, Sparks. But I've noticed that the longer you go chasing freedom, the more it dodges you. You can't find it. Can't grip it. The pursuit of freedom has always led me into captivity. Funny, eh? Into a profession, into the Air Force, into a marriage that never happened. Yet I thought each one would give me the freedom to know myself. It never did. The end of freedom is always the beginning of it. I got out of those institutions, and even then didn't find what I wanted. Do you know what freedom is, Adcock?'

His question surprised me. Though hardly listening, I took everything in while not caring to. I supposed freedom is not to worry about what the hell happens to you. I drank the coffee. He let his go cold, and smoked the cigar as if it were suckling him. 'In this flying boat I'm as close to freedom as I'll ever get. It's my natural state. But when the gold's been disposed of, I'll be free for the rest of my life. I won't live on Vortex Street anymore.'

He paused, his grey eyes staring at the photograph of the Lancaster. 'There's no more beautiful sight than that of an aircraft going across the sky. It's got engines, and fuel, and a crew on board. It's my reality.'

I wanted to sleep, or eat, or be at my wireless – anything but listen to a rambling I didn't understand.

'We are all inside that aircraft,' he said.

He's not well, I thought, determined to say nothing while he was talking to me. As long as he doesn't get stricken, and forget the drill when at the controls.

'I had an uncle who lived to be ninety. When I was on leave, the last time I saw him, he went for a walk. He seemed to have all his faculties, but he got lost, and the family had to search the streets for him.'

I knew younger people who would get lost if they went out alone. He only wanted me to listen, and I didn't think much of my luck in having been chosen.

'I'll never want to be taken away from myself, either by not being my own master, or by a senile old age. You understand?'

I said I did. And I did, though I wondered why he felt the matter important when he was so far from such a state. Everything happened for a purpose. He was sounding me out, to set us apart from the rest.

He thought I understood: 'I like my crew to function as one unit. Therein lies our survival. How do you get on with the others?'

'I've known them a fortnight.'

'You and I, Sparks, could get this aircraft from Point A to Point B on our own, if we had to.'

'I suppose we could.'

'I fly, and you navigate – by radio. Why do you think I picked an expert in direction-finding? Because you can get us home on wireless bearings, or at least make landfall, with me at the controls.'

He refilled his water glass. I was also thirsty. His words made me bone dry. Thoughts were rushing into my head that I didn't want. 'It wouldn't be impossible.'

'One has to anticipate all eventualities, that's what I'm saying. I want someone who is loyal, simple and clever.'

'Can anyone be simple and yet clever?'

He seemed out of touch. We were in the same aircraft, but of a different world.

'They can be, if they're loyal.'

'Loyal to what?' The question seemed important to my chances of getting out alive.

'To me.'

Self-preservation was paramount. 'You have all the loyalty I've got,' I heard myself saying.

He imagined it to be more than he needed. 'I expected no less. Getting to Kerguelen is easy enough, but knowing what we might find before we arrive – that's where you come in. I know you'll do it.'

The trunk of ash fell from his cigar.

'I'll try,' I said, having no idea what he meant.

9

Bull sat at the galley table and ordered slum-gullion. 'Every hour I'm in the air without eating seems as long as a day.'

I unwrapped my knife-fork-and-spoon. 'That's because you're cut off from mother earth.'

'I'd stay with her longer if she liked me.'

'You offend her with those obscene tattoos,' said Nash.

'I thought she was my friend, all the same.'

Rose dipped a biscuit into his scalding tomato soup. 'Friends are the easiest to offend. Enemies know where they stand.'

'Heads down,' said Appleyard cheerfully, 'or your steak and spuds'll get cold.'

'If it is' – Nash moved the peas and carrots around his plate – 'you'll go overboard, and no messing. You've got worse since the war. One thing I hate, and it's cold grub, especially in a flying boat.'

'Vegetables should be fresh, not out of a tin,' said Rose.

'Appleyard doesn't care,' Nash went on. 'His guts are like concrete, and we know why. He's never farted in his life. Oh yes, he did once, one frosty morning at Sullom Voe. He thought the bottom was dropping out of his world. The CO had him on the carpet because he sniffed lack of moral fibre. Took another ten trips to get him back on course – but it was a close-run thing.'

'You think this is the YMCA?' Appleyard felt genuinely

130

insulted at complaints about his cooking. 'I can't imagine why I came on this bloody trip. After leaving the mob I was so fed up with the Brylcreem Boys, I worked two years down a coalmine to get it out of my system. The money was good, the blokes were marvellous, and I was glad to be doing some proper work for a change. Now I'm back on this stunt.'

'Why are you, then?'

He looked contrite. 'Well, you need a change, don't you?'

Bull was unable to cut his steak. 'It makes the grub at the Driftwood seem like Mrs Beeton's best.'

'The past always looks good,' Rose drawled. 'The old Driftwood reminded me of the Jetsome Inn, a hostelry near Guildford where they even ruin black market food.'

Bull's eyes watered with nostalgia. 'I wish I was there, all the same.'

'I'm fed up with being duty cook,' Appleyard said, though no one took any notice.

'I think you-know-who's been boozing,' said Nash. 'I can smell it.'

Armatage ate the steak with his side teeth. 'When we get to Kerguelen, maybe a polar bear will make a meal out of you – though I expect the poor bugger'd sick its guts up if it did.'

'Your eyes look like piss-holes in the snow already,' said Nash. A scarf of cloud brushed by the porthole and turned the galley dim, with a grating sound under the hull, as if ropes that held us fast were being pulled loose. 'Can you cook seal meat?'

Appleyard levered a tin of Players from his jacket. 'We ate whale meat during the war.'

'You wouldn't cock a snook at anything,' said Rose.

'Or look a seahorse in the mouth.' Wilcox fought off another bout of coughing. The joke that he should get an

X-ray, or that the Kerguelen air would be as good a tonic as the best in Switzerland, had long been worn out, and we could only wonder how he managed to go on doing his job.

'Better get a move on, or your dessert will get hot,' said Appleyard as he dispensed bananas. Mine was too green, so I put it in my jacket pocket. He took each plate for washing up. 'I'll cook what you like, as long as I don't have to kill it.'

Armatage joked that for half a bottle of grog he'd kill anything.

'He'd cook his bloody firstborn for a swig of gut-rot,' said Bull. A fist flashed, as if powered by the jet of an obscene word, in an arc towards Bull's face, but collided with the palm of Nash's open hand, which stopped it dead. 'Wrap it up, the pair of you.'

A bump underfoot reminded us that we were moving on course to a place where none of us had been. Bull spat – nothing from a dry mouth, and reached for his mug of coffee. Wilcox coughed, his face pale and shining, a reddish spot in the middle of each cheek: 'We'll go hedge-hopping after seals, tally-bloody-hunting, like we did across Cambridgeshire when we chased a string of racehorses over the hill and down again. The skipper nearly lost his wings for that.'

Nash could hardly speak from laughter. 'And then there was that time when the old Sparks let go his trailing aerial and cut a cow in half. They couldn't decide which plane had done it, but the Air Ministry had to pay up – which was more than the cow could do!'

'We were bloody hell-bent in those days,' said Bull.

'If we mow down a few seals from the rear turret we'll live off the fat of the land, eh Nashie?' Armatage chipped in.

'There's even coal to cook on,' I said. 'And you don't have to get it from underground in a bucket. We'll find a whaler's hut for shelter. Stranded or not, we'll be snug.'

'I prefer civilization,' said Rose, 'on the whole.'

132

'Why not speculate on all possibilities?'

'Speculate, my arse,' said Bull.

Rose rinsed his irons in the bowl, dried them on the teatowel hanging from its hook, and put them into the top pocket of his jacket. 'I'll say no to that one, if you don't mind.'

I went back to the wireless with my mug of coffee, and wondered how we would survive if the flying boat couldn't take off. I was not so appalled at the idea as I should have been.

10

The plane was a workshop. Shottermill had obviously left a few packs of gaudy banknotes in the right places, otherwise how could we have set off with such lethal goods? I turned to see people lifting and carrying, serpentine belts of ammo around their necks. Curses were frequently shaped on their lips because the interior frame of the flying boat was lined with sharp corners.

Nash levered an assembled gun towards the rear turret. The *Aldebaran* was being set for defence, and it did not matter against whom or what. 'Something'll turn up, you can be sure. And if it don't, we ought to make it. Otherwise, what's life for?' But he was sweating and breathless, and put the gun down after a few feet. 'We had armourers to do this in the war, and I'm not as young as I was.'

Bennett need not have left the flight deck to see that work was up to scratch, because Armatage was sufficiently competent as an armourer to forget toothache, overcome his disability from drink, and rig twin guns in the mid-upper. The crew had been chosen well, and in our pre-lunch talk the skipper had made sure of me. Bull went to assist Nash, and they managed the labour between them.

I could make no sense out of the distant twittering on eight megacycles but, thinking that contact might come from that quarter, scoured to either side of the band. There was nothing for us. The plane was losing height. Cloud melted away except for what seemed like a line of grey bushes to the south. Hard to think of the Pole as being a point from where any straight line away from it went north. The cobalt sea glowed in the sun. My ears popped, playing a tune. Taking off the headset, a deep breath brought engine noise roaring back.

I looked out in the hope of seeing a ship. So much water was a transparent envelope around the earth, waiting only to be pierced by a spike of land. Maybe ships had been visible while I listened at the radio, but the world had now gone back to water, and our contraption was a flimsy habitation that might crumble any moment into a tangle of wreckage from which none of us would swim.

I returned to the friendly embrace of atmospherics, from whose noise some message of support might come, an item of interest or mystery to rejuvenate the brain. After a while cataracts of static became a form of elemental life, like being in the stomach of an animal big enough to contain the universe. If I closed my eyes there were colours, cobalt and magenta stippled with pale orange, a complicated pattern battling against itself, unharmonious because no morse impinged. The noise of the atmosphere was channelled into my headset via the aerials and receiver. In order to miss no signal lurking among the noise, I kept the volume high, the din almost overpowering.

I began to hear signals that did not exist, perhaps the bleep of a transmitter tuning in, or a string of dots and dashes that made no sense, coming and going but only to

134

tantalize. The next stream resembled bars of music, of no recognizable tune, and too fast to be intercepted. I was amused at how they could deceive an old hand like me. Rose glanced in my direction because he imagined I was listening to a broadcast of ITMA.

Figures and letters appeared on the notepad, my hand willing to write anything rather than be inactive; but all I produced was a dozen signs at most, and wondered what marcolin on the tailplane scratched signals into the atmospherics with webbed feet or clawed fingers. Perhaps a pair of stations on the Antarctic coast fifteen hundred miles south worked their two-way traffic, using callsigns in no handbook. Had they spotted us on a sophisticated form of long-distance radar? Only the continual brain-battering static could create such ludicrous ideas.

A garble of faint squawks resembled voices. I turned down the CW switch, but could not bring them clearer. My receiver, superheterodyned for wireless telegraphy, was not ideal for getting speech. Feedback and distortion made readability difficult. Given the static that deadened my eardrums and induced a kind of half sleep at my set, why did I think they were voices at all? And if I didn't hear them, what put the idea into my head? Craving company, perhaps I had conjured them out of the ether, suggesting I was losing my attachment to reality after barely six hours out. Voices or not, they were too garbled to decipher. If they had been understandable, what effect would they have had on our flying boat? That was the crux of the matter, if there was a crux, and if any matter existed, which I was beginning to doubt. Perhaps they were too far off to read, and it was only a question of time before the words became plain.

When I heard them again, slightly off frequency, I listened as if a needle had pierced my eardrums. I turned up the volume in the hope of surprising a word before the static became equally loud. It couldn't work, of course. But art is

135

often artfulness. A distant voice sounded like a slobbering idiot in the corner of a bare room trying to sing something he had heard twenty years ago. No amount of fine-tuning could get him to remember it. You try everything, however.

I couldn't delay informing Bennett of a mysterious harmonic or frequency echo from some far-off broadcasting station that had a twang of the radio-telephone in its tone. He left Wilcox at the controls, and stood near me. 'How far away?'

'Can't tell, Skipper. A few hundred. Or a thousand.'

Electric waves travel at 186,000 miles a second, so what's the odds? I thought.

'More than a thousand?'

'It could be.'

He gripped the receiver so tightly I thought he would yank it out of the fixture. 'It must be near the islands.'

'Might not be.'

'Did you get a bearing?'

'I tried. It's all over the place. Could be behind us – along the reciprocal.'

Sweat ran down his face. 'Why tell me, unless you're sure?'

'You asked me to notify you.'

He listened. The voices had gone. Pulling out a handkerchief to mop his forehead, a screw of paper drifted towards Rose's table. 'Keep at it. Next time, I want something definite.' He went back to the controls.

Would I tell him as quickly? He wanted to know. So did I. Then he'd know. God knows why he wanted to. The air around the world was full of noises. Pitting himself against that kind of play would get him either into a dead-end or a million fragments. The same with me, but I had to try, detach myself from the flying boat, become disembodied, attain a state of equilibrium, power of manoeuvre, and discrimination so that I would appear as an enigma to any outsider who might be trying to fox me with his intermittent sending. The difficulty in achieving any kind of success enthused me. To attempt the near hopeless induced humour, which gave way to a spirit of beneficial calm.

I must not seem anxious to begin measures for our defence. Hurry would create suspicion. I had to separate the imagined from the real and, having decided what was real, assuming I was in a fit state to do so, try to make sense from what I heard. If I hurried to find out, by tapping my morse key and asking direct, I would have little chance of success, and play right into their hands. Success was a term by which nothing could be measured, at this stage.

After a sunshot, and working out his spherical triangle – Rose sometimes liked to do things the hard way – he stood up and stretched himself. By a quarter turn I noted his movements, for any twitch within eye-shot was a marked event in our progress. There was a naval tidiness about a flying boat and, seeing the paper that had fallen from Bennett's pocket, Rose picked it up.

I measured time by my wrist watch set to Greenwich, other indications being the number of meridians crossed. Stations popped up from a quarter of the world but, being on radio silence, time ceased to exist as far as events were concerned. Locally, it was midday, but we were not due to sight Kerguelen till five in the morning. With a favourable wind we travelled south easterly at 120 knots air speed, the crackling ether so loud it sounded as if a giant saw was cutting the earth in two. No instructions tied me to my set, only a congenital burden of having to pass the time usefully, so when static threatened irreversible deafness (except when a message of 'Z' time landfall at Bombay was picked up from a Royal Mail ship) I went down to the galley for a stroll, where I expected to see Rose, because he was no longer at the chart table.

Armatage was putting the finishing touches to the mid-upper. Bull was completing installations in the front turret, and Nash was doing the same in the tail. Bennett and

137

Wilcox were on the flight deck. Appleyard slept in his bunk, a copy of *Lilliput* fallen onto his chest. I flipped through to the nude, then put it back.

The galley was empty, and on touching the handle of the door to Bennett's room I heard a noise. I acted like a somnambulist. My eyelids had two mattresses pressed on them, and sleep was my only wish, but as soon as the door began to open I awoke as if I had already dreamed of pushing it hard and had come out of the dream without knowing. Inside I saw Rose by the table holding a notebook and a sheet of paper. Both of us shivered as if stricken instantaneously with malaria. The good side of his face was as white as the paper, and I guessed he must have thought I was Bennett coming in.

He had only to say he had been sent to get something, and I would have retreated, for I was hardly inside. His shock was bigger, and a jolt underfoot made him lean on the table, and put the book back under the chart. But he kept the paper, and clutched my arm. His lips trembled, and he almost pushed me.

'What are you up to?'

'We've got to talk,' he said.

I clambered over heaps of stores and followed him halfway to the rear turret. We crouched by a pile of sacks, boxes and mooring tackle. 'What about?'

He waited, as if to get his breath after running half a mile, then he showed me the paper, on which the only thing written was a crew list. 'You can hear, but you haven't got eyes to see.'

I didn't understand till he pointed to three names with crosses pencilled against them. 'What are you talking about?'

'This paper fell from Bennett's pocket.'

'I know. I saw it.'

He took the paper back, as if afraid I would eat it. 'He's put a cross against your name, mine and Wilcox's.'

I lost patience. 'The bloody flight crew. But so what?'

'Not against his own.'

I still didn't get it.

'We're the ones he'll dispose of.'

Wireless operators face an occupational hazard of going off their heads for no known reason, but I had not so far seen anything similar happen to a navigator. 'Too many sunsights have done for you. Kick somebody out of their bunk and take an hour's snooze.' I felt I was in a flying lunatic asylum. 'He can't do without us, and you know it.'

'I thought so, too. But he's also a navigator. In that notebook it says we fly north to Ceylon. He wants to get rid of us. Maybe the gunners as well – even Nash. With all of us out of the way, no one will be able to say where he got his gold. There won't be any but him and Nash to share it with.'

I laughed. 'He used that notebook to work out every hypothetical getaway route, and it doesn't mean a thing. He's not a Roman emperor. You forget those who financed this expedition. He can't do them down – nor would he.'

He wondered, from his glare, what else you could expect from a Group Two Trade wireless operator. 'He'll give them the slip, as well.'

I was rocking. The scheme would make sense, if I could become sufficiently insane to believe in it. He said calmly: 'It fits as neatly as a cocked hat – the whole scheme.'

'Let's get back on duty.'

I needed to think. A wireless operator listening to static can do so, but a navigator can't, otherwise he makes mistakes, adding where he should subtract, or putting his pencil on the wrong column in the Book of Tables. He pushed me aside, and made his way through the plane.

In order to spare my brain the deadening drumfire of static I wondered if Bennett's idea really was to get home with only one other member of the crew. If so, who was the lucky man? The slip of paper need not have given any indication. Perhaps the final duo would be Bennett and Rose, or Bennett and Wilcox, or even Bennett and me. Even the person he marked down to live would not finally survive. The golden hoard would be Bennett's alone. If Bennett had chosen a gunner in taking over the flying boat, the obvious candidate was Nash, who could keep a secret better than any of the others.

The game might be carried a stage further. Should Bennett cease to exist, Wilcox could fly the plane. Rose also had the ability. Both could at least make some kind of pancake landing. But I doubted whether Rose or Wilcox had any notion of reducing the crew, sure that Bennett had wondered the same – if he had wondered anything at all. They were not that kind of people. Wilcox was ill, in spite of hectic optimism, and in no state to fly the plane for long. The others would not try to take the plane because they did not have the experience of command. They couldn't care less. As a crew they kept their feelings close, and lacked the personality to forge such a plan. Neither would they be accomplices of Bennett's.

Such a wonderful self-told tale kept me occupied while my ears flattened against the crackling emptiness of the ether. In no way was I distracted from listening. As a counterweight to deadness, the possibility sharpened the keenness of my ears. Once on civilized dry land, and the job finished, I would smile to recall such suspicions from inside and out, and laughingly remember it as if some tap-chatting card of the morse code fraternity had transmitted the latest joke about ice-cream vans at the South Pole.

My hand shook as it hovered over the key, knowing that an unnecessary contact might bring disaster. I was caught in the trap of being the only one able to open a window of our enclosed world and alter the turning wheel of fate. My suspicions were ludicrous, yet I couldn't let go the idea that I must take note of my feelings. The warnings from both sides were as clear as if they had come in at strength five from some guardian wireless station deep in myself, whose existence I had not known till this moment. Whatever words I keyed out, no one else on board would know what they meant. They read morse, but not at the speed I could send. The language was mine alone, and the responsibility belonged only to me.

But the sending could not be done in secret. I was visible to Rose and Wilcox, and my relays might be heard clicking over the intercom. I had to keep silent, but what did that matter when such feverish and lunatic speculations meant that there was no reason to send anything at all?

11

⚭

We were in a sunspot: duration unknown, dimensions beyond the scope of mensuration, not even a far-off coast station on which to focus the old needle, a feeling of timeless loss which made it easy to wonder whether Rose was out of his mind, or Bennett quietly loco, or Wilcox dying of TB, or Armatage about to pop down the chute from too much booze – or whether I ought to have my brains tested for trying to decide how many of us were, in fact, beyond the blue horizon. The eternal sandpaper of static rubbed the eardrums with little variation. The doldrums were in the ether rather than half over the sea.

Wilcox's cough was sawing through his windpipe. His eyes glittered, and a smile of confidence in God's benignity when the hacking paused made him appear that he would be almost grateful to go when the time came. Armatage was often drunk and hearing voices. Bull tended to be surly and quarrelsome, while the normally stolid Nash had been reinforcing his spirit with benzedrine pills since installing the Brownings, so that at least he and Appleyard seemed sufficiently level-headed to be trustworthy in a crisis.

For myself, the messages I intercepted went in circles, a snake whose tail was in its mouth, saying that if what Rose surmised turned out to be true, our worries were as good as over. We would be dead when the circle broke. Yet there was many a step between imagination and reality, though how could you expect anyone with a persecution complex to know that? The question I put to myself lacked subtlety. Born of distrust rather than enquiry, answers were unrewarding. Would we be killed on shore at Kerguelen? Or would the flying boat take off and leave us to fend for ourselves? Again, who was Bennett's accomplice besides Nash? More important, would I, Rose or Wilcox be the first to go?

Credence was not as firm as it ought to have been that Bennett would refrain from slaughtering his old crew on the last great flying boat journey for something so paltry as a bigger share in the profits. To ignore the evidence was stupidity or laziness, a way of hiding fear. Rose had passed his trepidations on to me, in whom continual static induced nightmares, and I wondered whether I should transfer them to Wilcox, and observe his reaction – supposing he wasn't too ill to notice.

The flying boat slipped, lifted, fell into another of God's pockets, then righted itself. I looked out of the port hole. Bennett descended through rain cloud to sea-level, overtaking the green and rolling combers to each crest and then down again. No wonder I couldn't get much range on the wireless. My guts were turning, but after a few minutes of such flip about, he held us straight, while the altimeter was checked for zero, leaving nothing to chance for the landing. Then we gained height.

I could only smile at Rose's fantasy that the best of flying boat skippers would put such a scheme in hand. But if Rose was mad, how far would we get with him in a straitjacket? All the way, if we worked hard. The paper had accidentally fallen from Bennett's pocket. I thought he had done it deliberately. Rose disagreed, apt to regard his own mistakes, however trivial, as mental deterioration. Even if temporary, no one was exempt, but when you dropped a clanger there was always a subtle warning to tell you that you had, and with concentration you could find it out. He whispered as much to me when we were back at our stations. When the sunspot over Bennett's consciousness cleared, and he discovered the loss of the paper, he would assume that one of us had picked it up.

We stood at the bottom of the ladder. 'I couldn't care less,' I said.

'That attitude will get you nowhere.'

'It got me here.'

'It'll keep you here. Or under the bog with a penguin pecking at your liver. The French claim Kerguelen, and to go there and recover the treasure from under their noses is illegal, old boy.'

'The mission's difficult enough, without Bennett disposing of people he'll need to get the plane to wherever he decides to head after his gold's stowed aboard.' I climbed up, and put on the earphones. I cared very much, not wanting to alarm Rose in case the others noticed his disturbance.

Static was less intense, and I swung the needle till a jazz band sounded like a juggernaut whose unoiled axles were squeaking and grinding over the stones. I got back onto my listening frequency, wondering if I should tell Bennett that we had his death list. He would think I was as much off my head as I considered Rose to be out of his. We would only know that the note had any significance if Bennett got up from his seat and carried out a square search for what he had lost.

We hadn't long to wait. He came loud and clear over the intercom, speaking calmly, yet seeming a shade on the still side of breathlessness.

'What I don't want is for any of you to keep a diary, or make notes, or start letters which you won't have the opportunity to finish – or post. Filling in diaries while on board will be frowned on, because all details of this trip must be kept secret. Your memories must black out whatever takes place. At the end of our journey, navigation and wireless logs will be handed in. Stray chits for calculation, or bits of paper containing call signs, or inside-out pieces of cigarette packets with engine performances or fuel consumptions scribbled on them will be handed in to me. In other words, whatever happens is not to be communicated to the press, nor any information given to people not permitted to receive it. Everything is restricted, and for official use only. That is to say: ours, and nobody else's. But mostly I'm talking about diaries and journals, because none of us want to be incriminated for minor breaches of the international navigation laws which we might inadvertently make. It's too easy for written evidence to be used against us in a court of law.'

He was talking to himself.

'Roger,' I said.

So did Rose.

Then Wilcox and the others gave their assent.

Nash added: 'I never wrote anything in my life, Skipper. It's not my style. If I don't keep a log, I don't have to cook it!'

Bennett laughed. 'Hi-di-hi!'

'Ho-di-ho!' said Nash.

I tucked the notes I had made into my left flying boot. If he expected me to eat them, or turn the wad in, he couldn't have been more wrong. He hoped one of us would produce that scrap of paper so mindlessly dropped. Rose winked, and I gave the thumbs-up.

144

I tapped out a few signals, hoping none of the crew would hear, but the contacts bled all over the intercom.

'Splashing a bag of Dolly Mixtures across the sky, Sparks?'

'Only testing, Skipper. I disconnected the aerial.'

'Didn't sound like it. If God gets a bearing on us, we're doomed. He's a sharp old bastard.'

'He'd have to be, to get that.'

'So pack it in. When I say we're on radio silence, don't play roulette with those nursery-coloured clickstops. Put the silencer on your heartbeats – like me. Everything provides a fix for some big-eared operator in the sky, or on the sea. Any more playing around and even the Radio Doctor won't get you going again. Just grow up, and do as I say. There's always someone in the world sharper than you.'

I saw his back, solid and unmoving, protecting his heart, keeping a straight course and constant speed, as if he didn't even trust the automatic pilot.

'Tore a strip off you, did he?' said Wilcox.

I gave him the fuck-off sign, and fished into my bag for the Smith and Wesson. With enough rounds for all emergencies, it nestled solidly among my possessions, the cold-comforter from Malaya that I was glad I'd got. Fired at Bennett, the great plane would cone into the sea before Rose and I (and maybe Wilcox) could get him out of the seat and set the kite back on an even keel.

My brain was no good. I had betrayed myself. To pit my endurance against the circling rush of electrified air was all I could manage. Murderous action was only fit for a theatre, preferably while I watched and, when excitement became too intense, hoped the curtain would descend and leave me with my own inactive reality.

Bennett inhabited the whole stage because, at one with his imagination, he felt no division such as that between the two that lurked in me. He sat at the controls of a world that was bigger to him than any other, as if not even God could break the unity of his cast-iron obsession. I contemplated destroying him before he could lead us into danger. But that would mean entering the zone of his obsession, where all thought would be clouded, and success elude me. The only way to fight was to get back to work, and establish a life-line to the outside world.

The more I searched, and found nothing, the more vulnerable I felt the flying boat to be. Instead of holding the loaded gun at Bennett's back I pinned myself to the tuning dials, knowing that nothing short of disaster could lift any of us from our private worlds. I heard Royal Navy ships sending to each other, and to Trincomalee in Ceylon. Their call signs seemed as far off as the Line of Capricorn, and pipingly distinct. They were the great morse-soloists of the age, brisk telegraphists whose machine-like rhythm was a pleasure to listen to. I noted their direction, and wanted to know whether they were frigates, destroyers or survey ships; whether they weren't caught in the flurrying tail of a monsoon, or smudges of smoke on the placid sea. What was the purpose of their manoeuvres? I looked out, as if beyond the earth's curvature, to force ship or plane into vision. But from the window of my flying radio shack, there was empty sea, and my effort at hallucination could not populate that vacant water.

I was glad to get back to my place, where the faintest squeak was backed by an intelligence that had initialled its duration and the leap of its distance – the Heaviside ricochet piercing the static racket. Whatever had diminished the power of its pure note, and furred the lines of clarity on its way from the transmitter, must be the same force that prevented me asking questions by which I might have bottled all problems up. Nothing could be done to cure my impotence, however, or resolve my ignorance. I had always been shifted by fate, something which I had known long ago.

Perhaps the Navy ships had nothing more to say. I

missed their robust precision. From our freebooting flying boat the tenuous connection of their signals had comforted me, and now their absence exaggerated my isolation. Rose called out a course correction, and Bennett took us a few degrees to port. The local time was ten minutes to five in the afternoon. A ceiling of highball cumulus, speckled cloud ragged at the edges of its denser parts, formed at twenty thousand feet, sun filtering through bars which kept us prisoners from the universe beyond.

I was divided between regret at having signed on, and enjoying the adventure I had let myself in for. Harmony could only be maintained by doing my job. But the split, being necessary, would need a third of me to keep them under control, which led me to wonder what other part of me would keep *them* in order? Only all states fusing into one, and fuelled by the conveniently forgotten split, could ensure self-preservation.

In the meantime, as dusk came on, I had to accept that there was no safety for one unless there was safety for all. The next moment I told myself again that I couldn't care less, but the part of me that knew better, earthed as much as it could be in such a place, continued to search the ether.

12

Dusk was gunmetal blue, and smelled of sulphur. There was an ominous wall of cloud to climb over, or fly under, or get around, and I could think of nothing except what we would find on the eastern side after travailing all night along the cone-like convergence. The new day would bring us to the island, and events beyond that were too much in the unknown to contemplate. But the darkness remained, and though my awareness of Bennett's intentions and Rose's fears had faded, and questions as to our future seemed irrelevant, I vacillated in mood between feeling entirely beleaguered and fitting in with the general pattern. I could not think why the night would demand all my attention, but decided that no matter what conflict erupted among the crew, I would remain as the radio operator whose duty it was to stay on watch for whatever information I could obtain to keep the plane secure. The flying boat was our world, and I did not want the world to end. Against the bumps of the elements it was flimsy, but the enclosed space was safe, and I was the ears of its inhabitants, doomed though they might be, able to hear from the outside, as well as having eyes with which to bear witness on the inside. Being the sort of person I knew myself to be was the extent of my power. I could fulfil my function, nothing more.

Bennett took off the automatic pilot and made a frontal attack on the looming battlements of cloud. Static became pandemonium at the airless pockets we fell into, and at the precipitous updraughts that sent us leaping. On the flight deck water beaded across the perspex. Through the turbulence I kept a grip so as not to be thrown off my feet.

At my set the static of the world converged for a conference at dusk, the worst time for reception. I searched for one clear voice of morse, however irrelevant, but every frequency was swamped. A rolling stone gathers no morse, I said to Rose, and settled on the 6500 HF DF frequency, sliding to one side or the other but getting little more than indecipherable squeaks.

The stars had gone, as if they had vanished with us into the spongy barrier of cloud. From the side hatch the propellers purred normally, seeming to make little noise. Grumbling underfoot felt like the earth giving way. I disregarded the yawing of our boat in the ocean-air, and my gyro-stomach took control. Swathes of rain and sleet slewed the canopy, and Bennett eased us through a series of alarming bounces, not yet over the top into clear air.

The lamp glowed, and I gladly returned to the semicircular window of my radio-face with its indicator lines of different colours. Someone stood nearby, and I pulled half a world of static from one ear to see Nash lighting a cigarette. 'The storm's very pretty. I watched it from the mid-upper, but every flash gave me a pain in the arse, so I came down.'

I tapped the set with my pencil. 'A storm like this makes me want to talk – about this one-eyed expedition, maybe.'

'If you'll stop listening to Dick Barton or Mrs Dale's Diary on that clapped out wireless, perhaps we will. Follow me to the rear turret. Tell Rose you're going for a kip, or he'll want to join in the pow-wow.'

Old fliers, with more than the five senses, can pick the air to pieces like a bird, and find a way through. Bennett pressed on regardless. The cloud ceiling rippled below, but in the distance was an archipelago of holes – dark pink and dirty grey, a purple band circling the sky, a well-advanced dusk I had never seen before and thought I wouldn't see again.

Darkness faded the rosy view. More cloud ranges bordered the northern sky. Streaks of white fire snaked themselves into the sea, one after the other, and no sooner did they hit water than they were as if by magic transferred back to the sky, to descend again, up and down, as if they would go on until the sky burned itself out. Closer to hand, Venus was rising, and shone on the sea.

I followed him down the temple of the fuselage. Half in and half out of the turret, his back to the guns, he resembled a gnome in spite of his bulk, outsized perhaps, and balancing to avoid too heavy a grip. His glint was amiable, but the lower lip showed anxiety. The boat grumbled underfoot as I crouched, and wondered how I would know if he was telling the truth, or whether there was any truth left to tell. Curiosity satisfied meant being told the worst more often than it meant knowing the best.

'The stars are flashing their peepers, so Rose can find out where we are. The skipper would like to know, I expect.' He shuffled his feet. 'I could never abide not seeing stars when we were on ops, even if it was dangerous. When I can't see stars or the ground, my level goes, if you see what I mean. Being in fog or cloud always scares me. I might see something I don't like, though I can't think what that would be. Or we might smash into a house, or a ship, or a cliff-face even though we are at ten thousand feet. My bloody sins coming back to haunt me, I expect, if it's anything at all.'

I moved to get at my cigarette case. 'Bit late to talk about our sins.'

He spat, though nothing came, then struck a match for our smoke. 'There's no time better than now when it comes to atonement.' The light which united us showed him to be smiling. 'But what I can't understand is why a young chap like you volunteered for this sort of job. What the heck have you got to atone for?'

'If I knew I wouldn't be here, though if you ask me where I would be if I weren't here I don't think I could tell you.' His jungle of atonement had no attraction for me, as he surmised, but I told him I was here because of money, adventure, work and a broken marriage. If he reversed the order he might well get it right.

'I thought there was more to you than met the eye.' We smoked, and listened to the test-bed grind of the engines rather than to our own thoughts. Darkness brought more ease, screened us from peril, and generated a denser element of companionship. 'Aren't you going to ask why I'm here?' he said at last.

'I thought religion and politics were out on this trip?'

'Well, we're not in the French Foreign Legion, either,' he

said. 'But *nothing* will be out before it's ended. Bennett's on a treasure-hunt, and there'll be no let-up till it's over. The gold's got to be lifted quick, because we aren't the only people after it. Someone knew enough to set another combine working against us, but we're on our way there first, as far as we know. If they should see our fuel ship and board it, they'll find nothing, because the stuff will already be away – by flying boat. Bloody neat, eh?'

We sat through the space of two cigarettes. 'The trouble is,' he went on, 'that Bennett lives in a world of his own. Nobody can get at him. But it's important to the rest of us that we know everything, so you've got to listen for any ship close enough to bash out morse so strong it parts your hair: it's bound to be on the same game as us, because no others get to where we're going – except maybe the odd whaler. Tell me as well as Bennett all you hear. You'll earn your keep, and our gratitude.'

It was wise not to show emotion or surprise at being plainly asked to divide my loyalty between him and Bennett. The reason did not seem clear, and if it had maybe I would have liked his advice even less. I was jolted as if, sitting in a room with a clock on the shelf, I began to hear its ticking again, when in fact it had never stopped. The noise of four engines rushed back into my ears as the war-surplus flying boat churned its airscrews through black sky, leaving a wake of exhaust fumes, the only roar for thousands of miles, and undetectable because no other vehicle was within range. We had the air to ourselves.

'There'll be hardly a pint of juice left in each engine by the time we get there,' he said. 'If these tail winds weren't pushing us along we'd have a ditching to look forward to. I'll certainly be glad when we're bobbing about on that fjord like a cork in the sink at Christmas!'

'I can't understand why we're so well-armed,' I said. 'Browning machine guns seem a bit excessive.'

He reached out and patted their grips. 'They aren't for

151

shelling peas. Nor are we going to make a wartime shit-picture. It might be all show, but it would be a shame if we got everything on board and somebody tried to pull it away from us.'

'But who?'

He stood up, about to push by me. 'I can't see into the future. But if anybody tries to get that gold from us, I'll blast 'em out of sky or water, let me tell you.'

I was aware of Bennett, immovable at the controls, mindless in his set purpose. Our lives were in his hands. But they had been in our own individual hands before we had delivered them into his. 'Are you glad to be on this trip, Nash?'

He turned, still stooping. 'I'd rather be here than in jail, which is where I was three months ago. I'll never go there again. It's paradise being here, compared to that.'

'Paradise can sink,' I said.

He grunted, and went on his way before me, saying: 'I'd rather go down from paradise than from any other place.'

13

When an aircraft on 6440 kilocycles informed Cape Town – ZSC – of his time of arrival from Durban – ZSD – his morse had a hollow tone, like someone clapping hands in the distance. I passed their messages to Bennett, but he stuffed the paper in his chart bag. 'No action.'

Caught by the hiss of ether, thermionic valves worked overtime trying to interpret the emptiness. The headset was my balaclava comforter, supplying atmospherics that sounded like a load of gravel shooting from the back of a tip-up lorry.

Another shadow dissolved mine under the angle-lamp. Bennett's eyes were surrounded by grey flesh. 'Tell me as soon as anything happens. You're the only one who can.'

Why me? There was no answer. He left Wilcox at the controls and went down the ladder. What plain talk entered the earphones would be pounded out myself, sending me through a black hole and searching along the space lanes, away from a world whose morse no longer made sense. Now that Bennett had gone to rest I could transmit. Wilcox was too concerned with keeping the artificial horizon and his splintering coughs in synchronization to notice, though what messages I would send, and to whom, I did not know. I could hear from further away than my signals would reach, but even with a more powerful transmitter my text would be distorted beyond readability.

Even so, I was tempted to put my hand on the key and try to contact another soul beyond the flying boat's periphery. Perhaps a ship was close, though few kept continual watch, while those that did were unlikely to come this way, and the frequency they listened on had little range. What would I say? I did not know, but maybe: Who are you? Where are you? Can you hear me? QRA? QTH? QRK? If he replied, I might enquire: Why am I here? But there was no 'Q' Signal for that. Never ask questions that cannot be answered, otherwise there will be no end to what you want to know. Yet an end was needed, was vital, though you may never get it. Emptiness is a desert, whether sky or water, and being in the wilderness tells you that there is no limit to sense or consciousness. Send that on your morse key and see how far it gets you! Mad bastard! Give us the proper griff, the pukka gen. Whatever there is to seek, you will not find it there. Your dots-and-dashes go into space, and vanish from weakness. The same with thoughts, unless there is a God to count the ricochets back into your heart and explain why you are alive.

Circular reflections induce fatigue. What grip is to be got on space? Nash asked why I had come, and I could have replied that if you have to there's no alternative. No one can tell why, though if a reason has indeed triggered off your impulse then you are faced with the fact that no reason can prevail against an impulse. It is useless to argue, or otherwise repine at the fundamental vagaries of fate. But do not come out the same as you went in.

'Some char, Sparks. It's the Relief of Mafeking. Everybody's nodding off. If it wasn't for Wilcox, the kite would have pranged by now.'

'Don't get that biscuit tin near the tapper,' I said, 'or a short circuit'll send a howl of pain through the sky.' Appleyard laid a stack of biscuits like a gambler's winnings on my log book. 'It'd sound as if somebody's stepped on a mongrel's leg, and Sirius would jump a mile. He wouldn't like it.'

'He'd have to lump it, then. One sugar, or four?'

'Is it strong?'

'Enough to rot a wedding ring. No bromide, though, like in the old days.'

'Put in a couple, then take your bucket to Rose. He can do with a drop before his next star sight. Tell him that the bright pointer of the Southern Cross is coming up abeam, if I'm not mistaken.'

The tea separated nerve wires at the back of my eyes. I heard them pinging, and was awake, thoughts once more in a Ben Hur race. Chasing gold was not for me, unless of another sort, but of what quality I hardly knew. My place was with Anne, though not in the state I had left her. She would never want what I craved. We couldn't exist together, so there was no point in hankering. I was as alone as everyone else in that airborne assembly of walking wounded.

Rose must have given Wilcox notice before getting star sights, because it felt as if we were cruising over black velvet. Every man froze at his station. If the engines went fatally and we were forced to ditch, we would know our position to within five miles or so, which was some comfort, providing Bennett allowed me to send an SOS before smacking the chop.

I pressed my finger to emit one dot – breaking radio silence by the single letter 'E'. What information would anyone get from that tick of electricity in their earphones? Only the fact, according to Bennett – who did not hear that shortest letter of the morse alphabet while he slept – that another transmitter was close by.

One part of me had surely known of my intention, but the other did not. That which knew had got the upper hand, while the other was aware of nothing. To accept responsibility for the error that had been committed, I needed to believe that the side which knew of my intentions had been to blame, but I could only feel guilty if that part of me which did not know had initiated the action.

I had been unconscious of outside phenomena for five minutes, proved by the last entry in my log. The crackle of atmospherics had been so deafening that no ear could have intercepted that single absconding dot – which vanished like a fish in muddy water. The only noise I can tolerate is static, out of which I gather information, or into which my thoughts melt. I prefer to be controlled by chaos rather than order. Whatever comes from order is written down and forgotten, whereas chaos rules by patience and subterfuge. When I was twelve I was walking home from school and hearing Handel's Largo still in my ears from the classroom. Wanting to sing the words on the street, I was unable to. I'd had to wait to make my own rhythms, and send them out in morse from a stricken flying boat plunging along the wind lanes of the Roaring Forties, Antarctica to the right, and space to the left as far as Asia. 'Where e'er you walk' played out the letter 'Q' of the eternal question, and I did not know what it signified – nor ever would.

155

From the mid-upper turret, beyond my D/F loop and across the bows, I saw the port and starboard wing broken only by an expanse of the leading edge which glowed in the darkness. Someone switched on the mike of his intercom and blew as if to cool a saucer of tea, glad to hear even the rush of his own breath.

Sirius, the brightest star, was behind us, and I picked out Canopus to the southeast. Far in front loomed another escarpment of bad weather, and the crate would soon begin a slow climb to get over the top. A blue glow came from the flame-dampened exhausts, and through the astrodome I could just make out, inside our huge flying belly, the dim light above Rose's navigation table, and the lamp of my wireless operator's position. A tug at my leg was a signal from Nash to climb down.

Rose on the flight deck wielded his sextant, and I recalled his rhyme sung in a drunken binge at the Driftwood:

> 'All places east
> By great circle bear best,
> All places west
> By great circle bear least – '

'You're all to cock,' he snapped. 'Stick to your own trade.'

I clamped my headphones on, informing Bennett, back at the controls, that the loop aerial indicated a stormy passage.

'I'll go right through. Can't afford to lose this flying wind. We'll be longer with the murk, but will overtake it in the end. So pull in the trailing aerial.'

If it was out, and lightning struck, I would be the first to get a knocking. A gutted set and a stunned operator might be the final safeguard for radio silence, but I didn't think Bennett would want to go that far. I got the trailing aerial in, but let it go again, thinking that maybe a dose of shock

156

would clear my head, and that wireless operator's roulette was a fair game to play.

Word came for safety belts, and I clipped myself in. Turning the page of my log book, I felt the secondhand aeroplane rear where no air was, then float as if on snow. The feeling underfoot was curious, as if we were held in the palm of some being to whom our flying boat was made of balsa wood. The electricity of anticipation ran through me, and my fingers moved without thought towards the morse key, which I would have pressed except that a sudden drop banged my knees at the table, and forced wide open eyes to witness every angled corner.

Rose, huddled over charts, grabbed the sextant, while his Dalton computer chased a perspex ruler down the ladder towards the galley. The good side of his face sheered by the bulkhead, and I felt a pang at the thought that he would be scarred there as well – till my neck was wrenched the other way and I saw the skipper holding grimly on, stability his sole aim. Rain splashed the windscreen, and we seemed under the ocean instead of two miles above. Over the intercom a steel door banged regularly on a wet plank, never tiring, till I thought to tighten the aerial connection. Nash was secure in his mid-upper, but when the plane levelled for a moment said: 'Do that again, Skipper!'

Which brought a curt response from Bull: 'Nearly broke my fucking elbow.'

While Bennett and Wilcox struggled to get out of a corkscrew descent, my hand gripped the morse key as if that action alone would bring us through the storm. I felt aileron wires and rudder joints cracking under the strain, and waited for that last ounce of pressure to pitch us hell-bent into the drink. I was otherwise too wary of losing equilibrium and being slammed against the click-stops to be afraid. Stresses and strains were matched to four engines, and there was no better plane in which to have a thirteen-rounder with the sky.

'If you believe that, you'll believe anything,' said Appleyard. My hand rested a couple of seconds on the key, making a letter 'T' which, if joined to the last symbol sent, would make ET. And what then? The floor slipped sideways and fell. I wanted to play the morse key like Niedzielski his piano, and instead of sending no more than a pip and a squeak bash out a heartache letter-telegram to Anne, explaining that my love for her was even more intense because I was in a situation where to think of it blunted my attitude to danger.

Bennett fought to get us higher, as if he had in mind a definite ceiling to the storm. Lightning danced along the wing, fixed by a trap of blue steel, which caused the plane to fall as if to get out of its way. 'Who gave us that weather forecast?' Nash croaked along the pipeline. 'I'll have his guts for garters.'

'They won't taste good.' I passed on a forecast which I had not taken down:

= SOUTH INDIAN OCEAN FROM 40 TO 50 SOUTH LATITUDE BETWEEN 50 TO 60 EAST LONGITUDE FOR NEXT TWELVE HOURS STOP FALLING 933 VEERING NORTH FORCE 9 OR 10 STOP VISIBILITY 1 TO 2 MILES = +

A cumulo-nimbus fist struck the hull, as if we were on a rough sea meeting an anvil-rock thought to be hundreds of miles away. 'There are tree trunks in the sky,' Nash said. 'Or army lorries, I can't tell which.'

The craft levelled like a dead log, and flew miraculously for half a minute. 'A monsoon in the wrong season,' Bennett said. 'Nothing to worry about.'

I composed the telegram and sent it out: *Once fall in love do not give up,* I told her, skip-distance and sunspots notwithstanding. *Listen to own voice only, stop. Look into nightsky for your face.* My sending sounded like fingernails scraping along a washboard, but there was no chance of being heard. Only the proper rhythmical thump of a real transmitter could get anywhere.

Could words of love break through by will alone? I sent a mixture of four short and three long signs, the Lucky Seven of her name going into the storm and getting nowhere, as the flying boat skated through black rain.

The night part of our trip was shortened by going easterly, yet seemed endless. Electricity hovered in and out. I felt like a fly which, primed by the good pickings of a long summer, and sensing an autumn death approaching, is filled with the strength to live forever.

The craft charged on, pushed without mercy by the wind. To move the body was a hazard. A descent to the galley might break a limb. Ordered to stay by my receiver, I searched for a significant message and, getting nothing, knew I would have to invent one. As long as operational gen was passed to Bennett, I could pluck down any telegrams and scan them for myself alone. Greetings from Anne who felt the pain of our separation would come in clear out of Portishead or Rugby:

Missing you. Come home as soon as you can. You did wrong to go. Why ever did you?

I didn't, I tapped back.

You did. Remember? I had big trouble finding where you were.

The ether was livid with the gibbet-rope of the question mark. Do you love me? Will you ever come back? Are you serious? You never were, were you? I don't think you ever really loved me.

I did.

You didn't.

Well, I love you now.

Do you? How can you be sure?

I'm sure because I know.

Whipcracks of recrimination decorated the sky – till I put a stop to it. My hand on the morse key sent HAPPY

BIRTHDAY. What did it matter whose? Only whales might hear, if they had the right antennae.

'All stations are forbidden to carry out the transmission of superfluous signals. Messages must not be transmitted to addresses on shore except through an official station. Private communications are strictly forbidden.' The rule book was peppered with such heavy type, but we were too far out for hand or eye or the ear of authority to reach, and though the power was mine, natural forces governed its effectiveness.

Rose, before being impelled to more work when we came again into the clear, dozed with his head resting on the chart table. He had put into abeyance the dread that if the overcast was higher than our service ceiling for a thousand miles in front he wouldn't be able to get a fix and find Kerguelen. Without stars, dead reckoning would put us out by such a margin we would miss our landfall, in spite of its spread. Beyond the point of no return in fuel, we would be all but lost if the stars stayed shut. Radio bearings on Durban or Mauritius, over two thousand miles away, were no substitute for an astro fix. In any case, with so much static, I could barely distinguish call signs.

Someone had picked up my foolish telegraphic greetings to Anne, because a strong signal through the atmospherics asked who was calling, which could only have meant me. I switched the aerial to D/F, ready to rotate the loop and find his general direction.

There were longer intervals between eruptions of static. I waited for a signal from whoever had heard me sending, so as to get a bearing. Had he already taken one on me? My doodling had lasted long enough. Perhaps he had been too surprised to act and, like me with him, was only waiting to hear me send again in order to confirm our direction. My hand stayed off the key, as no doubt did his. If he asked again who was calling, I would know that he was merely curious as to who or where I was. But if he didn't send, and waited for me to do so, he was someone to beware of.

160

A cold sweat clammed my forehead, and my heart thumped as if belonging to a drunken man about to zig-zag over a level-crossing with an express coming. We were flying straight, and everyone on board sighed with relief. The ship was less at the the whim of back-draughts and upcurrents. As if a work bell had sounded, Rose picked up his sextant and took readings from the astrodome. Bennett's voice came over the intercom: 'How's the radio silence, Sparks?'

'Thought I heard someone, Skipper.'

'Any idea who?'

'Too much interference.'

'What did he send?'

'Wanted to know if somebody was calling him.'

'And was anybody?'

'Not that I heard.'

'Did you hear, or didn't you?'

'There's nothing I don't hear if it's hearable. I'm waiting for him to come back. If he's somewhere close I'll get a decent bearing.'

'Let me know as soon as you can.'

I said something about the ungodly behaviour of skip-distance, to which he responded that, if we did but know it, skip-distance, like everything else, was anything but ungodly, though I was no doubt correct in assuming there was no method by which such phenomena could be tamed.

He left the controls, and stood close, the angles of his face emphasizing a funereal determination to push on at all costs, though it was plain that he wasn't as fit to pilot a flying boat on an exploratory haul over the ocean as he had seemed before setting out. I had never seen anyone with a deadly illness, which fact may have suggested that I was doing so now, but the glare of his right eye made it appear dead, as if struck by blow after blow from the inside. He's for the sick bay, I thought, but since we were still flying I supposed I must be wrong. My news of a ship somewhere

161

ahead may have been a shock, but he kept the composure that was expected of a skipper: 'Nail him with a bearing if you can. I'm going to the galley to see who's working on breakfast.'

Fully determined to do as I was told, I fell asleep.

14

I lay by a stream with no clothes on. Neither had Anne, and we laughed on the grass in the sunshine as she tried to pull a rusty blade out of my stomach. The water made a hissing sound, and tree branches crackled in the wind. The knife would not come loose, but I felt no pain. When the jaunty trilling of a bird said: 'Who is calling me?' she stopped tugging at the knife-handle. Why should a bird ask such a question?

Neither body nor spirit, half gone and half not, I was cushioned by dreams, shorn of care or will. But I awoke instantly to hear morse singing CQ CQ CQ DE ABCD ABCD = QRZ? QTH? QRA? QRK? QSA? QRU? = + K K K and got enough of a bearing out of his garrulousness to tell that he was east-north-east, though without knowing the distance.

Perhaps I had inadvertently pressed the key while dozing, and he was trying to discover whether I had been calling him. Rose was working out star shots for our position, locking us in a box of airspace among broken bars of cloud. By the time he knew where it was we'd be some miles further on – as if we had never been there. But from that vital fix an alteration of course would make for an accurate landfall, and leave a reserve of fuel so that we could search for our alighting place. We had been airborne seventeen hours, and Wilcox had long since got the pumps working to bring the second instalment from tanks in the hull.

A bluebottle-green in the sky came and went. Nash bumped me on the back. 'It's downhill from now on, Sparks.'

'I hope it's not too steep.' I felt grime at the eyes that only proper sleep would cure. With daylight beaming in at half past four, the hole we made in the sky moved as we moved, leaving a vacuum tadpole tail behind, a warm envelope refilled by sub-zero cold. A welcome smell of coffee spread from the galley. Appleyard was at the stoves preparing breakfast. A healthy hunger prevailed, but the skipper sent back his platter of chops and beans, and Bull who played the waiter stood by the ladder eating it with his fingers, mess-irons sticking out of his pocket. He wiped his mouth on Bennett's linen napkin. 'Two dinners are always better than one!'

The sky was empty, blue overhead but almost white to port where the sun stood on the horizon like the yolk of an egg looking cold enough to begrudge what warmth we might get when we landed. Morse rippled on every note of the musical scale, and there was nothing to do except let it settle, and wait for the nearby ship to ask again who was calling and why.

I had no will to track my tracker, if such he was, because the easy life was here, and for a few minutes, while breakfast was eaten, the duty I was paid to do lost its influence. If Bennett gave me a call to make I would sweat out a few pokes at the tapper, and the person I was supposed to find would no doubt come back loud and clear, wondering why the hell I had been sleeping my head off when we could have been playing an exciting game of wireless-telegraphic noughts-and-crosses.

The hollow-sounding signal began to bleed over my frequency, so I changed to the higher daytime band and reset the transmitter should I be asked to bleed back at him. I wanted to find out whether the other operator knew the day frequency. If he did, and called me, he was homing in and no mistake.

I listened, laughing to myself. The longer I waited, the more it was certain that he was exploring a few other frequencies first. We were sharpening our wits on each other.

Appleyard came up with breakfast, and a huge jug of coffee to fill our mugs. 'We'll soon be at Kerguelen,' I said.

'Where's that?'

'I never know where a place is when we fly there,' I told him. Nash bustled up the monkey climber to join the queue: 'Pull your finger out. I'm croaking.'

I winked. 'Do *you* know where Kerguelen is?'

He cleared his throat, and paused before drinking. 'I did ask the navigator, but he didn't know. When he asked somebody in Blighty, they told him all he had to do was to go to fifty degrees south latitude, then turn left for a couple of thousand miles, being sure to cut all meridians at the same angle. I expect he'll get us there.'

'Sounds like something from *Alice in Wonderland*,' I said.

Armatage looked up. 'I was born in Sunderland.'

'Didn't know there was such a place,' said Nash. 'Did you, Sparks?'

'Thought it was blown up in the war.'

'I left when I was eight,' said Armatage. 'The old man died, so we went south. My mother lived with her brother, and so did I. He was a real bastard.' His lower lip trembled as he reached for the plate of toast and eggs that came as a second course for those still hungry. 'Sunderland was a lovely place, all the same.'

Nash lifted his coffee mug. 'I'll drink to it, then.'

'So will I. It's near Cullercoats, isn't it? GCC, if I remember.'

164

After some talk, Nash set his empty mug on the tray and gave Armatage a nudge. 'Come on, then, get your nose out of that trough and let's give the guns another lookover.'

When the clandestine sender again trespassed on my beat, I jumped as if 250 volts had shocked up my spine, made worse by expecting him. He couldn't know that he had made contact, but he had, though he seemed too wily not to realize. His morse was off-whistle, clicks like the rattle of a cup and saucer carried upstairs by a man who did not want to wake his wife until she could see his wonderful surprise. I brought him on frequency and back to the usual bird-whistle. He called every five minutes, cued in to the second, but he was fishing blind. When I passed an account of his antics to the flight deck, Bennett said: 'Don't answer,' telling me that the ship certainly wasn't that which carried our fuel for the return journey.

15

∽∾

Oil pressure on the starboard inner had gone down. Wilcox wiped a red inkblot from his mouth. The engine was healthy enough. Must be the gauges. Nothing to worry about on that score. He would check oil and all contacts when we were moored. You do your job, I'll do mine, he said. We were touchy on that point.

Bennett came up the ladder, after resting in his stateroom, but with hardly the energy to mount each step. I turned in time to hear the same ship calling for an answer. His hand shook, holding a message sheet before me. 'Next time he fishes, send this.'

I was to use the callsign GZZZ, and make my position known as QTH 49 50 SOUTH 69 10 EAST. Bennett laughed, the dim light emphasizing his pallor. 'They'll search for a ship, not a flying boat: on the south side of the island instead of the north.'

Radio countermeasures had begun. All the same, he seemed unhealthily certain that they would work. 'They may get a bearing while I'm sending.'

'It won't occur to them the first time. They'll wait for a second message, which we'll never send. So just transmit.'

And shut up. We'll make rings around them. He thrust the paper into my hand. I'll lose my ticket for spreading false information. He couldn't care less. He had lost everything already, though God alone knew what it was. The rest of us didn't matter. I'd rather walk on top of the fuselage while the plane was in flight than pump out an inaccurate position.

My hand drew back from the morse key. There was an atmosphere of tension on board. Clouds lined up on the horizon resembled an escarpment of ice. Bennett's breath stank when, sensing my hesitation, he leaned closer. 'Not only does our getting the gold hinge on you sending that decoy position, but our lives are going to depend on it.'

If I obeyed, I would be up the creek, in a leaking canoe, and without a paddle. Should engine trouble force us to ditch, who would answer our distress call when we had already sent one fake message? The issue was as simple as that. To pay for a falsehood with our lives was not my idea of a bargain. There was no point in telling him. The captain's word is law. I knocked the morse key by way of assent as he returned to the cockpit, which brought such an immediate response that for a moment I believed the other operator's signal to be no more than a freak echo of my own.

His gleeful reply registered my surrender to an illegal act. If he was listening so intently, what chance had I of sending a false position without him taking a bearing on my message and knowing soon enough that I was not where I said I was? Our dirty tricks so early on would nudge them into their own deceptions. Perhaps snares were already spread, and Bennett was right to take precautions. Since they also were after the gold, dirty tricks would be a necessity rather than an exception. Thus I justified complying with the skipper's immoral request.

Their ship could not cover more than a single entrance or exit of the extensively indented islands. We had the location of the gold, and they would have to trace us before we could lead them to it. Because my bearing confirmed them to be north of the island, Bennett wanted me to give our QTH as being to the south, so that they would look for us in that area while we, unmolested in the northwest, could find the gold, load it, tank up from our supply ship, and take off into the wide blue yonder.

The plan made sense, but would they dance to our tune? If they already knew the location of our fuel vessel, they had only to keep it in view till we came close, as we would sooner or later have to do. Probably they had sighted nothing, but suspected that a ship (which might be us) was on its way, because my inadvertent tapping had advertised the fact to their alert operator.

To steel myself into carrying out Bennett's instruction, I sent two dots instead of one, and no sooner had they gone than two dots bounced from the Heaviside Layer as if in an attempt to meet mine before they got into his receiver – stabs of morse that set my brain going like a jelly. But I already had a bearing on him, and he did not know. Such was his speedy self-confident response to my tap of the key, that he could not believe me to have been so quick. We were already in contact. I wanted to take full advantage of his underestimation of me, and the best way was to make sure I would not make a similar assessment of him.

The multiplying strands of the situation were hard to disentangle. To strip down a transmitter, and disembowel a receiver, and put them together again, is a matter of following circuit diagrams; but the complexity of the relationship between myself and the other operator, and between the eight of us and whatever numbers he represented, would be impossible to illustrate by any blueprint.

The result of our kittenish game was that my scruples at sending Bennett's false position vanished, to the extent that I worried as to whether or not the one I had been ordered to transmit would get the most advantage out of our situation. Would it not be best, I thought, to hand out *two* position reports? First, I would send Bennett's, on which I hoped the other operator would not get a bearing. Then the second, which would be my own, would put us two hundred miles further away from the island than we were, and it wouldn't matter whether he got a bearing or not, because it wouldn't in any way confirm our distance.

For Bennett's message I would vary the note of my transmitter, and disguise the pulse of my sending to make the operator assume that we were a ship. The chart of the island showed that sixty miles separated one side from the other, with a six-thousand foot peak and sundry glaciers between. The signals of a ship on the southern shore would not bounce as evenly as those coming from a ship – especially a flying boat – approaching over level sea from the west. So apart from reducing the power of my transmitter for the first false message, I would also alter the tone, and make sure the rhythm of the morse bore no similarity to that which would bounce out the second false message to be sent later.

The scheme was like something cooked up in the officers' mess of RAF Bigglesworth, so simple that it would trick no one. And yet simplicity was the essence of duplicity, the first step towards success. When a plot begins to unfold, only direct moves can lead to subtlety. Effects might grow out of patience and cunning, and seem no moves at all, but certain doses of noise can have the desired result. A wireless operator is not a man of action, but an interpreter and manipulator of sounds, and however much our scheme was open to detection, it was the only confusion to which we could put them.

I would be going against the skipper's instructions in sending a message of my own, but I would do so because I was in two minds about entering into the scheme at all. Of those two minds, the primitive won, claimed acknowledgement and stated its price – which was that I should reserve the right to send a further decoy message. My own sensibility could cross from one mind to the other only at the orders of some force over which I had no control. One side of my brain deployed the values I believed in, of obedience to someone who knew more, who was older, perhaps stronger for that reason, who was rightly in command because of experience, and who deserved loyalty because not only my life but the safety of the aircraft depended on it. The other side of my brain was unpredictable and chaotic, yet equally fitted to deal with whatever seemed to be threatening us from the world beyond the flying boat.

I was also breaking the law on sending false data. Perhaps the other ship only wanted to make contact for reasons of mutual safety in an unpredictable sea thousands of miles from the depots of civilization. This I would not believe. Once the rules had been put aside, it seemed easy to disobey the skipper in our interests, and from there but a short step to deceiving another ship in the hope that it would be to our advantage.

The flying boat droned on, and I was never more part of it than now. I tapped the key twice, and the other operator, as expected, wanted to know who I was. Without preamble, and using the four letter ship's call sign that Bennett had given, I sent the decoy location in a jazzed and rapid rhythm: 49 50 SOUTH 69 10 EAST. When the operator requested further information, I jubilantly concluded that he had not taken my bearing and now wished he had. I

169

made as if to send what he needed to hear, at the same time diminishing my power into a natural fade out, and winding in the trailing aerial, as if the frying pan noise of atmospherics, as well as the glacier that was supposed to separate us, together with the uncertain bounce of the Heaviside Layer, had between them done for my signals.

16

The milky white of the sky was the kind from which visions came. We went through the air as if all sails were spread, but the ribs of actual green water raced each other towards land, while we were the umpire-clipper left behind. I remarked that I didn't yet have my airlegs, otherwise I would not have noticed when the boat lost its smooth ride and seemed to strike solid but invisible rocks underfoot, but Nash, the stubbled flesh slack at his cheeks, said every tremor registered because you were never up long enough to become deadened.

The following wind which had given a satisfactory groundspeed had saved much fuel, but such luck was too good and now, instead of the prevailing westerly on which Bennett had depended, the wind backed sufficient to clip our speed by almost thirty knots. When Rose had adjusted his airplot I reflected that the change of wind had worked to the advantage of the false message Bennett had induced me to send. I had transmitted almost at sea-level when the smoke flare was released to confirm the new bent of the wind, which helped the authenticity of my morse as coming from a surface ship, and the uncertain power of our signals

170

coincided with the supposedly intervening mountains and coastlines. Another advantage was that when our enemy (the only word I could use), believing the message to be genuine, went full steam ahead for that gold-taking vessel on the south side of the island, he would sensibly avoid the old whaling settlements on the east in case they were inhabited, and sail down the west coast instead, in which case there could be a danger of his seeing the *Aldebaran* approach from the west. But because the change of wind made us an hour late, there would be less chance of this.

Now that the time for my own false signal came, I wanted him to believe I was on a ship much further away, and that I was not the same person who had condescended to give him a position report twenty minutes ago. This illusion was helped by us being back at five thousand feet. Unlike his ham-fisted music, I rattled away in my own sharp style, giving him world enough and time for all the bearings he liked – though I wondered whether he had had sufficient wireless direction-finding experience to take the opportunity. His requests to make myself known – QRZ? QRA? QTH? – had been brash, the blade of his morse cutting sharply through the layer-cake of atmospherics, and so well pumped as to be almost aggressive.

Now that it was my turn, I knew that any attempt to match him would create suspicion, so I merely kept my signals healthy and distinct. No distance to travel, the flutey chirping came off a conveyor belt set into motion by my hand on the key, and I sent as if my only object was, out of courtesy and safety, to contact whoever was in the area.

A line of sun from between rolls of cloud marked my receiver. When he thanked me for my reply, I requested a weather report from his area, since I would be passing to the north on my way to Hobart. He told me to wait, meaning he had gone outside to cook one up, or was consulting with others as to whether or not I should have one. If he didn't send any gen, my suspicions that he was

171

not friendly would be confirmed – something he would want to avoid. But if he was not well-intentioned the report would be false, or at least unhelpful. He would reason, in the latter case, that since we were, as I had indicated, two or three days distant, it wouldn't matter if it was false or not, because weather changes so rapidly in this part of the world that we would never be able to accuse him of having lied. He could not know that we were in a flying boat, and barely an hour away.

While he was sending I got a rough bearing – though in the phase of minimum signal I missed the temperature – and afterwards jotted down: = WIND WEST 35 KTS .... VISIBILITY 10 CLOUD 2/10 AT 8000 SEA FRESH = + There was no certainty that close to the island the weather wasn't spinning around in circles, but from where we were visibility was half of what he said, and the cloud base four instead of eight thousand feet. His wind direction was the opposite to the one we had ascertained with the smoke flare. But what proved beyond doubt that he was lying was that the latitude and longitude he gave in no way tallied with the bearing I had taken – as approximate as it had been under the circumstances.

My work was done. I had him taped. He would not call me for a while, and I would not be calling him. Who had used who was hard to say, but I was beyond caring, and went to the bunks where I slept as one who had no interest in the future. The scarred side of Rose's face pushed me into sleep of a kind, and kept me away from billows of snow, but guilt with good reason weighed on me like a sack of bloody offal. I felt as if I had given up my soul.

17

We came through a three dimensional archipelago of cloud and sighted the jagged basalt of northern Kerguelen. From four thousand feet and twenty miles away, the black rock, three parts surrounded by turbulent water, acknowledged the accuracy of Rose's navigation. We cheered. Bennett had existed by the minute to get this view, keeping his impatience in check before entering the flying boat for a long grind over the water area of Mother Earth.

We had ten minutes to look at the black cone over whose summit course would be altered towards the Tucker Straits. I had visualized Mount Oben, on the thick paper chart, as rising to a seventeen-hundred foot peak above the three-sided blue sea, witnessing a benign image when confronted by hachures surrounding a dot. I got the coast right, and the hilly configuration more or less correct, but the elements were missing, and the black rock of desolation only came alive at the impact of reality.

Rose showed no pride at his navigational success, but Nash came up to tap him on the back: 'Bang-on! A bloody good show, Nav!' No more than a flicker passed Bennett's lips. His determination had driven luck before him like an explorer his dog team over the snow. From the moment he sighted Mount Oben he orientated himself by every islet and feature that he had studied four years on the chart. There were slight variations, but the view was tormented into conformity, and he hardly counted the nine main capes before turning into the allotted fjord. As each passed under the hull he felt as if he had taken part in creating the splashed shape of this island by the fact of his own birth, which he was revisiting after decades of painful absence.

173

Mine, all mine. We weren't meant to hear, his voice fainter over the intercom than the normal drone of instructions.

Ebony cliffs stood in yellowish vegetation along the starboard shore. Dark sand formed a moustache on either side of Elijah Cove, and shadows of brown kelp swayed in the water. The wind was feeling its way around the compass. Lines of foam streaked up the cliffs like desert religionists in white robes intent on making everyone in the world the same as themselves.

The plane bucked, and grated on its descent between rocks sticking out of the water like blunt pencils. I listened on 500 kc/s, setting the needle at the bottom left of the yellow semicircle, the volume two thirds over in spite of static, the filter button down, and the green eye glowing steadily because nothing came.

A thirteen-minute run on a bearing of 135 degrees from Elijah Cove took us by claw-like capes to where we turned south-south-easterly along narrowing straits. Headphones on a longer lead allowed me to see outside. Bennett announced action stations for Appleyard, Armatage and Bull, and I wondered why guns must be manned against such desolation, until recalling my inconclusive radio contacts at dawn.

Belly rolls of grey and white cloud hugged fjords that snaked their massive ways inland and seemed to vanish underground. Mist lifting from an island peak showed a glacier: snow lit by a gleam almost immediately doused. The plane turned ninety degrees on a southerly heading, and descended for its five-minute leg along Rhodes Bay. Cliffs with huge boulders at their feet glittered after a deluge of rain, and glacial water spread into a shallow bight.

It was impossible to tell one element from another, and I returned to search the band of hope on the radio, thinking that even to contact an enemy would be better than hearing no one. But when clipped morse spoke our signal letters, I let the magic eye wink on. Sweat melted as I got his zone of silence, the goniometer indicating him well to the south-west, where we hoped he was steaming towards the position given in our false report. I informed Bennett. The ship's call decreased in strength as the mountains faded his signals. Bennett laughed at the success of his ruse, then ordered me to close down the radio.

The boat was held steady while Nash took a back-bearing on Hallet Island. He subtracted 49 degrees magnetic variation, and passed it to the skipper, who centred the plane for the narrows leading to the Tucker Straits. Granite slabs shelved up fifteen hundred feet along both shores, and funnelled us towards the spectacular slopes of Mount Sinai. So formidable on the journey in its fight against storm clouds, the *Aldebaran* now felt like reinforced cardboard, and I expected to break through the floor when the cliff struck, feet following head to suffocation under water.

We went over brown tentacles of kelp, weaving along the sleeve of the fjord and unable to see out of it. The interior of the plane seemed to darken as Bennett coaxed our hundred-foot wingspan to where it looked impossible to get through, and instead of crumbling like cardboard the old kite was urged into a forty-degree turn. I noted gulls' nests built into the cliffs, the channel about to close forever. But Bennett flew as if he had all the space in the world, and my fear was subdued by a sudden and total confidence.

Nash came from the rear turret, and ambled up the ladder bearing the hand compass like an Olympic torch. Our way widened to an ample stretch of water, but one which seemed without exit, whose walls would cut us off from the rest of the world. We went to our stations. Veering to starboard, there were neither markers nor buoys to line up on. Rocks dotted the surface, the water calm in its protected state. We must get down without damage, or never lift off again. 'Don't make me cry,' said Nash. 'We've enough tools on board to rebuild the bloody thing if it prangs.'

175

Wilcox was going through the landing procedure with Bennett, free of his cough. Full flap and throttle back. There was no circuit, just a straight-in approach along the middle of the mile-wide water. Among the alien minefield, Bennett quipped. No rocks or snags. Going down. The channel widened. No side slip.

A wind struck beam on, rippling the water. There was one direction for landing. To try the opposite would set us among the whizz-bangs. 'Must have been there when the sub came in with its gold,' Nash added. 'But the sub went out by the back door, through which the fuel ship will come to us.'

'Can't see any door.'

'Nobody ever can.' He pointed: 'It's in the fold of that cliff, I expect.'

Use what run you need. Not too slow. Ease back. No side slip. A touch of power on the inners. Everyone held breath, as if giving more to Wilcox whose lungs were working over the intercom, said Bull, like a bilge pump on a sinking ship. Engines and water roared. A scrape tickled my feet, but getting down so soon was too much to hope for. A glance outside, and we were taxi-ing, full flap, inner engines cut, lost in a cloud of spray tracking along the surface.

Bennett kept her moving towards a patch of sand where the anchor might grip. Getting out would be no problem, said Nash. 'I've no intention of going for a Burton. Not on this bloody operation, anyway. We'd cut loose if need be.' A slight swell developed. There were black rocks under the surface, but Bennett had an eye for sand where a stream pushed its grit into the fjord, a bay for protection from swell and storms. The engines idled. A smell of fresh snow and wet slate rushed from high ground, and jackets were fastened. I pulled in the deepest breath of my life.

The island coastline, with scores of inlets, bays and zig-zagging fjords would make it impossible for anyone to find us. Bennett summed up our situation after he stopped

176

engines. He was laughing. So were we all. I thought he would do a dance of triumph. We heard our voices again, and laughed at the fact that we were shouting. Even if they suspect we're here it'll take weeks to find us, by which time we'll be away. He told Nash to let go the anchor, then passed an uncapped whisky flask to Wilcox, who doubled up from coughing and was unable to drink. So the rest of us had a stab at it.

Nash saw the heap of steel chain diminish into six fathoms. We drifted, and wondered whether the anchor had bitten. The shore receded. Anxiety was tangible as to whether the chain would snap, or the anchor drag. 'At this stage,' Nash said, 'there's no difference between mishap and catastrophe.'

With a slight tug, the boat was secure, and only then did I say to myself that we were safe.

PART III

1

Nash stayed on boat-watch with Wilcox and Armatage, and kept us covered from the mid-upper in case Bennett's party of Appleyard, Bull, Rose and myself were sniped at as we rowed ashore in one of the dinghies. The shelving beach of black and yellow sand was peculiar to stand on, as if the surface was covered with grains of rubber. Solid land did not seem as firm as I had imagined it when airborne, and I felt as uneasy as if I had just stepped out of a prison. My joke about D Day found no takers.

The steep slope to our left ended at a huge black cliff, while the rock-strewn land to the right, gentle at first, gathered itself sharply into the cleft of a watercourse. After the yellowing green of sparse vegetation, the sandy beach gave way to pumice and basalt. Only occasional groups of whalers and shipwrecked sailors had ever stayed on such terrain. No settled society had made a go of it, which was strange considering the world's turmoil, and the fact that the island provided coal and cabbage, fish and fowl in fair quantity. But I suppose that basic sustenance wasn't enough when contact with the rest of the world was lacking.

Bennett paced senselessly along the sand, occasionally stopping to kick at the gravel. He lifted his flying-booted foot up and down, as if exercising because of the cold wind, but I suppose he wanted to confirm that he stood on the island he had dreamed about for years. I wondered how his expectations tallied with reality, but they seemed to match neatly enough, judging by his expression. He picked up gravel and threw it down, then lifted a piece of rock and looked at it so intently I couldn't tell whether he would kiss or eat it.

We pulled the dinghy up the beach and unloaded a rifle, primus stove, food, spades, two surveyor's poles and the theodolite with its tripod. Bull examined the re-entrant through binoculars. 'I hope we don't have to scramble up that.' Low cloud brought a north-east drizzle, and we shivered around the tarpaulin sheet as if the stores it covered would give warmth. Surf bumped against the beach, and Bennett, in his grit-kicking demoniac progress, was beyond recall in the rising wind, cap on, back hunched and – the only encouraging sign – jacket collar turned up for warmth. Every minute or two he ranged in a wider circle, then shook his head and went on.

The world was empty of voices till Appleyard said: 'It might take him days. Pity there's nothing to get a fire going with.'

Rose up to now had seemed oblivious to all of us: 'You want a coal fire in a lovely grate, do you?'

'Your bloody voice grates.'

'You'd like to turn the dinghy upside down and make a hut out of it, and get it snug inside and play castaways till some nice sailing ship comes by for the rescue? Wouldn't we all?'

Appleyard sat on a slab of rock, but the surface was running with water, so he leapt upright as if nipped by a crab. He looked away from Rose, unable for the moment to face the terrible scar. I regretted their antagonism, yet it was a comforting reminder of human warmth still among us, stuck as we were in the raw air which seemed to peel off the emotional protection we had known in the flying boat. I wanted to be back on board and listening to my radio. Rose was irritated at having to undo his flying jacket to reach pipe and tobacco.

'You'll never get it lit,' Appleyard grinned.

A pair of giant petrels came over the water, and separated when they got close. As they swept low on either side of our party and went by, I noted the downturning bill and scavenging eye, and the flash of white along the body between head and tail. They circled back on dark brown wings, flying lower on their hunt for food, scissor-beaks set for us. I wielded a surveying pole, but they went odoriferously by, wings clicking into a thermal lift at sensing we were dangerous. When they alighted behind some tussocks up the watercourse, Appleyard let off the safety catch of the rifle: 'I ought to get something tasty for the pot.'

'Shoot, and you'll be for the pot – for the big chop, in fact.' Rose lit his pipe. 'It'll make so much clatter that everybody for a hundred miles will be on our necks. And that's not what the skipper wants, believe you me.'

'It's too much of a stinker, anyway,' said Bull. 'It walks on water, so it stinks.'

'What have we got a rifle for, then?'

'In case somebody comes up on us.' He fastened his clothes against the wind. 'I knew we had a sea-cook among the crew, but not a poacher.'

'I'm supposed to look after our bellies. We can't live out of tins forever.'

I observed Bennett's interminable booting at the sand. An insane person would have given up by now.

Rose spoke with the pipe in his mouth, a line of smoke from his injured face. 'He was always one for taking his time about things. Straight through the flak on our flying bombrack. He never wavered.'

'None of us did,' said Appleyard. 'We were with him.'

'All the way,' said Bull. 'That's why we won. It was all or nothing.'

Where the beach turned north, Bennett fell on his knees, and bent over to scrape at the gravel with both hands. The wind took his shout out of our direction, but I picked it up like a wireless signal half murdered by atmospherics. Two skuas cried their way by, eyeing us hungrily. 'He wants us to go to him.'

Rose ordered Bull and myself forward. We crunched over

the gravel, the effort sweating and winding us as if we hadn't walked for years. Bennett looked up when we stopped halfway. 'What the hell are you crawling for? Run!'

Quickening the pace, we got off the beach and went through mossy grass and a sort of dirty brown plant. Our boots slopped into the pools between, so we returned to the gravel which at least was dry.

He laid his cap on the ground and pointed to a ring of steel by his feet. A circle of sand had been cleared from the few inches of unmistakable fixture. He scraped mould and rust from the rim of the wide calibre pipe with his penknife, like discovering traces of a factory on the moon. He stroked the edges without looking: 'Bull, go to the dinghy and bring a surveying pole. Adcock – you stay here.'

He pulled off his silk scarf to wipe sweat and rain from his face. He was so pale I thought he was cast in lime, and not of the slow sort. His hand shook as he lit a white cigar with the third match, holding a cupped flame close till a whiff of smoke for a moment civilized the air. 'This is the first point of the base line. I allowed us a day, and we find it an hour after touching the beach.' He stood, and rested his boot on the circumference of the pipe, but gently in case it was pushed under and never found again. 'The other point is three hundred metres away at 109 degrees. A piece of cake, Sparks. We're in luck.'

Frozen and foot-soaked, I was glad to hear it. He bellowed again into my ear. 'When Bull comes back, slot the pole into this pipe. Get it absolutely upright, then fix it firm with rocks and sand. Do you understand?'

At three hundred pounds a month, plus an unspecified amount of bonus yet to come, I had no thought of neglecting to do exactly as I was told.

'When the two points are flagged up, and the theodolite gets the cross-bearings, we'll be right on target.'

He set off with head down, counting paces at such a rate he almost beat Bull to the dinghy. A wall of mist moved

184

upwater as if pushed from behind by a mob. The flying boat off shore was soon covered, as was the dinghy on the beach, and Bennett in his rapid walk towards it.

If silence was trapped under my feet I need only move to release noise. Reason told me to do so and go back to the others, but I wanted to be alone. Every action needed a decision, so I did nothing, and unwittingly obeyed instinct. A circle of gravelly sand was visible, and the half-buried pipe in which the surveying post would be fixed. If I walked, and kept the hiss of water to my left, that shape and area would remain behind. Not to move would leave me with a known pattern of gravel and moss within whose misty circumference I was safe. Familiarity induces a comfort which prescribes its own duty – that it shall not be glibly abandoned.

Should weather come from glacial heights to rampage in earnest, I might follow the beach back to the others, but in the meantime I was a target marker, and until the ten-foot pole was fixed in place I would not leave, in case gravel, water and natural subsidence covered it again.

There was the sound of birds, and the noise of cascading water, and the crunch of boots as I walked a tight circle around the embedded pipe to keep warm.

2

Only a fool, on an uninhabited island, would take it for granted that he was alone, and to pass the time till the mist cleared and Bull came back I played a mental tactical game, using the disintegrating aspect of the island's map as a board, a picture-map as splashed out as if someone had thrown a coconut full speed at a watermelon. Bull, seeing the map on Bennett's table, had likened it to a patch of vomit on Saturday night outside a pub.

For tokens I had the *Aldebaran*, the ship I had contacted, and the vessel which was to meet us at our anchorage with high octane fuel. Manoeuvres became a game of dodge-and-run in numerous places of concealment. Throws of dice concerned bad weather, or colliding head-on while getting closer to the buried gold which I, naturally, was the first to find.

Another factor in the game came without any wanting, and caused a shudder which sent me more cold for the moment than climate ever could. Intuition placed Shottermill as a vital counter among the players. He stood before me, and in one move dominated the board. The question as to why a ship was waiting could be answered only by him. I hadn't realized – perhaps because I had not been sufficiently alone to meditate with advantage – that he was playing his hand for more than one side. Bennett thought it beneath his dignity to distrust a mere chandler who sold rotten cigars, but at least I hoped – the notion made me colder still – he had kept Shottermill away from any information as to where our landing place would be. He knew little more than that we were going to the Kerguelen Islands, and when. Bennett's caution was only fully operational when he was actually flying. On the ground he was easier to deceive. No wonder Shottermill was worried by a wireless operator being carried, who could give early warning of anything heard.

My eyes were closed but I was wide awake, hearing boots on gravel when the wind had lessened its howl, and the snort of an old man about to talk. At a shuffling in the mist I looked for the rifle I had not brought. I must have been heard leaping to my feet.

A hawking and honking reverberated, but I was afraid to

186

make myself harder to find in case I never got back to the same place. I stood close to the pipe to prevent its being noticed and saw, as I started to sweat with fear, a penguin with head high and breast gleaming, even in the mist. I ran until it fell back trumpeting, and then with its loitering mate walked off with flappers going as if I was too disgusting an object to contend with. Their cries had so many echoes, I thought there were dozens, but the grumbling diminished and I settled to guarding our home-made trigonometrical point.

A ration of chocolate revived me in the clammy damp. I supposed Wilcox on the *Aldebaran* to be running an engine to check the oil pressure, but the sound was far off, and too light in tone. Distortion caused by the configuration of the land couldn't tell me from which direction it came, and as much as I cared to disbelieve my ears, I knew the sound to be that of an aeroplane above the blanket of mist which still concealed our flying boat.

From the southwest it sawed unevenly as if buffeted by currents stronger than the wind which pushed against me. The mist was no longer thick, only molecules hiding the light. Others also had an aircraft, though it was obviously single-engined and could not have flown to the island as ours had. The plane, however, was looking for us, suggesting that this was to be no unmolested treasure search, and my heart beat fast as I realized how much our fragile flying boat was in danger.

I doubted my ears. Perhaps the noise was from a motorboat, searching for us nonetheless, exploring inlets on the off-chance of finding our base. In this glacial hiding place any engine could sound like that of an aeroplane, distorting itself into whatever meaning the imagination concocted.

The sewing-machine purr diminished, having given up the search. Then, distinct and lower, it returned to hem another frayed edge of the sky, a tinny rattle of disappointment yet sounding as if determined to have a more serious go some other time. Its persistent motor noise finally departed.

I went back to my tactical game. The ship that my signals had sent to the southern part of the island had catapulted its seaplane to explore the northern side which was, after all, only twenty minutes' flying time away. Bad weather would keep us hidden for a while, but good weather would reveal us sooner or later, though perhaps not before we were airborne and carrying the loot. The game was still open for all contestants, and I wondered if anyone would finally win. I was plagued by Shottermill's features, but decided he was not in the game at all. Then it seemed obvious that he was.

Bull came out of the mist with the pole on his shoulder. 'How's the forgotten army?'

The plane was like a bee in my ear, dying but never dead. The dropped pole struck my boot. 'If you damage it' –angry, yet glad to see him – 'the skipper will push you out of the hatch from ten thousand feet.'

'Wouldn't be the first time he's done such a thing.'

I slotted the pole into place, telling him to hold it upright so that I could pack gravel around. 'What do you mean?'

'He's that sort. Do anybody in who stood in his way.'

I made as neat a mound as could be done without tape, ruler and scalpel. He patted the structure as if it were his own work. 'You don't need a war to make that sort.'

I took the offered cigarette. 'What does make 'em?'

'You're born like it.'

It was time to get back to the dinghy. 'Did you hear that plane?'

'What plane?'

'One of those funny bird things with two wings and an engine that goes phut-phut and travels in the sky.'

My sarcasm made no impression. 'Oh yes,' he said, and as if recollecting an event from stone-ages ago: 'It's gone, though, hasn't it?'

With my back to the damp air I felt the mist dispersing,

pressure higher on my left. The increasing wind played a peculiar chanson, its booming voice coming down the mountain and channelled into a flute as it hit the fjord, which acted like an everfilling bagpipe and sent a banshee wail through to my bones. Our white flying boat was half a mile away against a mountain background, on blue water so clear its replica wavered into the deeps. Such beauty made it seem fragile, and I felt an affection close to love because it was the only vehicle which would take us back to civilization. The sun illuminated its fluted hull and port float which, though of different sizes, were waterdynamic twins, graceful lines meeting at the stems but with shadow between. Three propeller blades in each nacelle had 1200 horse power behind them, four units joined by the leading edge.

The slightly ponderous fuselage, with its line of portholes retreating under the wing, was eighty-five feet from nose to tail, where the rear turret was angled high above the water. If the flying boat was on shore its height would have been nearly thirty feet, and it was no wonder that, once you were inside its body, everything outside lost significance. The last obscuring mist withdrew. The flying boat would take us back to a world in which I at any rate had no option but to belong. I would have to make sure, however, that what Shottermill might have told them had not been enough.

3

Cool air in the sunshine steamed our clothes as we walked over moss and sank into pools at each step. The dark shape of a bird hedge-hopped rocks in front, a skua with a four-foot wingspan wafting the air, whose eyes in a wicked head gazed like the blades of twin axes.

'I'd trade my right arm for the pop-gun,' Bull said as the bird came round again but swept wide towards the cliffs. 'I'm not used to having animals fly at me.' We struggled through potholes of black slush, boots and trousers saturated. If I were stranded like Robinson Crusoe, how long would it be before I got myself to the highest cliff and dropped off in despair? Skuas would pick out my lights before I touched bottom. It was no life for a death. Not a tree in sight. No tools, matches, gunpowder, the flying boat gone to pieces, and little to pick from its equipment. Crusoe did well, but I wanted our work done, and to quit the island.

Appleyard's cartridge-belt sagged around his middle. He stood by the upturned boat with the gun crooked as if he were a gamekeeper ready to plug the guts of stealthy marauders. 'You should have peppered those birds,' Bull told him.

'What birds?'

'Or salted 'em. I thought the buggers would peck us to bits.'

'Rose told me I was only to shoot people.' He leaned the gun, and took off a glove to scratch his nose. 'Nash is in the mid-upper, ready to spray the hills. Or the sky, come to that. We take no chances. Good job it was foggy when that plane went over. The skipper wouldn't even let us speak. We had to stand as if on parade. Nash would have got him though, if he'd come down for a proper dekko.'

Bull opened the theodolite box as if hoping to find food. 'They're looking for us, right enough.' He closed the lid on the delicate instrument inside.

'Bound to find us with a seaplane,' Appleyard said, 'sooner or later.' In the distance Bennett and Rose slotted the second surveying pole in place.

'He hasn't found anything yet,' said Bull. 'Only the indications. And there's nothing priceless about them. We'll need to stand on the loot before we know we've earned our pay. I'd rather have a bottle of whisky than a handful of gold. Feels like ten years since I had a drink.'

'If you don't keep off it,' said Appleyard, 'you'll see two kites instead of one.'

'And hit neither,' I said.

'You should have shot them gannets, all the same,' Bull complained.

'Skuas,' I said.

'That mountain's about a one-in-two gradient.' Bull lifted his legs high as if chary of stepping in the unavoidable mud. 'A walk to the knocking-shop every night of the week just wasn't good enough training to shin up that.'

'You should have stayed on board if you don't like it out of doors,' Appleyard said. 'Before the war I used to run up Kinder Scout like a jackrabbit.'

'Life was a piece of cake ten years ago,' said Bull.

The slope was less steep where the watercourse descended. Maybe what we were looking for was in that direction, but whichever way, the clock would turn against us if the seaplane spotted us in daylight.

Rose was breathless when he came back from working with Bennett. 'Bring the theodolite. Skipper wants to sight the angles.'

I humped the twenty-pound box onto my shoulder, and Bull carried the tripod which weighed almost as much. Rose turned from his path-finder's position in front. 'Don't drop your load, Sparks, or you'll have to go all the way back to Blighty to steal another from the stores.'

The distance was less to Bennett's second station, though far enough on puddled terrain. I looked intently at the moss to make sure I didn't step into an unexpected hole. 'Mind you, ' Rose said, 'I think a box sextant would have done just as well, and you could have carried that in a haversack.'

191

Bull reshouldered the weighty tripod, and told him to embark on a course of action which, Rose realized before turning to me, was all the nastier for being suggested among such superb scenery. It was uncalled for, and best ignored, and hard to say whether he was being serious till he went on: 'It's a pity we have to be so super-accurate to get anywhere or find anything. Takes the sport out of life. I lost something when I became a navigator, Adcock.'

I felt pain at his baleful tone. 'Maybe you gained something as well.'

'Not very much. As we get older we lose more than we gain, however much we change.'

'I don't like to think so.'

'No one does,' he said. 'We're the end of the line.'

'Speak for yourself. I'm not a fish on the end of any line.' Even while I spoke I had a strong impression I was wrong and that Rose, detecting my lack of conviction, knew why there was no need to answer.

I changed pressure to another shoulder, for in spite of my padded jacket the box had a fine time grinding the bone. Bennett's voice came on the strengthening wind. 'Pull your bloody fingers out. Come on! We'll have the fog back soon.'

Gravel had worked into my left boot, and grated the skin off my heel. Hurry was impossible if I was to avoid dropping the theodolite and spoiling its accuracy. Cloud covered the mountaintops. Rose said that the peak to the north – though Bull cursed him for a schoolmaster – was over two thousand feet. Skuas stayed high, enraged that we had invaded their territory, making a noise as if calling for reinforcements to drive us away.

Bennett worked his computations on a small drawing board and, having fixed the length of the base line and its angle, took the surveyor's pole from the pipe and set up the tripod, gauging the perpendicular with a plumb line from the box. He and Rose then clamped the theodolite onto the base plate.

192

We stood aside while they aligned on the pole which I had installed, and then set the sights according to the bearing which Bennett extrapolated from his notes. I wondered whether the German hadn't scribbled a few jottings in order to play a joke on anyone foolish enough to be taken in. Perhaps he had buried a mine which, at the greedy touch of an exploring spade, would blow any treasure-seekers into pieces-of-eight and back again.

Bull and I smoked in silence while the drill of checking for collimation went on. Sundry technical terms floated away on the wind, and I wondered what surprises the other party had for rendering our efforts null. They had no directions for getting at the treasure, but maybe there was more than one vessel to bottle up the *Aldebaran* once they located us. I mulled on our plight, supposing such thoughts to be better than brooding about Anne and why we had left each other – as for some reason I began to do, convinced by now that the separation had been good for us both.

Thinking of her took me away from the activity around. The landscape was no longer inspiring. A feeling of vulnerability replaced the sense of adventure. Questions cracked the structure of our group. My sending of false signals had disordered the edifice, so that from now on I could only live as the moments came, which didn't seem like living at all.

'Adcock! Come out of that ten-foot hole!' He pointed at the theodolite telescope, and then along the line of its bearing. Parallel to a turn of the coast, and a thousand yards southwest, was a short ridge of black rock, green and yellow vegetation at the summit. A watercourse beyond streaked down the re-entrant and ran into the sea. 'It's on that rise.'

I was to station myself there with the surveyor's pole, and find the line of the bearing according to Bennett's signals, which Bull would observe through binoculars. It sounded a plain enough routine, and I set off over the rocks and moss with the pole on my shoulder, cheerful now that I had a task which needed a good eye and some activity. The wind from the port quarter did not let me hear myself whistling. The sun was as high as it would get that day. Bennett worked against the storm, having a good idea from where it might come. I'd have felt safer if any of us could know where danger from men was likely to appear – who were perhaps a worse part of Nature's wrath.

The ridge, separated from the main line of the mountains, lost itself for a while in the general undulations, and I maintained track by counting the paces, releasing one digit from a clenched hand every hundred, knowing I would be more or less there when both hands were open. I kept my steps as even as possible, and though many fell short and I zigzagged to avoid large rocks, I realized the eminence was under my feet when the land sloped down before me and I could see the hidden section of the watercourse.

The hill was four hundred feet high, sea nearly a mile away. Bennett and Rose were waving their arms. Appleyard sat by the dinghy like a statue, as if marooned until death. Our flying boat heaved on the water: if the roaming seaplane came close it would soon find how spiky she was. Bull focused the binoculars. 'They want you to go to the right.'

I hoisted the pole so that they could mark me, and moved ten paces.

'A bit more '

I walked twenty.

He laughed. 'They're having fits. You're to go back.'

I went, two by two.

'Stop!'

The wind whistled, and pushed hard, but I kept the pole vertical. 'Now what?'

'Left,' he said. 'But creep. None of your bloody two-step, or they'll have your guts for garters.'

I took half a pace.

'Stop again. You're spot on – I think.'

194

I scooped a circle in the mossy ground, and stabbed the pole in. Bull grinned at my useless work. 'They want you to move to the right.'

The hole I dug filled with water. A cold wind beat on my jacket. If this was summer, I preferred Singapore. He put down the field glasses and hammered the stave which, though bolstered with rocks, nothing would make firm. 'You'd better sit on top.'

'You're not my bloody oppo,' I told him.

We carried stones, and though the first hundredweight displaced water, even on a hilltop, we gradually erected a pyramid.

'They're giving the thumbs-up. Rose is making semaphore signals. Flag-wagging isn't up my street.'

I preferred lamp-work, but was able to read semaphore slowly, which was all right because Rose couldn't send quickly. Arms outstretched meant R. The left at one o'clock said E. The same over the head, and the right at ten o'clock signified T. 'V' of the arms added U to the word that was coming. Two arms fully horizontal again denoted R. And both at the inverted 'V' position ended the word with N.

'Return,' I said to Bull.

'Where to?'

B was indicated, so I sent C to say I'd got the message.

'Return to B. They want us back with them.'

He marvelled. 'Communication's a wonderful thing. No chance of a quiet skive with a bod like you in the party.'

Being downhill, the way back was quicker. Bull's leather soles sent him skidding on the moss, legs flailing so that he resembled a figure of matchsticks stuck in an unpeeled potato, except that a spud couldn't yell such foul language. He tried a cat walk after the first come-uppance. All was well, till he imagined no more spills likely and hastened his pace a little, smiling at the success of each careful footstep. Then cozened into optimism, down he flashed, no vegetation to grab, rolling like a baby and bumped like a kitten.

195

When he struck his elbow on a rock and was in real pain he forgot to curse. The hillside was made of black lard, and he was shod in roller skates. He ended more out of breath going down than he had after the climb.

4

'What did you find to talk about?' He glared on his way by. 'There's too much dawdling and gassing. We want *speed* in this operation.'

Rose packed the theodolite and handed it to me. No time had been lost, and Bennett's hurry, though understandable, was futile. Heaps of cloud inched from the sky, giving total coverage up the fjord and on the opposite shore. Bull fancied he caught a whiff of frying sausages from the flying boat, and complained that he was starving. We had more important things on our plate than food, said Rose. 'If we aren't on target in the next half hour we'll be staggering around in the mist for days.'

I held the theodolite in my arms like a wounded bird that had to be kept alive. The white flying boat was pressed between black water and the sky's ebony ceiling. While Bennett and Rose set up the theodolite on the end of the base line, Bull and I ascended the hill carrying a spade and pole each. Accustomed to the terrain, and though the skin on my heel was worn away, the thousand yards seemed little distance. A flight of skuas threatened, as if they guarded some secret at the summit and were warning of the fate which would befall any who solved it. They dive-bombed, coming at low-level with prominent wings and avaricious beaks. Bull swung his heart-shaped spade. 'Looks as if they mean business.'

They lost interest halfway and soared towards the beach. The triangulation, given bearings and distances, was a matter of alignment on the surveyor's poles. Providing the theodolite was accurate, all should fall into place.

The summit was familiar, but weather changed the view. Bennett wanted to get the treasure while the mist held off, but once found, the same concealment would be an advantage. If God was on Bennett's side – and nothing had so far happened to suggest that he was not – there was no more perfect scheme.

We aligned our poles on their separate bearings and walked forward along them until we met. That would be the spot on which to dig. The difficulty was to place ourselves on the exact bearing from the two ends of the base line. Bull unstrapped his binoculars. 'They're having a bit of an argy-bargy. The skipper's tearing a strip off poor old Rose.'

I was as interested in helping to solve the problem of intersection as I had been in plotting decoy signals from the flying boat. Trying to create order out of confusion made me feel like a gambler. Every act – from a minor diversion to a matter of life and death – involved risk. Conscience had no say. My element had been found, and a safe life was impossible to imagine.

The flying boat bobbed on the water, white chops around the hull. Wind stung like clouds of flying pepper and brought tears from Bull's eyes when he lowered the field glasses. 'You've got to shift.'

'Which way?' I stood by the centre pole.

'Left. No. What the hell are they on with? Right, I think. Yes, smartly to the right.'

I didn't know whether the continual roar came from wind, or walls of water breaking at cliffs beyond the headland. We had a better view of the flying boat than Bennett got from below, and it was nearer the shore than a few minutes ago.

'Back a bit,' Bull said.

The flying boat was about to be pounded to aluminium and plywood, while Nash, Wilcox and Armatage ate themselves senseless in the galley, or yarned by the bunks over a quiet smoke.

'Another pace to the right.'

We had no world but the flying boat, and the rocks were a row of rotten yet still strong teeth waiting to bite. Appleyard was waving for help, but no one could see. The roar of the wind choked my shout.

'Right on the market place!' Bull was keen. 'Stay till we fix it.' If I ran into the wilds there would be the problem of rediscovering that hallowed spot, and the hurry of recouping time lost. I wanted to abandon the post which I had a duty to maintain, but could not do so even to save my own life. I refused to follow instinct in order to see what happened. Instinct and sense might well be in agreement, but if I 'did the right thing' I would deny myself the excitement of wondering whether or not I would survive if I 'did the wrong thing'.

I stayed, and with Bull's help made a neat bench mark on the spot under which we assumed the gold to be. But the part of me that had been decisively overridden nevertheless pictured what it would be like to flee down the immediate slope and turn left up the water-course, scrambling out of sight before anyone could shout or shoot. With such a good start, I would reach the two thousand foot summit a free man. The thickening mist would cover me.

I was diverted by Bennett who, aware of the flying boat's difficulties, ran to that part of the beach where Appleyard guarded the dinghy. His small figure appeared to move slowly, till flurries of rain took much of the clarity away. It seemed a bad sign that the skipper should run to try and save the flying boat. The hull was glancing against the rocks. Even if Bennett had been able to help I would not have expected him to run. It did not matter that I had sent

198

out my own false radio signals. I wouldn't have run myself, and maybe that's why I was alarmed at him doing so. He only discovered what we on the hilltop knew, that on such terrain you couldn't run. He fell, and lay still. 'He's kissing the earth.'

Bull's voice came out of the wind noise. 'There ain't much else he can do. Maybe you and me should do the same, Sparks – pray that the *Aldebaran* doesn't go to bits.'

I would witness the disaster standing up. Nash, Wilcox and Armatage wouldn't get ashore if the boat broke in pieces. They were some way from the rocks, though how close or far was hard to say. The obscuring rain flung itself against our faces like needles of ice. Distances deceived. The wall across the fjord seemed as if it could be touched, yet the flying boat in turmoil by the shore was out of sight. Bennett winged his arms to where he had last seen it.

We turned our collars up and crouched over the point we had been sent to mark. My hands covered my ears and met on the top of my head. If the flying boat disappeared we would be staked out in the wind till we died – or were spotted and rescued, which was unlikely. I brought my hands down. Rain penetrated. The gorge of the straits was blocked to the east by a dark wall advancing towards our cove like a cork being pushed home to bottle us up. I imagined the splintering of the thin hull.

I needed to know the worst, but the loud wind created silence. My ears craved to hear the tinny noise of disaster, as at my radio I had extracted the faint squeak of a vital message, except that now our lives depended on it. No wind could hide the sound of the flying boat's rending contest with rocks and gravel, and neither did it have the power to negate an irritated drone which came first from the mountains, then from another direction, and again out of the sky as if its own peculiar accelerating roar was being bounced slow-motion between the clouds.

199

I knew what it was, but Bull shouted first. 'They've started the engines to keep it off shore.'

'Let's hope they can.'

He didn't hear. 'Good lads! Hold tight! Get it away!' or some such words, to judge by the way he jumped up and down.

Unable to see, our ears were attuned even more to the engine, and we became part of the struggle in the cove. The wind moaned as if signalling the death-rattle from the four-stroke throat. But the engines roared around us, ears and eyelids shivering as they overcame the bang of the wind. I almost expected to see the portly flank of the flying boat go by on take-off.

It was hard to stay still, but to pace in circles to the wind's screech, and the engines that fought marvellously against it, might be to lose the position we had worked so hard to find. Bull did not feel the same obligation, and there was no response to my call. I shouted full strength but hardly heard my voice – only the rattle of it in my head. Visibility wasn't more than a few yards, and I supposed he had descended the hill to find a better view through the mist.

The engines cut, but I continued to hear them. Either better times had come or the worst had taken place. How long ago they had stopped I couldn't know, and I fought to stay calm, seeing no one and hearing only the cosmic shutterbang of the gale. I sat and imagined Bull lost, never to return, that Bennett, Appleyard and Rose had been drowned trying to reach the flying boat in the dinghy, and that those on board had gone down with the ship. But my face was wet from rain not tears.

I might have assumed that the engines had been cut because the flying boat had found a secure anchorage, and that those on shore were sitting out the storm before coming up the hill to me. All was well in the world. I talked to Bennett as if our small globe of visibility had enough

200

warmth to keep us alive. The only time I could attempt communication was when he was not present, and so I took to pieces the reasons for coming here, and put them back together in a way that suggested we had made a futile journey, but to show also that I had understood our motives sufficiently to remember them for the future.

It didn't wash. The rain did that. I felt like a stump of wood being worn away. He said: '*You* don't talk to me, erk. I do the talking, if I care to. And what have I to say to a superannuated Backtune who wasn't even on active service when he got his Dear John letter? On this stunt we not only do our jobs, but that little bit extra as well. The *Aldebaran* needs you, don't forget. Remember also that the skipper takes an interest in your work.'

There was little either of us could say. I was pulled into a trance. If I had not been acting as marker for the gold I would have walked to keep myself warm, but having given my word I was obliged to stay no matter how numb I became. I didn't think about the possibility of death approaching as quickly as Appleyard said later that it might. Having sent the false signals made it obvious that I would now do as ordered. If I had not sent them I might have weakened, abandoned my position under the excuse of survival, and lost the location of the treasure, so that refinding it after the storm – the guide poles having been swept away by the wind – would have left us no time to get the gold up before we were discovered by those who wanted it for themselves. An unpleasant course of action was always seen as crucial.

But the matter went deeper than doing what was obviously my duty. I would have stayed in any case, acceptance being composed of pride, tradition, greed, honour and a desire to explore my nature to the utmost. There was nothing more attractive to me at that time. I thought of fate as the unbreakable spider's web, but did not know whether by being drawn to it I was the spider or the

201

victim. In my imaginary conversation I told Bennett none of this.

I sat on the ground and dozed. The lack of visibility was a sort of darkness, within whose protection I grew less cold.

5

~∞~

If Bennett had been authorized to recommend any of his crew for medals, or to be mentioned in despatches, he would surely have honoured Nash for saving the headquarters of the expedition. It was not that he had been uninterested in the fact of our superbly winged vessel being poised for a fatal collision with the shore, but that he had got his priorities right. With one good man on board, and four prime engines, he felt no concern for the flying boat. He exercised fine tuning over his tactics, Rose said to me later. It was his strategy that had been out of control from the beginning.

He sheltered under cover of the dinghy, for to try reaching us on the hill in such a tempest would have risked his party being scattered and perhaps lost. They stayed together till the wind died sufficiently for him to take a compass bearing and follow Rose and Appleyard up the hillside, keeping them in line-ahead.

In the dream I banged my shoulder against a crenellated wall forty feet high and fell towards the ditch, pursued by half-bird and half-flying boat, nature's work and man's which, within the dreamscape, seemed absolute reality. A blow at the shoulder caused me to topple as if hollow, the dream sliced through. Appleyard thought I might be dead, but Rose knew better. Bennett's demand as to where Bull had gone came above the rattle of the wind.

I reached for the mound of stones and sat up, angry because unable to continue falling into the moat below the crenellations. After a trumpet call the wall would descend on me, and I would sleep forever after an endless drop not of my making.

Bennett kicked around the area as if spoiling an invisible sandcastle before the tide came in. 'I asked where Bull was.'

'Gone for a walk.' I spoke three times before he understood. They had brought food and coffee from the dinghy, and the quick meal opened my eyes. Bull could be miles up the mountain. Perhaps he had fallen. He was bound to be lost. He didn't need defending. Anyone with sense would have done the same. 'He couldn't stay put, and freeze to death.'

'He'll be court-martialled for dereliction of duty.'

Appleyard worked as if excavating a slit trench for protection against artillery. He considered the air bracing – as I had a few hours ago. 'No worse than a summer's stroll in the Lake District.'

'He deserves to be shot.' Bennett laughed, but I didn't like his humour.

Maybe the bearings had been inaccurate. Perhaps they were false. The exploration was shallow, and there was no sign. I wondered whether I had moved without being aware. The soft and peaty soil was striated by occasional gravel. When Appleyard's spade struck, Bennett took it from him and dug furiously, then gave the loosened boulder a kick to burst any toes.

Rose and I had a turn, keeping our backs to the flurries of rain and sleet. Bennett gazed into the mire and listened to every tap of the spades. We could see further down the slope, and while I wanted the sky to clear sufficiently for a search party to go up the mountain, the others hoped that the mist would stay so that we could dig in safety. The low rampart shielded an area three yards square and a foot deep. I enjoyed the work, in spite of the ache to limbs and spine, and the heat on my palms preceding blisters. The depth of our excavation increased. 'Anyone from a distance might think we're digging our graves.'

Appleyard told me to shut up and get-bloody-on with it. His spade met a hard object, but he pushed with his boot as if it were a temporary aberration in the composition of the soil. Bennett, on the edge of our visibility, was engrossed in the uncertainties of the weather. I also reached solid metal. 'Something here, Skipper.'

My feelings were out of contact with reality. The boxes or tins could have been filled with stones for all I cared. Unable to appreciate the great moment, we were exhausted and silent, but continued our slow-motion poking about the soil as more rectangular shapes became apparent. Bennett strolled over from the gloom, and saw how we were getting on. I lacked enthusiasm, but my memory was good, both qualities uppermost at the sight of him in muddy soil pulling boxes which weighed nearly sixty pounds. He drew one to the edge of the diggings as if it were a celluloid replica, and we gathered around like keen types as he hammered at rust-encrusted bolts and lifted a lid.

The inside was lined with oilcloth. He took off his gloves for the occasion, hands looking more delicate and pink than during the unrolling of a chart, or when at the controls of the *Aldebaran*. He scooped up dull coins, and we were treated to the unforgettable sound of gold tumbling against gold, which I had never heard before and have not heard since.

Soil and treasure produced a peculiar smell, a mixture of metal and mushrooms. The gold was not ours, nor any Bennett's till it was transported to where the share-out would take place. Nevertheless, I think we all wanted to dip into the mess of pottage, and perhaps one of us, unwilling to miss a unique experience, would have done so if we hadn't heard, in the declining wind, the echo of a full-throated scream.

It was uncalled for, an intrusion at the wrong moment, causing more irritation than alarm. None of us moved, perhaps for as long as half a minute, to hear if the cry came again. My direction-finding ears got a fair bearing, and I stood up to point the way. 'It came from the watercourse.'

Bird cries filtered through the mist. 'We'll go and get him,' Appleyard said.

'Your work is here,' Bennett said coolly, 'not searching for a fool who should have stayed at his post.'

I knew how cold the body could be, as ice went to my stomach and seemed to freeze it solid. But I felt incapable of a long hike up the mountains. 'He's injured. We can't let him die.'

'He's had it already.' Bennett was adamant. 'If we go off searching for him we'll be lost in no time – or fall down some precipice.' The day's rain sent enormous falls of water rushing to the sea. When the wind dropped, the sound of the torrent was unmistakable. 'I'm responsible for holding this expedition together, and it's already split between here and the ship, so I can't send another two of you into this kind of countryside. If I had twice the crew, I wouldn't sanction it without fair weather. To look for Bull now – even if it was him we heard – is to risk a real cock-up.'

I'll never know if he was right, yet he sounded reasonable. We got back to work and, still in daylight, stacked forty boxes like so many bricks on solid ground.

6

We huddled, eating, smoking, swigging whisky from Bennett's flask, and hoping that the moment to begin our donkey-work would never come. We were to get the gold down to the beach, but in the meantime the last daylight was drawn from the sky like bleach out of a bottle encrusted by the detritus of a wasteland: clouds of swarf, rolls of gunmetal, wisps of green mould, puffs of damp blue, the strangest ochre-coloured sunset I ever saw from a pure-air part of the world. 'God is up to some funny stuff.'

Rose shielded his eyes. 'Isn't He always?'

Appleyard spat. 'You shouldn't take His name in vain.'

With darkness the mist drew back. Bennett put a large torch into my hand and looked into the luminous gradations of his prismatic compass. 'Face the same direction, and when you find the signal-button get in touch with Nash on the flight deck. Tell him to come ashore in the second dinghy with Armatage. Make it as short as you can. We want no interception.'

I held a steady light on the downhill bearing and sent a series of AAAs. Bennett paced behind. 'Keep on. They'll see it.'

I lifted my eyes. 'There's a star in the sky.'

He had faith, and everything to gain by persistence. 'We want foul weather. The fouler the better.'

I thought of Bull, dead or dying on the hillside, and hoped for the good of us all that he was alive. After a further string of AAAs , the steady white flash of an answer came, and I sent slowly so that Wilcox or Nash could interpret with ease. 'O K ERE STOP NASH AND ARM CUM SHORE THEN WAIT O K ?'

QSL showed that Nash had worked it out and would comply.

'Send a second signal.' Bennett spoke as if we were in station headquarters, and I had a full-scale wireless section to look after his traffic. 'Tell them to beam on us every five minutes.'

Rose was to stay on the hill with the torch and guide us back, while the occasional flash from the flying boat would enable us to locate our beachhead on the way down. Bennett had spent so many weeks working out the drill that he didn't have to think. He had netted the landscape with pre-computed vertical and horizontal triangles, devising an intricate movement and communications procedure. It was hard to think that slide rule or compass would lead him astray, though with so many stitches in the fabric it was also difficult to see how the pattern could hold.

Nash was as clumsy with a signal lamp as I would have been in a four-Browning turret – but he was effective. The opening and closing lights fused into letters, then words, and the second message was received and understood.

We started, and pressure on my ankles due to humping a half hundredweight metal box made the stint with the theodolite seem like a carefree brush with a football. Bennett, as became his rank, carried nothing, his job being to locate the dinghy and the reinforcements from the flying boat. He frequently stopped to make sure no one spun headlong on the slow descent, or wandered off track with such precious cargo. If I vanished and was picked up by a whaler in six months I'd be richer by twelve thousand pounds. Invest that, and I would live modestly without working for the rest of my life. The haul for Bennett and his backers was a quarter of a million, and the cost of getting it, including the hire of the fuel steamer, could not be above thirty thousand. The well lit picture of a happy share-out in a Hong Kong or Singapore hotel was hard to credit as I stumbled in waterlogged clothes behind Bennett's shadowy back, which now and again stooped as – counting the paces – he consulted the compass to keep us in the right direction.

A reassuring light winked off-shore. Low clouds held their rain, and the sharp air was sweet. I had forgotten what it was like to move without being breathless. Wandering unladen over such landscape might be pleasant. But like a pack animal I dwelt on nothing, determined that never again would I indulge in such work.

Forty boxes would mean twenty trips uphill and down. The Duke of York's army would have nothing on us. Even if reinforcements doubled the number of hard shoulders, ten trips would still be needed, which would take fifteen miles of humpbacked walking. Soldiers or mountaineers had done as much, and the daunting prospect was forgotten when a light flickered and we heard Nash's voice at the beach. 'You've got it?'

Bennett nodded. 'All we do is fetch it down, and tuck it up on board before daylight.'

'Not at this rate you won't. Where's Bull?'

'He went missing.'

'In this place? Couldn't you stop him?'

'He just wandered off.'

I took a few seconds to realize who Bennett meant when he said: 'The wireless operator stayed at his post.'

Nash peered into the darkness. 'We'd better get going. How far is it?'

Bennett told him. 'One man will stay here, to guide us in.'

Nash waved his arm. 'To hell with that, Skipper. The quicker it's down, the better.' He lashed a switched-on torch to a surveying pole stuck in the sand. 'What's the angle? We can beam on this. Don't need a man to hold it. The battery will last. The more of us at work the sooner we get back on board to a bucket of cocoa and a ham sandwich!'

We set off towards Rose's intermittent light on the hilltop. When Armatage stumbled, Nash told him to move sharp or he'd get a boot at his arse. I expected a barney, but Armatage grumbled at the slippery ground and went forward.

At the summit Nash took the torch and matched a similar beacon to the one at the beach, which was so dim that only his rear-gunner's eyes could see it. 'You can hump your share like the rest of us,' he said to Rose. 'It'll keep you warm.'

When we picked up our loads he said: 'Put the buggers down again. I haven't run a building site for nothing. We need a few labourers from Lincolnshire on this stunt. If I promised a bonus they'd have this lot down the hill in ten minutes. See what I do, then follow me. We'll adapt our tactics to the terrain. But be careful not to bust any of the boxes or there'll be a few slit throats for the birds to fly into.' He turned. 'Eh, Skipper? If you feel inclined, Mr Bennett, you can join the party as well.'

'I'll stay with the boxes. They shouldn't be left unguarded.'

'As you say, sir, but Wilcox has the mid-upper guns trained on the beach in case of funny business.' He took two boxes by their handles and, walking almost at ground level, like a truncated dwarf, slid them over the turf and set off downhill. The heavy metal moved as if on ice, not keeping a straight course, yet heading towards the lighted dinghy. Appleyard followed, then Armatage, brought up by Rose, and rearguarded by me, so that we had ten boxes in motion at the same time.

Not five yards apart, we were covered in mud. Curving around boulders created a splash-track that shot moss and black liquid up our arms – which met spray coming from boots dug in to prevent overturning. Halfway, we were close enough to hear Appleyard say: 'On our next job I'll bring a couple of mud-sledges, and fifty black huskies!'

Nash enjoyed being the foreman. 'Your time-sheets are going to look pretty before the night's out.' Stooped and moving, only the hard work stopped it being comical. We were his dog-team, but didn't mind because he also was in harness. Bennett sat on the hill to guard the fast diminishing cargo. Now that the gold was found he had lost interest. The quest was over – so we thought. All we had to do was depart from the place and collect our wages. Bennett had brought us here, but Nash, it seemed to me, would get us back.

7

If our energy came from the sight of the gold, we were spending freely. None stinted his basic resource, and in three hours the boxes were at the beach. While Nash and Bennett discussed the best way of getting the cargo on board, we ate what was left of the rations.

The flying boat rose and fell. Wind played in the aerials, moaning above the slop of water on the beach. There was a smell of seaweed, half burnt vegetables, bird droppings and fish, odours coming and going between prolonged alcoholic gusts of sweet air. The sense of adventure was almost carnal, a sentimental attachment which was nevertheless profound and lasting. Standing in the open, tired and splashed with mud, on an island in a part of the world which did not seem connected to any other, the feeling was wholly a part of me because the wind and the smells said so, as also did whatever hazards were brewing before the light of day came on.

Waves lapped their creamy phosphorus over black shingle, and our pale flying boat dominated the cove. I was as far from home and what had made me as it was possible to get and yet be on earth. It was where I had always wanted to be, though whether I would learn anything of the half of myself that had got me here was doubtful. I only knew that whenever I took one step to alter my life, Fate took two. Now it had taken three, and I was lost in more ways than one, and if I couldn't make the effort to care it was because I did not think there was anything on earth that could do me harm.

We put out our cigarettes, and Rose who hammered his pipe against the heel of his boot swore as the stem flew away from the bowl. Being in the second boat, he could have sat for another ten minutes. 'It was a present from my mother. I've a spare one in my kit, but I get nervous if I don't have a reserve.'

'Why not try to fix it?' Appleyard, thinking it important that our navigator be consoled, found the two pieces. 'I'll have a go later.'

Nash shouted, as the icy water struck up to his waist. Armatage went head first, legs waving till Nash put a hand on his back. 'Dive in, for God's sake. It ain't a concrete mixer. Do you think your mother's going to come out of bed and pull you on board?'

He steadied the motions of the dinghy so that Bennett could get on. Armatage fixed the oars in the rowlocks, then caught hold of a spare oar and pushed from the shore into the calm water of the fjord. Nash's voice carried over the water. 'Hold the bloody thing still!'

Appleyard dragged boxes to the water's edge so that they could be lifted as soon as Nash returned. A light from the flying boat was set to guide us. I was roused by the click of rowlocks and, down from my dream on the hilltop, ran into the water and caught the rope, pulling till I heard the hull scraping.

211

Four boxes made the boat unwieldy once we were on the water, but I pulled hard at the oars, spraying Nash at the tiller. Our eyes were used to the darkness, and the flying boat was close inshore. Craving sleep, I wished for the labour to be over. 'I'll take it on the next trip,' Nash said. 'Can you manage the tiller?'

I nodded. 'The palms of my hands are giving me jip.'

'Just keep on. We'll beat 'em yet!'

Night and day had been pulled from the passage of time. There was neither. We were nowhere, attached only to the passing moments. 'Do we look for Bull, or not?'

I had forgotten the question by the time he replied. 'After this effort,' he said, 'we've got to have sleep. We'll be no good without it. And to look for Bull we also need daylight, and fair weather. Then we'll see what can be done. Go a bit to port. I'll square it with the Skipper.'

The starboard float was suspended in the darkness and, feeling that the rig might fall, I rowed quickly under it. Nash told me to steady-on, and make for the hatchway. Water chopped against us, but we reached the side. Wilcox threw a rope. 'Another mud-pie gang!'

We tied close, and I set a box up on my shoulder. Bennett looked out from the promised land of the flying boat, from which wafted the warm smell of fuel and stale food. I wanted nothing more than to get in and sleep. Any surface would do. 'Keep it close, Mr Nash,' the skipper called. 'Keep that dinghy in. No space between.'

The weight came from my shoulder. Nash hoisted the second box. 'Wakey-wakey, Sparks! Let's have the third.'

I struggled to lift, but the box was pulled from me by Armatage when about to slip into the water. Nash told me it wasn't necessary to heave them onto my shoulder. If I used both hands and levered as far as my knees, the handles could be reached from the hatchway. 'It's also safer. You won't get a hernia.'

We pushed off to let Rose's dinghy unload. Exhaustion

had seemed so final that I was unprepared for a return of energy. After the first load it became, as Nash said, a piece of cake. Knowing the distance helped. Technique improved. He was right. At unloading I would bend my knee and ledge a box on it so that Armatage could reach from the more stable platform of the flying boat.

We dreaded a rough sea, the snapping of a rope, and the slipping of a heavy box into the dark sandwich of water between dinghy and fuselage. So I was careful. Every plunge of the oars while rowing was like dipping pens in ink to skim us through the shine of water. The blend of hurry and absolute attention carried us from the hatchway and around the rear of the port float which, looming above, served as a circuit marker, giving the second dinghy a clear way in.

Nash worked the oars and I steered for the light on the beach. My back was to the flying boat, his view of it blocked by me as he moved us in unruffled transmission over the water. Out of a half dream came a yell and a splash which brought me back into consciousness. The responding shout from Appleyard caused me to wonder what had gone wrong, but I blocked speculation so as to make the run-in to shore. 'Something's happened. Do we turn?'

'Keep on. We've got work to do.' His pace didn't alter, but he was out of breath. 'We'll know soon enough.' Distance muffled the noise of shouting as I leapt onto the beach with the rope in my hand.

The pile of boxes diminished. I set the last of our load in the boat, my feet swollen from wading. 'We'll take some getting dry.'

'Sea water's good, unless you swallow the stuff.' He went ashore for his customary piss, and when the boxes lay like dominoes on the bottom of the dinghy I placed myself at the oars.

'Push off.' And felt the gentle lift as we were waterborne. 'You'll make a sailor yet.'

213

'Does Davy Jones want me that badly?'

'You're lucky if somebody does. My wife left me when I went to jail, and none of my family would talk to me anymore. They loved me during the war. I'm best out of it.' I rowed more quickly. 'That's the way of the world,' he said. 'But take it easy. You'll get there, soon enough.'

'They may need help.'

'You'll be no good if you knacker yourself.'

It was easier to hurry when exhausted. But our passage took longer than usual. We neared the float. 'What's wrong?'

Wilcox had gone overboard.

'He slipped, and let go of the rope,' Armatage shouted. 'But the box was all right.'

'You'd better give him a cup of the hot stuff,' Nash called. 'This water's too cold for a midnight dip.'

'And where's Appleyard?'

'In the drink, looking for Wilcox.'

My clothes felt like tissue paper in the wind. Rose's dinghy came round by the nose. 'We tried to get him out.' There was an explosion of water from which a hand and head surfaced between the side and Rose's boat. Nash leapt on board and stretched his arms out of the hatch, while I nudged the dinghy so as to push Appleyard close. While the rest looked on, silence during the actual lift was more awesome than any activity. The body seemed waterlogged, a dead weight. But he was alive, a hand moving across his marbled face as Nash rolled him like a carpet till there was no danger of him tipping back into the drink.

Bennett came out of his room. 'Why have we stopped work?'

'One man missing, believed drowned.' Nash didn't look up. 'Wilcox, the flight engineer. Another man half dead searching for him. Appleyard, the gunner.'

Bennett looked as if such an event wasn't worth his attention, the lines of his gaunt face set hard by the fact

214

that, whatever it cost, nothing was going to stop him being rich. But in the dim light of the door his mouth was twisted by uncertainty – which a further touch of callousness put right. 'I rely on you to keep everybody working.'

Neither the sea nor the basaltic lava of the mountainside would give up their dead. I stood in the dinghy, balancing to stay upright. Above were the birds, and below voracious fish. In between were castaways. 'The wireless operator and Mr Rose will get the next lot in, sir.' There was a wheedling in Nash's tone, but from diplomacy rather than nature. 'I'll look after Appleyard. Armatage can unload the boat when it comes back.'

I waited for an order from one or the other.

'Both boats are needed to finish the job.'

Nash's tone, from being respectful, turned comradely. 'Can't do it, Skipper. We can't afford to lose Appleyard. But I promise to get everything in before daylight.'

Rose and I would have to ferry another five loads, instead of three. It was easier said than done. 'I'll take care of him,' Bennett said, 'and stow the boxes when they come aboard.'

The raw wind blasted us. Even the cry of the birds would have been company. Nash looked up from his patient. 'Oh yes, I know you will.'

His sarcasm made a clear picture of Bennett pushing the half-conscious man back into the water. I couldn't believe it, but knew that Nash thought it more than likely.

In the lighted hatchway I saw Bennett's revolver touching Nash's temple. 'Get back to your boat, or this will be the one trip you won't come back from.'

The face that turned to him was green with a sickness that had nothing to do with fear of death. Confidence had been broken. The fight between sense and power was back, but Nash could not give in easily to either, though when he spoke his lips had become thinner. He tried to camouflage the revelation with a smile. 'The sound of the shot will travel for miles, Skipper, and may be heard by those who are looking for us. If I go for a Burton, so may Appleyard. That'll make four off the ration strength. You'll be short-handed when trouble starts. I can't believe you want that.'

I lacked the comforting hump of the Smith and Wesson under my jacket. If Nash was killed, the rest of the gold would stay ashore, buried by seaweed and birdshit till God Almighty claimed it for his own. I pulled the dinghy close, ready to leap aboard.

The gun was aimed at my face, and the chances were small that in the next few seconds I would continue to feel miserable and exhausted. I did not care whether I lived or died when Nash missed his chance to knock Bennett down.

'I'll tell you what' – his voice was as friendly and familiar as during a discussion at the Driftwood Hotel – 'I'll get Appleyard on his feet, and when the boat comes back make up two crews again. We'll finish stowing those boxes before you can turn round.'

Bennett nodded curtly, and walked to his room. Rose and I each took an oar so as to get away quickly. Beyond the float he moved to the tiller. 'What did you make of that?'

I was pulling too hard to talk.

'We'll have to lock him up,' he said.

'Nash knows how to deal with him. If we go for Bennett, he'll be on his side, believe you me.'

We landed, and began loading. 'I'll have cramp in my fingers forever,' he said. 'I might not be able to work my slide rule or sextant with sufficient dexterity to find our way.'

The oars seemed bigger with every trip. 'I don't suppose I'll be able to tap my morse key, either.'

'Wilcox just slipped into the drink. Came up twice, and none of us could get him, though it looked easy enough. When he went down for the third time Appleyard dived in. The whole thing happened in slow motion. He was our co-pilot.'

I asked Rose if he could fly the plane.

'Me? No more than you can. And I know you can't.'

'You'd better not think of doing anything to Bennett, then.'

'That's all very well, as far as it goes. But it might be our turn next.'

'How is he going to get the kite back on his own?'

'He'll have Nash. Nash got his wings. He went right through to OTU, then was grounded for something or other. He remustered as a gunner.'

'He never said anything to me about it.'

'Why should he?'

Armatage was at the flying boat. 'He's as right as rain. Wants to get back on the job already, but Nash won't let him.'

I lifted the first box. 'And the skipper?'

He winked. 'All jolly and bright.'

When we were empty Nash got into my boat. 'I'll row both ways, Sparks. Give you a break. I'm for finishing the job quick.'

So were we all. Zest was apparent, with the end in sight. The second dinghy was a few yards behind. Halfway to the shore he said: 'If there's any further argy-bargy between me and the skipper, you keep out of it, see?'

I nodded.

'I'll take care of him. I've known him a sight longer than you, and we've been through a fair bit together.'

'If you want it that way.'

'It's the only way it'll work.' With the mooring rope over his shoulder he leapt onto the beach. He worked quickly, passing the boxes to me, and we were away before the others landed. He rowed our last trip as well. We made the boat fast and, once on board, I stayed close to the hatchway, my dissociation from the world complete. But when Rose came I lifted the final boxes from Armatage, and while stacking them Bennett said: 'I'll see you get a campaign medal for this, Sparks – which is more than we poor aircrew got from the war!'

217

Appleyard volunteered for guard in the mid-upper, and Bennett sat on the flight deck. After a hot drink we slept – as they say – in our own footprints.

8

Easier said than done. Sometimes in sleep I go under and die, don't remember dreams growing out of bedrock. I'd like to know what's there, but my faculties have hooks that won't grapple. I belong to another world so absolutely that during the time of contact I do not exist. What I endure while in that world is impossible to know. Or so I understand. I woke after an hour as if called up by radio even though the set was switched off.

Where Rose's head pressed on the chart table, a tideline of sweat stained his pre-computed altitude curves. He breathed evenly and, without waking, though his eyes opened for a second, turned his head to lay the scarred cheek down. Perhaps he dreamed someone was trying to kill him. On the other hand, maybe while sleeping he was at peace.

Bennett, enthroned at the controls, sat up stiffly but fast asleep. Darkness beyond the canopy was thick with ground-level cloud in which anything could move without being seen. Whatever happened would be to our disadvantage. Appleyard slept in the mid-upper. The boat rocked unattended, hatches battened, tanks almost empty. Wilcox wouldn't work his knobs and levers, or cough unspoken thoughts into the intercom – or play slot-machines anymore. We were also a gunner short, but did it matter with a ton of gold on board? The metal meant no more to me than a cargo of cement or wheat. Bennett was part-owner and skipper, but we were merely employees of the carriers.

The atmosphere was eerie. I put down the button of my radio and waited for the magic eye to dawn. Atmospherics drowned everything in the hour before daylight. Mountains closed in on the medium frequency and limited our range. Fragmentary weather reports on short wave bounced from too far to be of use. I switched off and stepped down the ladder, circumventing Armatage who was curled up like a baby. Nash snored in the bunk, bare toes pointing in the air. Mugs and plates were everywhere, tea towels spread, a box of apples going rotten. I lit the primus and put the huge kettle on. The smell of carbolic made me hungry when I used a handful of water to wash my face. I rifled the biscuit tin, and sat drinking coffee at the table.

'I thought you'd died.' Armatage woke me two hours later. 'You didn't even hear me shouting when I dropped a plate. I wouldn't mind being twenty-five again!'

'You never will be,' said Nash, 'and that's a fact.'

Intensive sleep had oven-dried my clothes. Daylight air billowed in. Nash stripped to his underpants by the hatchway, did half a dozen knee-bends, then lowered a canvas bucket and emptied water over himself. He shook and danced, shot the contents of his nose into the drink and wiped the final sleep from his eyes with the corner of a towel. A corpse edged between the dinghy and the hull. The shoulders went under. One arm ended at gnawed and mangled flesh. However it had been trapped, the motion of the rope and bucket caused its release. Perhaps Wilcox had fought himself to death in the kelp. Nash got a boat hook under the belt and we heaved to get him out, except Armatage who went chalk-white and sat at the bottom of the ladder with his face turned away.

The open eyes looked up, as if the possibility of seeing

219

horizontally would elude him for ever and he was doomed to view only the blank sky. The corpse stank of seawater as a cat's fur stinks of rain.

Bennett took off his cap, and pulled at his dry springy hair – unlike Wilcox's which was short and pasted to the skull like a dummy's. 'We must give him a decent burial.'

It would be kinder to fasten an anchor and let him go overboard, Nash said. He would sink to the bottom and stay put. 'Wouldn't mind such a resting place myself.'

But Bennett found a canvas sack where the towing pennant was stored, and Appleyard stitched the body in. We lowered our cargo into the dinghy with as much care as if we had charge of Lord Nelson himself. Nash stayed on watch, and we rowed ashore.

I had hoped never to leave the flying boat again, but was learning to respect the unexpected. Its homely confines were settled sparely on the water when I glanced round. We hauled at ropes through the mire, sledging the body uphill. So much for our day of rest. Wilcox hadn't weighed more than seven stone, and though the mailbag slid well enough, we went slowly up the gradient, Bennett in front with a book under his arm, cap on and appearing taller than any of us at reaching higher ground first.

The path had been worn already by transporting the gold, and in an hour we reached our former diggings. Bennett manoeuvred a stone as if worrying a football, to the point from which the most central box had been taken. With spades and entrenching tools we shovelled sufficiently to demarcate an oblong hole. The displaced soil eased our job of getting the grave deep enough. Armatage wiped his sweat with a handkerchief. 'He might have picked a better place to die.'

Rose picked up an earthworm, and dropped it. 'Who can choose?'

'I don't suppose his next of kin will come with flowers.' Appleyard's shoulders were level with the surface, and only one man could work at a time. When Bennett signalled, he climbed over the parapet. We stood facing the skipper, hats in hands, senses blunted by geological layer-cakes at all points but for the slit of water on which the plane floated. 'We shan't do well without him,' Appleyard said. 'He was one of the best.'

Bennett nodded. 'No more talking. And throw those cigarettes down.' I expected him to remind us that we were on parade. All he needed to complete the scene was a gatling gun and a pack of natives coming up the hill to dispute our claim. He paced the flattened surface of the ridge, and perused his slim book to decide what portions should be read. I anticipated a few mumbled words, though dragging Wilcox's body to this spot obviously called for something more.

'After the war I lost touch with him, and went to a lot of trouble to find him. I finally reached him through his mother, who told me he'd had tuberculosis, and had just left a sanatorium. I didn't know he'd walked out without being cured. When I told him our plans, he produced a certificate to say he was fit for work. Where he got it I don't know, but there seemed no reason to believe it wasn't genuine. He was dead keen to come, and I was just as keen to have him. By the time I found out that he'd been given only a short time to live it was too late for me to replace him with anyone else. It was hard to believe he wouldn't last the trip, and I'm sure he would if it hadn't been for the accident.

'He wasn't your ordinary everyday knobs-and-levers merchant. Not Wilcox. During the war we went through some hair-raising moments, as you know – except Mr Adcock – but we were part of a team, of which Wilcox was the perfect member. He would never hold back from doing more than his bit. We were all or nothing, and we came out with everything. On the other hand, we should never forget those who didn't come out, who gave more than everything.

221

But when we said goodbye at the end of the war none of us knew we'd meet again, and come to a place like this. Nor did I know that when we did, Wilcox would be killed in action. There were dozens of times when he could have gone, which leads me to wonder at the reason why God chooses the time and how He decides the place.'

He turned a few pages of the book. 'Blessed be the Lord, our God, King of the Universe, who formed you in judgement, who nourished and sustained you in judgement, who brought death on you in judgement, who knoweth the number of you all in judgement, and will hereafter restore you to life in judgement. May David Samuel Wilcox come to this place in peace.'

In spite of such grand words, I felt he believed nothing of what he was reading, till in one pause came the faintest smile, a moment perhaps when he sensed the biting relevance of his text, suggesting that this ritual of getting Wilcox to such a burial spot was an attempt to work something human back into himself. Why else would he have done it? I recognized his peculiar smile as a mark of pain, which spread into every fibre of his body and soul.

'He that dwelleth in the shelter of the Most High abideth under the shadow of the Almighty. I say of the Lord. He is my refuge and my fortress. Thou favourest man with knowledge, and teachest mortals understanding. Forgive us, O our Father, for we have sinned; pardon us, O our King, for we have transgressed. Look upon our affliction and plead our cause, and redeem us speedily for Thy name's sake. Vouchsafe a perfect healing to all our wounds.'

Appleyard wept.

'As for man, his days are as grass; as the flower of the field so he flourisheth. For the wind passeth over it, and it is gone; and the place thereof shall know it no more.'

Heads down, we saw a world of grit and ash. Whoever cannot weep is damned because he will not. But I couldn't.

Stinging wind made tears. I felt the power of desolation, in a country I had never known. The most unreal comes to be the most real, a truth apparent as I listened to the Ninetieth Psalm and the whine of the uprising gale behind each line. Death drummed us into a silence that was not bitter, but neutral. The only good was that the words of the Book rooted us in a common past, and held promise of a common future, provided we could get out with no more dead.

'Lay him to rest. He's better off than we are.'

'God gave him a Blighty one,' Appleyard murmured. Unable to deny it, I rolled the body to one side. We drew the rope under the middle, them steadied the sack down.

Bennett set his cap on and stuffed the book inside his jacket. 'Put plenty of stones on top.'

We made a cairn on the hump of ground so that the location was unmistakable – which was what Bennett wanted. 'A trig point,' said Rose. 'Let's hope all of us get one.'

Beyond the reverse slope a stream descended from the re-entrant. A cloud of birds wheeled clockwise above rushing water near the beach. We were close enough for the crying skuas to overlap the sky and investigate us. Distaste blighted Bennett's expression when he lowered the field-glasses from what he had seen.

Out of its wide circuit a skua came close. We avoided its scything beak. Black eyes glittered, swooping on a wide span of wing with proprietary rage, a flash of white near each tip. Armatage hurled his spade like a javelin. 'I'd like to twist its bloody neck.'

'Our necks would be bloody if it had half the chance,' Appleyard said. I saw no advantage in such a fray. To know when to stop is vital. A step forward due to curiosity, or because you move without realizing, makes you a plaything of some force which is beyond explanation.

Bennett was halfway down. Other predatory outriders of the feast swirled about. Probably a seal, said Rose. There's no animal protection society in these parts. I never liked birds. Nothing's safe from them. Our voices became crazed as we advanced in line with spades and entrenching tools. 'It may be king of the air,' said Appleyard, 'but if the bugger comes close, it's had it.'

They wheeled in pairs, riled that we would compete at their feed. I felt the wind of one sweep by, and swung at another coming near. Appleyard sicked them with salvoes of gravel, and stung the most daring which, unsuspecting, got it full against the head, swerving not to come back. There were a dozen by the river, and we fought off those which would not move. Armatage enjoyed the skirmishing. 'They're bloody game birds!'

I ran to unseat the last pair. What they had been dining on was scattered by the water, red flesh on black gravel. A bar of rock held gobbets at its rim, but most had been pulled ashore – cloth, a hat, a familiar boot, and pieces of kit as if thrown by some St Vitus-stricken murderer, discernible because soaked blood made them like wads of flesh.

At another rush of air I cut with the spade, striking the head as a beak swept by. It crashed and flapped, and tried to run. The sight of Bull's eyeless decapitation settled by green flies sent me chopping at the wings, cries mixing with the flash of nearby water, till I was pulled from my mad hacking.

I wanted to be alone, block off their gloating and congratulations, to slaughter what other birds came close. Bennett's command from his own world had no effect. He stood to one side while Armatage wrapped the wallet in his scarf.

We would go back along the beach rather than over Wilcox Hill. Across a headland, thousands of white-chested penguins moved like the surface of a lake with indistinguishable shores. A pigeon-coop smell came on the breeze. Fate was intent on us dying like flies at the end of summer – till nothing was left but an oil stain on a sea without end. Rose said we should deposit Bull's remains in the same grave as Wilcox. Bennett told him they could stay where they were. It was no more than he deserved for having deserted his post. We had work to do. And common graves were bad omens.

9

Bad luck, I muttered on our way back to the dinghy, till the others, realizing that anguish shared is anguish doubled, asked me to belt-up. How much bad luck can you have when two people die for no good reason? 'Maybe we'll have more.' Rose walked along the beach with me. 'And that'll be worse.'

I wanted to outpace him, but he kept up. 'We'll batten the hatches and have some respite against the island, even if the kite sinks under us, or falls from the clouds when we take off.'

'Respite!' he shouted, burned by the word. A lone bird lifted from a rock as if to take a bite out of the sky. No birds can penetrate the flying boat, or compete once we get into the air. We're impervious to their evil eye. Bennett laughed at such logic. I was close, but he wouldn't respond. Appleyard pressed my arm. 'Hold off, or he'll kill you. He's no more responsible for what he does than you are for what happens to you. Shake yourself back into one piece.'

Rocks and tussocks were alive. When I turned, a king penguin, out from the rookery, wondered who I was. His white breast blocked my way. I stood bemused, then stepped aside at the smell. The others laughed as it waddled away grumbling.

I went in the second dinghy with Appleyard. 'Row hard. Pull your guts out. It's the only thing to do.' The air was soft, no breeze. Each oar met its own image as it touched water, the boat sliding along the surface of a mirror. 'Accidents happen, Sparks. You see a good many down the pit. And you never get used to them. There's little you can do. That was a nasty one back there, though. Can't say I've seen anything as bad. But such pictures rub off. Like those transfers we used to put on our arms as kids, that we thought would stay forever. Everything goes, sooner than you think. You don't even know it's worn off, and that's the truth. I thought I'd had my chips this morning when I went into the drink after Wilcox, but I feel bang-on now.'

Back at my wireless, half the day had gone. The Heaviside Layer was a band of spinning water, and I was a babe new born with a deafening overdose as I sensed a storm towards the prevailing wind. I told Bennett that weather could hit us within the hour.

He poured a glass of brandy, which I drank straight off. 'Shouldn't bother us, in this anchorage. A few ups and downs. It might blow itself out before it gets here. Or change its mind at the last minute. Such things have been known.'

'We'll be carrying less weight back. Of the human sort, anyway.' He pressed a clutch of fingers at his forehead, and on taking them away looked relaxed. Two men were dead, but the gold was aboard. What else mattered? 'Stop worrying. Bull and Wilcox were careless. Luckily they only harmed themselves. I'm sorry, believe you me, but we can't let their deaths interfere with our purpose.' He pointed to a chair. 'I've got more radio gen for you.'

'Will we be able to take off with so much weight, and more than a full load of fuel?' I couldn't let the topic alone.

His left eye was bloodshot, and his smile became a scowl.

226

'Has Rose been talking? A good navigator – who's losing his grip. He's been tainted by four years of civvy life.'

I sat down. 'So have we all. But he got us here.'

'Too true. And he'll get us back. We're a team, Sparks, and I need you all, because' a hundred things can go wrong – though there's no reason why they should. The task is straightforward, but the execution is complicated. There's no mystery. When the goods are delivered we'll set up a pay parade, and everyone will be on a first class boat back to Blighty. Or you can hitch the flying boat service – if you still have the stomach for it!'

I topped up the next glass with water. 'I suppose you wanted Wilcox's grave to be visible for miles, as a decoy? The seaplane looking for us yesterday was after the site of the gold diggings. And now they might assume that's where it is.'

He laughed. 'Any ruse in a storm. You're right, Sparks. A man after my own heart. They may think we haven't got the stuff out, and concentrate on that spot rather than on us. Wilcox wouldn't mind. With a bit of luck, such as bad visibility for another fifteen hours, we'll be up and away.'

'And if the weather clears?'

'We shoot our way out of trouble. Take off on a wing and a prayer, if need be. But that's speculation. I've no time for it. Our fuel ship should now be near the northwest corner of the island, at 48 45 South and 69 15 East. The schedule was worked out three months ago. It's a single deck 600-tonner built in 1928, 145 feet long, manned by the captain, two mates, chief engineer, nine sailors and a radio operator. It's carrying the best aviation juice money can buy. The master will bring it through the bay at 4 knots, on a zig-zag course for 24 nautical miles, and then he'll do 2 knots for 96 minutes while negotiating the tricky bits – before picking us up on his radar. It's the smartest piece of navigation in uncharted waters without a pilot as any captain who's lost his ticket is ever likely to undertake.'

227

'What's the ship called?'

'My memory seems to have gone for a Burton.'

'Where's it registered?'

He gave that Dambuster smile. 'Where hasn't it been registered? The last name painted on its stern was the *Difda*. Not much of a star, but we'll call it that, shall we?'

Dizzy from the brandy, I pressed my eyes back into alertness with such force I thought they would stay stuck to the plates of my cranium forever. When they shook loose I looked at him. 'Do you want me to give him a call?'

'This is what you'll do: send the letter K every hour on the half hour, on 425 kilocycles. If you don't hear the answering letter L, tap it out again after five minutes. But if there's no response don't bother for 55 minutes. Carry on till you get something back. But no call signs. Nothing except that single letter. When you finally get an L in answer to your K, send nothing for another hour. Then send K again, and wait for the answering L. When you get the first response, let me know. And tell me, on the hour, when the other answers come.'

'What if I don't hear anything?'

He gripped my shoulder. 'We're in trouble. But we'll talk about that if it happens.'

10

ை∂ை

There was a while to go before the half hour struck, but I knew that the bell had gonged for Bennett. The barren world had a more human aspect than the wilderness in him. I felt dead in his presence, and alive out of it. I did not expect him to tear his hair or cover himself with ashes about Bull and Wilcox. We were beyond that. No deaths could interfere with a dream that had turned real. It was easy to understand. The presence of an alien metal aboard the flying boat infected us all. I glanced at the boxes as if each held human remains, musing that a few more dead would make no difference as far as Bennett was concerned.

Rose bent over his chart, working out a course for Perth. 'Do we have the petrol?'

'We will.' He closed his dividers. 'Though without Wilcox to work his fruit machines we'll be lucky. And that old wind god will have to blow hard at our tail.'

From the astrodome I looked east to the steep-sided channel in which we had landed. Like a fly in a bottle, could we get out? A kelp patch lay under the southern cliffs. Where the throat widened, the waters were mined. The north-south channel which we could use for take-off was hidden by a headland. Mist swirled along the water. Bays, capes, glaciers and mountains were weather-pots continually boiling. When a squall peppered the glass I got back to my radio and listened so intently for that bit of short-long-short-short squeaking that I heard it coming when it wasn't there. Would I recognize the sounds if they suddenly turned up? I sent the letter K five minutes later, but at no answer leaping back I stayed by the set as if my sanity was bolstered by the glowing button of its magic eye.

The mist protected us but, after an hour, showed us up for miles. The starboard float, suspended from the wing, was the last man-made object between us and India. Mist turned into rain. I put out my hand to feel the patter. No one could speak without being heard. A cough or heavy breath was audible. The world beyond my earphones was a tap of footsteps on aluminium ladders, a spanner falling, a garbled song, the call of seabirds, a clatter of tins from the galley. Water slopped and gurgled at the hull. The peace was accentuated because I no longer felt unsteady underfoot.

229

Damp air swept through open hatchways, and Nash at the draught called for wood to be put in the hole. Appleyard threw a cigarette end into the water. 'When the weather clears we'll be spotted because of this cloud of birds. They'll do for us yet, if we're not careful. They're like flies over a dead cat, a beacon that can be seen for miles.' He claimed to distinguish between cries of skuas, penguins, petrels and seals. He would guess at their distance, saying that while some were across the water, other sounds carried from far off.

I felt a pang of desire for sight of the sun as I went to my radio for the next schedule, wondering how high one need go to reach blue without limit. I wanted to be airborne and away from this sub-Antarctic envelope. Checking the time with Rose, and hoping I was spot-on frequency, I sent the letter K. Perhaps the other man was not listening, or our signals lacked strength to cross the void. The laws of power and distance were inexorably fixed, and maligning the operator of the *Difda* for laxity had no effect. Maybe the 600-tonner was swamped already – the SS Maelstrom with its berserking crew caught in the switchback of the Roaring Forties. Perhaps it was a postage-stamp picture of Bennett's imagination and didn't exist at all. Nothing seemed real or possible in this world of the anchored flying boat.

Then I heard a callsign loud and clear, which I read but did not recognize for what it was. The volume startled me, each beat scraping my eardrums with brash familiarity. The sender requested that I get in touch with him. My false call sign from what seemed years ago had come home to roost. He had sensed I was listening, as if my transmitter created sounds I didn't know about. I was checking the leads when he called again, confident and close – but how close I could not know. A bearing put him due south, while the *Difda* coming to refuel us should be northwest.

He seemed to know where I was, or at least that I was *there*, and I fought not to rap the key and make contact.

Radio silence was a negative weapon, but our one salvation. I waited for him to come on again, but heard nothing, so closed down and told Bennett of the rogue transmitter.

Out of the hatchway, Appleyard in the dinghy held a rod over the water. Two fish were already flapping in the bottom. He made a motion of silence, pulled another into the air and took the hook from its mouth. 'I thought we needed fresh grub. The water's full of them.'

'You'd better emigrate.'

'I wouldn't starve, and that's a fact.'

He threw his cigarette-end towards the float. 'I found this gear in the survival box. No point not using it.'

I asked where the other dinghy was.

'Armatage slipped ashore with a butcher's knife to get some meat. That was hours ago, but Nash gave permission. We'll have fish and fowl for breakfast.' He gutted the fish with his black-handled service knife, and slopped the pieces overboard. A bird flew between the struts of the float and gobbled them, then returned to its perch to wait for more.

'I hope he comes back.'

He laughed. 'Armatage will be all right.'

'I'm glad to hear it.'

'After he left the mob he worked on trawlers around Iceland. Coalmining's a picnic compared to that job. And this one's a Sunday School outing. Bennett contacted him at Hull when he was at a loose end, so he was all gung-ho for this operation. He'd come back out of hell itself, though I expect you'd see the scorch marks. Not that there's anywhere he can go on shore, unless he finds a nice cosy settlement with a few women and a barrel of whisky inside. Armatage was pissed on every op we went on, and nobody knew where he got the booze. Out of the bloody compass, I expect. Didn't stop him doing his work, though. He was a gunner we could rely on.'

231

He recognized the noise in the sky sooner than I did and, netting his fish, leapt back inside and trod on my foot as he went by. 'Action stations! Get moving!'

The pilot of the plane was scared to come below the mist and risk hitting shore or water. They'd obviously studied the chart and noticed that the area was good for concealment. Nash took the rear turret, and Appleyard climbed to the mid-upper. 'No gun to fire without good cause,' said Bennett. Clutching his computer like a packet of sandwiches during an air raid, Rose came down the ladder and went to the front turret.

The high-pitched engine seemed directly overhead, but there was another at a greater height going back and forth above the northern side of the fjord. Bennett was on the flight deck, and I tuned my receiver for any signals. Perhaps they were hoping to pick up some from me. Nash's voice came over the intercom:

'Can't see 'em, Skip.'

'They can't see us, that's why,' growled Appleyard.

'Shut up, and look,' said Rose.

'No talking,' Bennett ordered. Would their radar pick up the *Difda* steaming towards us in the next fjord? 'They don't have it,' I was told.

When the time came I didn't send my one-letter call sign in case the *Difda* returned the contact and gave the game away.

'We're up shit's creek,' said Nash.

'Without a paddle,' Appleyard added.

'Pack it in,' Bennett called.

The engine roared as the plane flew above the water. 'Bloody good altimeter,' said Rose. 'Can't be more than a hundred feet.'

After two more runs the engine noises diminished, and went silent.

'Be dark soon.'

'I hope so.'

Bennett ordered stand-down. Appleyard imitated the wail of an all-clear over the intercom, then went to the galley and lay out fish in the big pan. 'They must have got our number.'

'And we've got theirs,' Nash put in.

'They won't be back tonight.'

But we knew that they'd be back sometime. Such certainty was better left unsaid, and there was nothing at which a crew were more adept.

Because food was abundant, it was assumed that the more we consumed the lighter our load would be on take-off. Nash as our quartermaster supplied plenty to cook: steak, potatoes, sausages and beans, to be eaten by whoever had the appetite. Bread was baked in the oven. Appleyard produced loaves. They were old hands at good living in the confines of a flying boat. From the ice chest he took tomatoes, and a cucumber which he cut so thinly that the monogram on the knife-blade was visible through each slice.

Bennett complained that the place stank like a black market restaurant. Tea and coffee were brewed in urns. The Elsan worked overtime, though Nash walked onto a dinghy and hung unashamedly over the side. After two days of hard work we ate much. A friendly routine fixed the domestic workings of our community.

'Smells like Friday,' said Rose. 'Where's Armatage?'

'The bastard's overstayed his pass,' said Nash. 'I told him not to take more than an hour or two. I'll ram the bloody Pole Star down his throat when he gets back.'

'Jankers, at least.' Appleyard set pieces of lemon on a plate of fish: 'Life must go on' – and took it to Bennett's room.

'And then we were five.'

Nash turned on me. 'It's a piss-poor show, all the same. Far too serious for levity!'

I spun the coffee tap. 'You've lost your sense of humour.'

He sat by the table to eat. 'I never had any.'

'No chips?' said Rose.

Appleyard came back. 'You've had 'em. I'm not frying tonight, but if you've got any complaints, tell 'em to the orderly officer.'

11

∾∾∾

On time, I tapped my signal, and the responding letter almost pierced my ears.

When I told them on my way to the skipper's room, Appleyard gave the V-sign. 'If we're up the creek, at least we have a paddle.'

'We'll drink a bottle of steam to it,' Nash said.

Bennett's voice stayed so leaden at the news that I felt halfway between obsolescence and being surplus to requirements. Then a flicker of relief crossed his lips as he whitened a cigar between his palms. 'I suppose you realize that in this world it's every man for himself?'

Before he could roll the chart away, I noticed a line joining our present position to Negombo in Ceylon. 'I expect it is.'

'The world's gone bang, Sparks. No freedom left. Even when you harm no one, you can't do what you like.'

I wondered whether things had ever been that way. I had also thought we were going to Perth, not Ceylon.

'I trust this aeroplane to fly, and the radio to get the news I'm waiting for. It's the technical stuff that keeps us going. Otherwise, watch out for the devil.'

'What devil?'

He drank off his glass of white wine. 'The devil who tells us what to do – and expects us to do it. The world's full of them, and you've got to stop that type from making contact with your own devil.' He tapped his chest, but not over the heart. 'When they meet, it's mayhem. So be on your guard – like I am. They create slavery – the greatest evil of all. Piss on that kind of devil, Sparks. It's the only way to put him out. I've fought him all my life, but in this flying boat I'm as free as I'll ever be.' He was quiet for a while, then: 'God is on the side of those who try to be free of anyone but Him.'

I suppose I contributed to his freedom by not reminding him that it was usually acquired at the expense of somebody else. I needed a tot of Nash's brandy to pin my eyelids back.

He waved a fly off the table. 'Keep contact with the ship.'

'I will.'

'Every hour.' He looked around the small room, as if surprised at its reality. 'Is Armatage back?'

'Not yet.'

His grimace was a positive reaction. 'The flying boat isn't large enough to accommodate a guardroom, but he won't just get a strip torn off him. He's deserted while on active service.'

I should have walked out. 'He's only been gone three hours.'

'Four.' He sweated as if starting to rot. 'Have you ever seen an execution?'

He knew the devil intimately, and I was listening to him. 'I can't see that I'm going to.'

'You may well, before this trip is out. There's no discipline. Without it we won't survive.'

I laughed. 'Is it that bad?'

His eyes maintained a steadiness that was without life. 'It is. And I can't have that. You'd better get back on watch.'

I wondered whether I shouldn't send an SOS, and not

care who heard as long as he was put somewhere safe. This engine-house of precision was no longer where I wanted to be. It was as if chaos and order had declared on each other the war to end wars, and I was being crushed in between, and fed into a darkness out of which I could not possibly return. I went down the steps to the galley.

'I suppose the news made him happy?' said Nash, trying to complete a crossword puzzle he'd started three weeks ago.

'He asked if Armatage was back. I said he wasn't, but would be soon. It's best if he stays away. Bennett intends to kill him.'

Appleyard gripped the plate, while he ate with the other hand. 'He'll kill nobody.'

The skipper was under a strain, Nash said, and who could blame him? I've only two more clues left. It was bound to show. He was surprised at me repeating what I had been told in confidence, but I argued that Bennett wouldn't have spilled anything that he expected to be kept secret. Nash agreed, and said I should attach no importance to it. Bennett had been known in the squadron for practical jokes. That's a fact, said Appleyard. He would say things just to observe the reaction.

'Apart from that,' Nash went on, and I wondered why he was going on at such length, 'he might not be feeling all that well. Can you imagine the pressure this trip puts him under? You can rely on him doing the right thing as far as his job is concerned, which is fair enough when you think of where we are. Bennett's only fault is his talent for organizing forlorn hopes. He could set up an asylum tea party on the far side of the moon and bring everybody back without a scratch! Only Bennett could have done this job, believe you me. You've got to play God a bit to pull this thing off. Stands to reason. He used to be a shade like that in the old days, but it never got out of hand. Nor will it now. Anyway, we'll be off in the morning, and twenty-four hours later

236

we ll make a landfall and be our old selves again. I can't bloody wait, I can tell you.'

Appleyard lit a cigarette. 'I don't believe anything I can't see, and I wouldn't mind seeing a good football match right now.'

'Like when Charlton beat Burnley, you mean?' Rose came down from his exertions at the navigation table.

'They needed extra bloody time, though, didn't they?' He only ever lost his temper in arguments about football.

'They rubbed their noses in the shit, all the same.'

'I'd prefer a good boxing match.' Nash filled in the penultimate answer.

I left them talking. On Rose's desk courses were drawn, and dead reckonings calculated, to get us to Perth, and I thought what a shame to have worked so much for nothing. No doubt people were waiting there to take over the gold, but Bennett, with his especial flair, had probably organized a stunt to keep it for himself. He could no more vanish and live like a millionaire in a place of his choosing than a pools winner who had been interviewed by all the papers. And if he did give the slip to those who had put up the money to get the gold from this godforsaken ashcan of the earth, they would surely not rest until they had it back, and killed one by one those who had helped him to – as they would suppose – steal it. Yet I found his audacity exhilarating, knowing that we had no option but to relish the same mad dream.

Armatage was missing, and I wondered if he had contacted those who were so anxious to locate us that they had equipped themselves with seaplanes. Was he in league with Shottermill? In which case even the innocent scheme of going to Perth would be perilous, never mind that of making for Ceylon. Bennett perhaps assumed that Armatage had climbed above the mist and signalled the planes, reason enough to think that he should die. The reward for Armatage would be far bigger than that promised by

Bennett – and with a safe exit guaranteed. Now that Bull and Wilcox were dead, we were unable to go out and bring him back.

Though Bennett might be a more than competent captain, he knew little about people as human beings, otherwise how could he imagine that another member of our crew would betray us? Armatage had gone too far on his foraging, and stayed longer than he should. In such visibility he might have overshot the flying boat on his way back from the shore. Nothing more than that.

As soon as I let my next K sign loose, the letter L sprang onto its back, and both went off into the ether like grasshoppers mating, a perfect meeting that led me to disregard all misgivings and feel glad to be a member of the *Aldebaran*'s crew.

12

❧

They were determined to find us.

'Who can blame them?' asked Nash. We did not question who or what controlled the weather, which had so far been on our side. There would have been no point. Such a force was beyond discovery. 'We'll shoot 'em out of the sky.' He rubbed his large hands together, as if he'd only come for the fireworks.

'They'll have a go at doing the same to us.'

'And see the gold sink to the bottom of the sea?'

Rose looked up from writing on small sheets of blue paper. 'Time is getting short, that's all I know.'

No one took him up on that fact, so he went back to his

letter, as if to be finished before the post left at six o'clock. The complicated form of the land was also in our favour, and as for who had made that, none of us cared to speculate. To say we couldn't care less to each other was as far as we'd go.

'Do you know what the skipper used to say?' Nash mused.

'Tell me.'

'He used to say: "Anything's possible that's happened."'

A grunt of scepticism came from Rose.

'That's why he don't say much now,' said Appleyard.

'He doesn't need to,' said Nash. 'You can only say so much. Anyway, we know it all.'

'I don't know about that.' Appleyard passed around tea and sandwiches. 'He said a lot more in the old days, and we liked it better, if I remember.'

'He did a lot more, as well,' said Nash.

Rose scooped up his closely-written letter and threw it in the trash bin. 'He'd take us through the Valley of the Shadow, and we, being other ranks, non-substantive anyway, had perforce to follow. They referred to him as "Jack Flak".'

'They called him other things,' said Nash. 'But for my part I never worried till it was necessary. By then you were walking on stilts and trying to stay alive!'

Time was also short for our pursuers, who could not decide which nook to comb. But they were persistent, and had plenty of fuel. Even before the whine of their engines, Bennett ordered Appleyard to the mid-upper, Nash to the tail and Rose to the front guns. Headphones got the buzz of swift aircraft out of my ears. Perhaps they'd return through the sunset, alight nearby and shoot their way on board while we were empty of fuel. Every minute of life was a God-given bonus, and the fact that nothing in my past seemed important more than paid for any danger I might be in.

239

A blackening cape blocked our view into the next stretch of water, like a prison-grille never to lift. Above, streaks of blood poured between bands of luminous green, letting in wind that scattered the mist. 'Pray for half an hour of good visibility tomorrow.' We told Nash we would do our best.

Fishes ruffling the water, and a few birds overflying. All I wanted to see was Armatage rowing from the shore, dinghy awash with brains, heart, tongue and liver of a leopard seal slain with his knobkerrie. We hoped our trackers weren't adept at night-flying. In their place, Bennett would have been. Some light was bound to show while refuelling from the *Difda*. Nor did I like to think of any disruption to our tricky performance of getting airborne with over three thousand gallons of fuel on board.

A further letter K from me was responded to by '1/2' – meaning a half hour to go before sighting. Passing the message to Bennett, I supposed that our signals, however brief, were being monitored, thus giving unmistakable confirmation of our presence in one of the island's indentations. Effective radio silence was impossible on either side, for they too had revealed themselves.

Bennett said I would have to take an occasional turn at the knobs-and-levers now that we had lost Wilcox, and proceeded to instruct me in the duties of flight engineer. He produced papers and manuals and, after explaining a diagram of the fuel system – amended in red to include the tanks installed for extra long range – showed me the relevant gauges on the panel, the fuel pressure warning lights and oil temperature gauges, as well as items that I only half understood, and would not be able to remember. I was left with the *Pilot's and Flight Engineer's Notes*, and various other dog-eared publications, and told to gen up between now and morning. If anything puzzled me, I had only to ask. 'Nash could do the job, but he's likely to be more use as a gunner.'

I wondered whether such a flying boat had ever been

flown by so few, and found it hard to believe that Wilcox
could be effectively replaced.

13

∽∾

When our supply ship moved around the headland as if lit
up for VE Day Bennett ordered turrets to be manned.
Darkness wasn't down, and we could see each other without
lights: whoever skippered the *Difda* must have thought his
navigational feat in threading the fjord in such visibility
deserved a campaign ribbon – and clasp. 'Call the bloody
fool up on the flashbox and ask him to show essential lights
only – with my compliments. If he doesn't pour water on
'em, we've had it. Sight on the bridge – if you can find it.
I've never seen such a rotten old bucket.'

She had two masts, flagless rigging culled from a rubbish
yard on the Medway, and funnel salvaged from a factory
boiler after an air raid. All of us commented on such a
random assembly of spare parts. Yet she had survived her
journey and brought our juice. She seemed little bigger than
the flying boat, but the distance was deceptive, and her size
increased as she rolled on her way in calm water towards
us.

I clicked Ks till the answering flash came, feeling a
spillage of tension as soon as my fingers were still. Bennett
was split between gratitude that the relief ship had arrived,
and being ready to meet any treachery by having our
machine guns sighted on her decks, as if he expected to see
an Oerlikon spit shells, or boats rowed towards us by
cutlass-toting jailbirds commanded by Long John Silver.

241

Acknowledgements from the *Difda* were prompt between each word. The signalman began his message with a light twice as powerful as my twelve-volt twinkle, proving by speed and rhythm that he was also a founder member of the Best Bent Wire brigade – acid test words which, if got through without a mistake, show that the ink on your ticket is not only dry but has long ago turned brown with age.

'What does he say?'

'He'll comply – and sends his greetings.'

'Tell 'em to anchor as close as need be for transfer of fuel.'

'CLOSE IN FOR FUEL FEED,' I sent.

Back came: 'WE KNOW OUR JOB.'

'What was that, Sparks?'

'They'll do it.'

'What's he saying now?'

'The captain's coming over to say hello as soon as they've anchored.'

'Tell him he's welcome.'

He flashed back thanks – TKS printed on my mind before reason separated each letter. I pictured a bearded old captain standing by the operator, a hook in place of his left hand, perhaps a corrugated cap whose crown had been worn through by his bald head, an obviously fierce gaze, and certainly a stubby pipe fouling the air but keeping his insides primrose-fresh. He gauged their way perfectly along the water, maintaining an exact position in mid-channel.

'He knows how to take no chances.' There was admiration in Bennett's tone. The manoeuvres needed no passing of texts, so the operator flash-chatted gossip meant for us alone: 'ONE OF YOUR BLOKES SIGNED ON.'

Bennett talked refuelling procedures with Nash at the top of the ladder, and neither saw me sweat:

'NAME?'

'SMITH.'

I sent back the wireless operator's laugh, and he responded with: 'NNNPD' – meaning 'no names no pack drill'. I pelted him with another laugh.

'PICKED HIM UP FROM WATER.'

Must have rowed miles. Bennett stood by my shoulder, but the man was sending too fast for him to read. 'What's he saying?'

'Only chatting, Skipper.'

'Watch the plain language. Just tell them to get a move on.'

'PROCEED SOONEST POSSIBLE.' Then, as if repeating the message: 'KEEP HIM STOP DEAD IF HE COMES HERE.'

'DEAD ALREADY – DRUNK. DA DA DI DI DI DI DA DA.'

I laughed back, and imagined the blow-up if Bennett discovered Armatage to be nearer than was supposed – after his deft transfer of allegiance.

They took care not to foul our moorings, and Bennett considered them close enough at two hundred yards. From the ship's bulk, exaggerated in new-born darkness, a message announced that Captain Ellis, the master, was on his way over. 'DONT CROSS HIM OR HE WILL KNIFE YOU – LAUGH LAUGH.'

I visualized the shaking of hands as he stepped on board, one chief meeting another. The two men with him stayed in their boat, as if for a quick getaway. Going to the top of the steps I saw a small sandy-haired man of about forty wearing rimless glasses and smoking a cigarette, carrying an attaché case with initials on the side that were not his own. He looked around our domain. 'Nice little world you've got. Bit like the inside of a cardboard giant. How many crew?'

Bennett told him.

His laugh was forced, and dry. 'A one-watch ship, eh?

243

Show me over the place. It's my first time on a thing like this.' He was an agile ladder-climber, and I moved out of his track so that Bennett could explain the flight deck panels. He drew his finger across the chart table, as if it were covered in dust, and glanced at my radio place as if I weren't sitting there. 'How is your survey work?'

'All we need is the fuel to get back.'

He descended the ladder. 'My chaps'll get it on by midnight. When I promise 'em a bonus they work like blacks.' His face was bland, but his hands twitched. 'I heard a plane nosing about this afternoon, so I want to be at sea by dawn. I'd get shot of the place as well, if I were you. I think you have rivals in your line of business.'

Bennett wasn't made for talk, so Ellis had to provide his own, which seemed no hardship. 'Funny thing but, do you know, we have a stowaway on board. God knows where he came from. Maybe a castaway. Took him on this afternoon. He was well fed and decently dressed.'

'A castaway?'

'Must have been. All he needed was drink. He's drunk now, in fact. No sense in him – like Europe after the war.'

Nash was close by, and we both wanted to throttle him. He stopped, as if remembering. 'He's a Norwegian – came off one of their whalers. That's all I got out of him, before my chief engineer put a keg of booze in his paws. Took ticket of leave, I suppose. Funny things happen, south of the Line.'

I looked out of the porthole, as if uninterested. Bennett's frame unclenched. But he must have known. 'Which reminds me,' Ellis said, 'maybe we should take a glass before we set to. I usually have a drop about this time.'

Bennett's room was out of range. Engines vibrated from the nearby ship that seemed to own the fjord. The bridge was vacant, and I supposed the signaller was back in his cabin with a plate of supper. Nash came to the flight deck. 'You heard what Captain Windbag said?'

'Sure.'

'And what did Wankers-doom with the magic flashlight say?'

'The same. He's over there, as pissed as a newt. They'll keep it quiet, though.'

'I hope he knows he's left us in the lurch. I'd like to break his neck, but we can't risk a shindy. Bennett'd want a drumhead court martial, and we haven't got time.'

I'd have been a fool to keep such forebodings to myself. 'Maybe Armatage sensed something.'

'Don't talk tripe. He just got the wind up.'

'I thought blokes like him never did.'

'You're not worth much if you don't. None of us were sworn in,' he said by way of apology. 'Not properly, anyway. Not this time.'

He didn't want to go on, and neither did I.

Captain Ellis was merrier than when he stepped aboard, and less loquacious. Also, his briefcase weighed more. He shook Bennett's hand, and passed the money to the man in the boat, advising him not to drop it if he valued his next hundred years' pay. I watched them leave for their rusting but trusty ship, sharply visible against the side of the fjord.

So many tanks were filled that nothing less than a flying bowser would take to the air. For a few hours Rose and I were, as Appleyard said, *superfluous* to requirements. Barrels were derricked two by two over the side and brought across in a lifeboat whose motor smoked like a matelot's briar. I went to the galley to make coffee, but Nash pushed me from the stove saying did I want to blow them all to kingdom come? I felt slightly less stupid when he laid into Appleyard who had pulled out a box of matches to light up between consignments. Nash raged that he had nothing but lunatics for a crew and, taking no chances, went into the rest room where Rose was lying on the bunk making smoke-rings from his repaired pipe.

On the flight deck I was hoping to get in touch with

Armatage, to find out why he had committed an act which filled me with awe. To abandon what you had pledged to serve was to lose a world and go into the wilderness. Must one be sworn in before doing one's duty? Couldn't one live without taking an oath? It was imaginable, but frightening, and my feeling for him was of pity rather than condemnation.

There was no movement on board the *Difda*. All interest was on traffic between ship and flying boat. Perhaps Armatage was not drunk. Maybe Captain Ellis needed an extra man for his crew, which was why he had connived in keeping him there. He had rendered us more vulnerable than we cared to believe. With three people less, our flying boat seemed forlorn, so I sat at my receiver to imagine I was among company.

The mild antics of atmospherics on 500 kilocycles separated me from the surrounding industry. Then my call sign thumped all speculation aside, came as loud as if emitted from the nearby ship. My hand went forward to respond. I refrained. It was dangerous to doze. I might send without thinking. Someone kept a listening watch, and tapped my call sign in the hope that I would give myself away.

He called again. Please do, I said. Just as the postman always knocks twice, so a telegraphist will tap his request two or three times in the hope of getting through. By his bearing I could tell that their ship was coming north.

Bennett counted barrels by the hatchway as they swung over. I informed him of what I knew, and returned to my wireless. Those who listened so diligently for me could not know what happened on the four megacycle band where the fast steely morse of coded messages passed between Royal Navy ships to the north. On short wave such signals could be hundreds, even thousands of miles distant. I was tempted to retune and get in touch, resisting only because my signals might bleed onto the frequency of the other ship and give our presence away. If they already suspected where we were I had nothing to lose, but to introduce a new element into the equation might mean the end of our flying boat and its cargo of gold. I was beginning to believe that we were surrounded by enemies, and that they were closing in.

Bennett would decide what was to be done. I switched off the set, and slept with my head resting on the desk.

14

Nash and Appleyard reeked like leaking faglighters. We all did, said Rose. Whether we had worked or not. One spark, and the expedition would vanish. For a while anyone looking on would have thought we had swallowed a half bottle of whisky each, such were our high spirits as we larked about.

But a breeze cleared the air. Nash's body flashed under the wingtip as he swam in circles, and he stuck up two fingers at Appleyard's: 'Come back! We don't want to lose *you* as well!'

He pulled himself in and splashed us with cold water, then searched his kitbag for dry clothes because we were expected to spruce up for departure. I put on a clean shirt and shaved, and used half a tin of blacking on my shoes. Appleyard dipped his dental plate in the sea, and slotted it back with a shiver.

I was stationed on the flight deck with the signal lamp.

'Tell them thank you,' Bennett said. 'And wish them good luck.'

I sent in full as their anchors rattled up.

'SAME TO U,' their operator replied. 'WILL LOOK AFTER YOUR BLOKE.'

'Look after who?'

I cursed his slow sending. Perhaps he hadn't slept for days. 'I asked him to remember me to a friend of mine.'

There were times when Bennett, able to do every crew member's job, did not make things easier for himself or the rest of us. I moved aside, out of his bloodshot gaze. He pulled the lamp away. 'Unofficial plain language is forbidden.'

Impossible to say what he suspected. His sensibility was sufficiently acute for him to know, and if he did, something stopped him taking action. 'From now on, send only messages that originate from me.' He thrust the lamp back. 'Is that clear?'

Once around Black Cape, the fuel ship would be seen no more. I wanted to be with Armatage, looking back at our immobile crate that would stay behind as a decoy in the fulsome visibility of dawn.

Fuel cocks were checked and fuel contents gauges registered as full. The priming pumps were in working order, and the oil system was OK'd by Nash and Bennett. The galley was sufficiently aired to light a stove for supper, and Appleyard used the last eggs to make omelettes. We sat at table, hatches battened against the cold. Whisky was poured into steaming tea, so we drank to our take-off in the morning. I couldn't envisage the event but neither, it turned out, could anyone else, and we finished our meal in silence.

Nash and Appleyard were rewarded with four hours' sleep for their labour of refuelling, so the nightwatch was split between Rose doing the first stint and me the second. During my two hours free I envied those who weren't kept awake by the nagging of anxiety. Nash, our mainstay, lay at peace, hands clasped behind his head, his pruning-saw snore forming a duet with Bennett's tread around his small room. Appleyard kipped by the stove, under a blanket which he'd acquired during his recruit training and had never been without.

I could cut off from the sounds of people by turning on my

radio, an extension of the senses which connected me to the spheres. I wanted to be in both worlds at once: one with ordinary life, and also float through the atmospherics of the heavens. But the two would not exist together, and I could only blunder from one to the other until such time as I found a way of combining the attractions of both.

As in everything, one had to make a choice. But those I had so far made had taken refuge behind the phrase 'I couldn't care less', because to care would demand too much energy, too much thought, too much consideration for others, too much anxiety about our fate, thus creating unnecessary (and unwanted) disturbance. To gather wisdom from those experiences in which I had been forced by fate to take part, and to combine that wisdom with speculation and intelligence gathered from the ether, were two areas of the same necessity. Craving both, I could deny neither one nor the other, though for the moment I couldn't put up with Bennett's obsessive footfall or Nash's grinding snores.

I trod soundlessly to the flight deck, passing boxes covered in tarpaulin and well lashed down so that none would move when airborne. Rose at the controls was so still that I thought he too was asleep, until a finger by the throttle-levers twitched. I sat on the arm of the other seat. 'What were you thinking about, before I came up?'

Such a question couldn't bring a serious reply, but he. answered with a weariness that lack of sleep alone hadn't given. 'I was meditating on the benefits of a new face.'

The unexpected response had nothing to do with our plight. 'What the hell for?'

'I'd like to get rid of the personality that gave it to me.'

Anger was pushed out by curiosity. 'We'd all like to do that.'

'You'll be telling me I have to live with it next.'

'That's right.'

'But I'm not sure I want to.'

'You don't have much choice.'

'I think you're wrong. Can man make something as perfect and beautiful as a flying boat, and not have choice?' His emotion surprised me. He pushed the throttle lever of the port inner slightly forward, then drew it back again. 'I've known since I was born that I could end it whenever I liked. But there's nothing more calculated to make one live forever! I suppose it helped me to survive all those ops over Germany.'

'What about the rest of the crew?'

'They were lucky, perhaps. Skilful, to a certain extent. That we were brave goes without saying. So were those who didn't come back.'

It was hard to talk sense in the gloom. 'Fate decides everything, I suppose.'

'If you let it.'

'There's no option.'

After a silence he said: 'Oh yes, there is.'

It was useless to deny it. 'You'll feel different once we're airborne.'

He shifted in his seat. 'When I'm in England, wherever I am, I feel that if I stretch my arms I'll touch walls. It's comforting. But here, even inside the flying boat, there are neither walls nor limits. I don't like it.'

'That's just what makes me glad to be here.'

He wasn't interested. 'It's a long night. Low cloud, not much visibility, no stars to guide us. Like life itself.'

'You'll see plenty of stars on the way to Colombo. Good fixes all the way.'

Was it a mistake? It depends on what you believe. Fate may be cruel, but he who blames it must be guilty of something, a thought which justified what I had said. In the dim light I watched his various grimaces registering the fact that I had blurted out the truth when I mentioned Colombo.

Or some such place, I was about to add. But I had too

250

much respect. To make good with false words was unworthy, by which I meant to imply that it would have been less worthy of myself. That second more distant pucker of his face wanted me to admit that I had made a mistake, but any half-hearted statement would not be acceptable. My paralysis lasted until speaking would do no good, and it was too late in any case. When he had waited too long to feel any benefit, and his features had settled into the permanent expression of a disappointed child, I said: 'At least it looked like Colombo.'

His flicker of gratitude was broken by a bitter smile, which seemed unconnected to my error of saying we were going to Colombo when he had assumed that we would set course for Perth. I should have kept my mouth shut, but it wasn't me who had spoken – or so I could not but assume. There was something pathetic in his anguish. Nothing could justify it, and anger with myself turned to annoyance at Rose being upset because he thought that such common knowledge among the lesser grades of the crew had not been passed to him first. I could not say that my information was only a faint line seen before Bennett had time to get the chart out of my sight. The glimpse was enough to show, however, that between Kerguelen and Perth no track was drawn at all.

'How do you know it's Colombo?' The fight to ask this took time, and by not volunteering the gen, and forcing the effort out of him, I had at last done what was right.

'No one knows except you and me.'

He leaned over the chart table, as if to read a description of how his life had been wasted. 'Nash must.'

'I don't see why. But does it matter?'

He didn't answer. I was to wish he had. In the gap before responding lay the waste of his life – and its loss. The two hour watch was up. 'I'm going to find a place to sleep,' he said. 'We're a pretty clapped-out lot, aren't we?'

'Depends which way you look at it.'

'The last of the many, if you ask me.' He scribbled calculations, erased them, wrote a couple of lines, then threw the pencil down. I thought he was making too much fuss and was glad when my turn for watch came because, though tired, and not knowing when I would sleep again, the radio waves would keep me alert.

15

~

Every few minutes I detached myself from the ambrosia of static and walked to the flight deck, hardly able to imagine the cold flying boat coming to life and getting us beyond the surrounding wall of night and rock. I was cheered by the magic eye of the Marconi, and knew that inevitably the darkness would lift and my watch reach its end. I felt some trepidation, for when it did, with a ton of gold and such a quantity of fuel, we would need limitless visibility and the longest run for take-off that a flying boat ever had. At supper we agreed that only Bennett could get the *Aldebaran* airborne. 'A good captain never reflects on danger until he is right near it,' said Nash. We needed luck, however, and who in the history of the world had as much as they needed? The bold prospered, the just progressed, the skilful succeeded, but now and again someone fell from on high because his luck ran out, no matter what qualities he had.

On my way to the wireless I examined Rose's chart, and saw that his sharp pencil had written: 'Not enough petrol for Colombo. God no longer with us.'

I laughed at such effrontery, wondering how long it was since God had been with anyone, never mind us. It seemed to me you had to be with Him, not Him with you. Rose didn't think so, and I hoped his madness wasn't catching. Was Bennett passing his insanity onto him via me, and was Rose, in sensing this, trying to push it back down my throat? Of course we had enough fuel for Colombo, if Bennett said so.

Perhaps the night was eating into my soul because it was the last through which I would live. I did not believe it. We were a cohesive crew, whether or not we had attempted one operation too many. Those bombing trips in the war had been undertaken from different motives and in another spirit, but what happened to one ricocheted through all, to test the strength of our mutual dependence. We were a pilot, navigator, wireless operator and two gunners, a competent team to work the plane on its final leg to safety. Wherever we set out for did not matter, and I couldn't believe that Bennett would take risks with treasure that had already cost so much blood. To cut things fine was another matter. We had all done that a time or two in our lives.

I dozed, twiddled at the receiver and smoked a cigarette, walked to the galley and back, looked through the astro-dome and saw one star above the gully in which we were stranded. Otherwise, I listened on the common frequency of distress and waited for the dawn. Though at peace, there was no understanding.

The naval operators swapped the strength of their signals, but on my own low frequency no one called. Whoever the other ship was, why did it observe radio silence? Silence was more ominous than a manifestation of sound. To the ear it was a lack, but a positive one, and had qualities which sound could never know about. With sound you had a clue to what was going on. Silence, though it kept you guessing, was a tactical weapon which could be used with double the effect of sound. All the same, silence worried me more than noise.

I kept my personal belongings in a hold-all by the radio,

feet sometimes resting on it while at work. The Smith and Wesson was wrapped in underwear and spare clothes, and should Bennett call me to a duty that would transcend the rules of human behaviour – as it were – the gun might be of use. The body of the flying boat was cold, and after a premonitory pre-dawn shiver I reached to take out the gun. Having been much thrown about since beginning the trip, and rummaged in for changes of clothes, the bag was not in a tidy state. Allowed only one piece of luggage, it was also large, and wondering why the pistol was not there, I heard an ear-splitting clap of noise in the distance which sounded like a salvo of anti-aircraft fire in the war.

Meteorologically, nothing surprised me. On the line of the Antarctic Convergence two antipathetic systems produced weather quick to change and impossible to predict. A summer thunderstorm, at whatever part of the day, caused no surprise. Those with more experience believed it to be no such thing and, as I wondered why the revolver I had packed so carefully was missing, several more echoing clouts erupted which could be nothing less than cannonfire.

'Somebody's hitting the flak,' Nash shouted. I fumbled in my kit, unable to imagine what was happening till I heard the awesome rhythm of an SOS coming out of the earphones.

Appleyard, with the reflection that some poor sod was getting it over Hamburg, levered himself into the mid-upper in the hope that the view might explain where the gunfire was coming from. The clack and follow-up along the fjord and over the heights was like trains leaving a station and going in different directions across the sky. There was six-tenths cloud at 4000 feet, and visibility was good for take-off. A floorcloth of cloud was about to wipe the ridgeline of the mountains clean.

My hand shook as I wrote. The operator was separating the SOS letters instead of running the dots and dashes together, indicating that he had not sent one before, and

254

probably not heard one, either. 'SHIP FIRED AT STOP SHOTS ACROSS BOWS STOP BUT NOT STOPPING STOP POSITION 4901 SOUTH 6910 EAST WAIT WAIT WAIT' – a sense of humour to the end.

A fast modern steamer came out of the dawn and ordered the *Difda* by lamp to heave-to and accept a boarding party. Captain Ellis told his flash-man to send something he wouldn't dare say in front of his mother, and the operator added a few unprintabilities of his own, which puzzled the other ship whose signaller didn't understand that kind of English.

I tore the sheet from the pad and took it to Bennett in his room. He shaved before a mirror, insistent to the end, in spite of the gunfire, on being the smart captain, while the *Difda*, having kept her part of the bargain, was being pounded to ashes in the next fjord. 'I should at least tell him we're getting the message, Skipper.'

'You'll do no such thing. He's being attacked because it's thought he has the gold on board. They don't know about us. They have their suspicions, but won't know for certain unless you do something bloody silly.' He laughed at how the play was working to our advantage. His luck could not have been better if he had planned everything with God Almighty. There is no one more cynical than he who is always lucky – at least so he seems to those who get in his way. That he never thinks himself merely fortunate is part of his cynicism. 'Isn't there anything we can do for them?'

When he wiped his face a fleck of soap fell across the dead dragonfly not yet removed. 'We have neither bombs nor depth charges. They've got an 88-millimetre by the sound of it, not to mention a couple of seaplanes. You should be glad we've got the *Difda* as a decoy. While it's being dealt with we'll up anchor and away. When they find that the *Difda* has no gold they'll come for us with greed and murder in their hearts. It's time to get weaving.'

I too wanted the scheme to work, and caught his smile of

satisfaction in the mirror as he ringed his neck with collar and tie. His expression said that each move had been planned. While knowing that Fate could not work eternally in anyone's favour, he may well have sat down months ago and plotted as far forward as possible. Optimism and hard work made each event come to pass, and so drew me as much under his spell as the rest of the crew.

But I refused to believe in him, and maintained a small area of freedom by telling my fellow operator on the *Difda* that he was being heard. If Bennett and all of us paid the price of my disobedience, or stupidity, or integrity, it was because my actions were as much out of my control as Bennett's were out of his.

I continued to search my hold-all, and had to conclude that the revolver was missing, which meant that if Bennett told me to account for my actions (in the same way that Armatage might have been ordered to say his prayers before the promised execution) I would be defenceless. Perhaps Armatage had taken the pistol, in which case he would be able to look after himself, a solacing thought as I worked at my radio to receive what details I could of the *Difda*'s tribulation.

Bennett did not think to ask why the ship continued sending, otherwise he might have guessed that it was because I encouraged the operator to do so. In any case, did he really expect me to put a bit of cardboard between the contacts of the key? My occasional letter R was not a long enough exposure for our direction to be fixed, and the *Difda* was not sending for my benefit alone, but to any other ship which might hear and go to his assistance.

'STRUCK AMIDSHIPS STOP MAKING FOR COVE 485930 SOUTH STOP BOARDING PARTY ON WAY STOP GUN FIRING FROM DECK TWO SEAPLANES ALSO ON DECK STOP WAIT WAIT WAIT.' Then came the request: 'DO SOMETHING STOP GET GOING.'

I felt a kind of triumph at handing the message to Bennett. That I listen and send nothing in return was the cry of someone who still relied on chance to protect him. The drill of departure left no flexibility of manoeuvre. Seaplanes would reconnoitre for whatever vessel acknowledged each message from the *Difda*. If Bennett's luck held and the attacker, assuming the *Difda* to be the only ship in the area, ceased all W/T listening – hearing neither their pleas for help nor my responses – they would only look for us on finding no gold on the fuel ship, by which time it would be too late because we would be away.

I handed in the message. 'Who are they?'

He let the paper drop. 'A rival company. They want the stuff too. Who wouldn't? I thought we would beat them to it by a few days. But you can't win every leg on the chart.'

'You knew we'd bump into them?'

'I supposed there was a chance.'

'It seems we're trapped.'

He was grey at the face. 'I wouldn't say so. The sum of the probability of errors has usually managed to avoid the fickle finger of fate – at least in my experience. So get back to your box of tricks, and leave the cogitations to me.'

The pennant showed little wind, and the sky had the markings of a fine morning. We had a sufficient stretch of water to get airborne, despite our perilous overload, but the latter part of our long runway ended in a minefield. To avoid this by going around the headland into the western fjord for take-off, where there were no mines, would bring us against the armed ship still in the process of persuading the *Difda* to heave-to. We would be blown to pieces by mines or blasted by shell-fire. Either way would mean an enormous fireball when several thousand gallons of high octane spirit exploded. And yet the enemy would not fire once it was realized that we carried the gold. Again, Bennett had them nailed, but we had to get airborne because if they caught us on the water they would force us into surrender. Five of us would be no match for them, and the gold would be theirs. Fate's finger was never more fickle than at that moment.

Bennett called from the top of the steps that he wanted to see Rose for a navigation briefing. The dinghy had been hauled aboard, and I helped Nash rope it down. Sweat poured from him after the effort. He wiped his chest with a rag and stood up to reach his shirt which lay across one of the boxes. 'I haven't seen him, sir.'

'Then where the devil is he?'

'He was in the tail, at stand-to.'

'Get him.' He went back into his room.

There was no crawling on your belly to reach a thimble-sized turret – as at the end of a bomber. The flying boat had a cat-walk and you could go in comfort. The door was half open, Rose slumped over the guns inside. Sleep was our only escape, and I hesitated to wake him. The strain of going out on a limb, forever forward and with no prospect of return, had shagged us utterly. All the same, I reached forward and gripped his shoulder.

An inch of tongue protruded from between his teeth. He fell to one side and grinned at me. Getting the turret door open, I pulled him free. The Smith and Wesson clattered. Accustomed to pinpointing the stars, he had made no mistake in finding his heart. I felt more dead for a few moments than he could ever be. The vast scar which we thought he had learned to live with looked as if he had merely slept awhile with his face against the corrugations of a heavily embroidered cushion. In another half hour, if he had been alive, all marks would have disappeared.

An explosion of cannonfire must have hidden the sound of his last star sight. The heavenly body came down to the horizon. Flak got him, I told myself. He's been killed in action as we all might be, so shed no tears while there's work to be done. Who wants a memorial service that you can't take part in? I put the gun, wet with Rose's blood, into my jacket and made my way back to the flight deck.

16

~~~~

Bennett reasoned – if you could call it that – that the dead were dead. Fair enough. Old times would not return. If you mourned the dead by letting them disrupt your life, new and better days would never come. Even so, Nash said, I thought the skipper had had it when I told him. He asked for an apple, but there were none left. He had to chew on something else. Shouted he was surrounded by desertion, treachery and incompetence – as he lit a cigar. There would be a Court of Enquiry when we got back. Count on it. He would notify all concerned, taking care to record illegal absences, accidental deaths, deficiencies in property, oaths taken and not kept. Separate courts would be convened to account for sub-headings yet to be defined. Nothing would be left out to prevent the court from putting together the true state of affairs. If I didn't know the skipper, said Nash, I'd have thought he was off his rocker.

In the meantime, Mr Nash, there's work to be done. The late navigator perished in the highest traditions of the Service. Bring his effects to me so that I can put them in a special box. As soon as practicable the next of kin of those men lost must be informed, and you may be sure I shall write proper letters of condolence, explaining how they died doing their duty while on active service. As there is no time to inter Flying Officer Rose on land we shall do it now, since we have to shed unnecessary cargo in order to get away. Find a weight to help him under the water.

It was action stations, and we prepared to cast off. A message was halfway through when I got back to the radio: ... 'HEMMED IN COVE STOP LIFEBOAT HIT STOP YOUR CHAP KILLED SLEEPING IN STOP TWO OTHERS DOWN WAIT WAIT WAIT.'

Bennett carried out pre-flight checks: controls free and fuel cocks off while the exactors were bled. Should I tell him about Armatage? He's had it, Skipper. A shell struck the lifeboat and gave their ship a coat of paint. He couldn't escape the net of God Almighty. Nor would I talk to Nash, or let lack of moral fibre take me over.

Vibrations from the port outer brought back life, and a willingness to do the utmost. Not to question showed pure health: stiff upper lip and press on regardless. The sound of propellers beating the air beyond the portholes set us breathing freely in our separate corners. The starboard outer roared its music up as if to push the cliffs further apart and reach the rest of the world so that even the deaf would hear. Bennett signalled Nash in the bows to slip our moorings. Outers and inners were run up in pairs, and we moved from the shore.

'BOARDING PARTY ON US STOP SHIP GOING SOUTH TO YOU.'

I passed the chit to Bennett who, involved in the complications of take-off, relayed the info over the intercom. Nash responded from the tail, blood still wet. 'Who forgot to swab the turret, then?'

Bennett was calm. 'We'll turn the cape, and take off as they come towards us.'

'Mind their gun, Skipper.'

'Will do.'

'As we pass over their heads we'll rake their decks.'

'Good show, Nash.'

'We've been in hotter spots, Skipper.'

'You there, Appleyard?'

'Yes, sir.'

'See what you can do from the front turret.'

'I'll shoot 'em with shit.'

'Sparks?'

'Skipper?'

'What's going on?'

Atmospherics raged like the noise of a forest fire. 'I'm listening.'

'Roger-dodger.'

'Hi-di-hi,' said Nash.

'Ho-di-ho,' Bennett said.

We taxied towards the water-runway of the straits. The *Difda* operator sent: 'NOTHING TO BE DONE STOP CHEERIO QRU QRT.' I tapped 'GOOD LUCK' – thinking it deserved to be our turn next but hoping for no such downfall. He pounded SOS three times, then screwed his key onto a continuous note so that anyone with a mind for rescue could home in on the bearing. After a few seconds his penny-whistle stopped.

The tail banged into a trough as we picked up speed. An odd chop shook the aircraft, and the subtle but deadly winds of dawn were set for a rampage. Bennett slowed his taxi-ing, and I felt a steady washboard grating under the hull. A blade of weak sun lit the nose of the south-pointing promontory. The water was speckled white towards our turning point, faint breakers creaming both shores. The low hill where we had buried Wilcox was outlined.

Maybe Bennett waved goodbye. 'What news, Sparks?'

We turned to starboard, under the lee of the cape. 'Sounds like they got aboard and signed him off. Smashed his gear. They're coming for us.'

'Press on remorseless,' Nash said.

'Remorseless it is.'

A pale grey glacier rose between the flanks of two basaltic

mountains, a broken expanse of other glaciers beyond, in places pink, and merging into a semicircle of cloud. Crevasses, ice ridges, solidified waterfalls stretched to the south as far as we could see. 'Better than the view from Boston Stump,' Nash said. 'It was worth coming this far for!'

The sea was calm, straits widening. Engines on full power muffled the bang and drowned the whistling shell which preceded a waterspout in front. The earphone-lead enabled me to look out and see a ship coming from behind an indentation of the western coast.

'Two miles,' Appleyard said, 'and it ain't made of cardboard.'

'Nor is that 88-millimetre screwed on the deck,' Nash told him. 'And I've just got the last clue.'

'What is it?' I asked.

'Perseverance – it must be.'

'Congratulations,' said Bennett. 'We're back on form.'

Another shell exploded so close that a wall of water swept the canopy. 'Third one has it, Skipper.'

I was flung at the navigating table while Bennett did as tight a circle as he dared without smashing the port float, the hull in a cloud of shooting spray. I grabbed the radio handle as if to wrench it from the fitting.

'They should be put on a charge for dumb insolence,' said Appleyard. 'They're trying to drown us.'

'Kilroy was here,' said Nash. A shell exploded to port. 'Give 'em the figure of eight, Skipper. We can take it.'

'Get on your radio, Sparks, and tell them that if we go up in flames, everything on board will sink to the bottom.'

He turned to starboard, and another half circle took us so close we could no longer be seen by the ship's gunners. Bennett hurled back up the straits, and when he drew level with our old mooring place and saw the way clear for five miles ahead, let all engines have full throttle and began moving for take-off.

During these manoeuvres it had been impossible to send

his signal, but when on the straight I was about to do so he told me to scrub it.

'Prepare for take-off.'

'Minefield starts at four thousand yards,' said Nash.

'Give or take the odd furlong,' Appleyard added.

'Fact noted,' Bennett said.

'Is our new address to be Carnage Cottage, then, or the "Old Bull and Bush"?'

Rather than give up the gold, he would kill us and send it to the bottom. Morse from the *Nemesis* (or whatever name the other ship had) was fast, but so faulty in rhythm that it was difficult to tell dots from dashes, though the message was unmistakable. 'WE HAVE YOU CORNERED STOP SURRENDER HEAVE TO.'

They knew we were hellbent for a minefield, but I told them to get stuffed as we flogged up speed – tactically flexible, and versatile unto death.

'Salt water for breakfast,' Nash said.

'On toast,' laughed Appleyard.

Expecting flak from above and below, we trusted Bennett to get us clear. He saw no reason not to proceed, and sped by the cliffs. But there was no lift, meaning we'd get through the minefield only to crash into the hill blocking the end of the channel. The same text from the *Nemesis* was repeated, demanding capitulation. They imagined us skulking behind the headland, contemplating the damage they had caused, and debating what to do next while we adjusted our reading glasses. 'We'll get up,' said Nash. 'We aren't in a bloody railway carriage, and that's a fact.'

We seemed to be travelling between the sleeve of the cliffs forever, pounding forward too slowly for our ominous weight. There was little wind to help. No one spoke. For better or worse, Bennett's fight was ours and we left him to it, sat tight and prayed to get airborne without suddenly ceasing to exist. I looked out of the porthole to see, if only

263

for a second, the nipple or big apple of a mine that would demob us for good and take us into a dream impossible to wake from. Supposition as to life after death watered my fear while we went through a zone marked on the chart as dangerous, and I wondered whether they were as thickly sown as eyes in a plate of sago, or as thinly as balls on a wet-day bowling green.

The *Nemesis* wouldn't follow, and that was certain, but with a long-range gun it didn't need to, though the dilemma of boarding was for them to crack. Their ship had not yet turned the final headland to watch either our spectacular fireball demise, or see us wiggle our tail as we lifted into the wide blue yonder. Bennett was too much locked in his fight to wonder about the seaplanes. Every rivet spar and panel vibrated as if, should we put on another knot of speed, we'd come to pieces.

The shakes diminished, but the hull scraped against the carborundum wheel of the water which seemed intent on grinding us down to the extinction of a wafer. In spite of the universal thrust, our boat was dead if it couldn't lift – and so were we. Disintegration beamed on us, but a hummed tune came through the intercom and while I mulled on an end to our history, I recognized words which I joined in though only under my breath so as not to break our luck. Why that song rang out I'll never know, nor who was the instigator, but in that couple of minutes I loved it for melting the wax of menace from us all.

Perhaps it was a case of spiritual buffoonery carried to its greatest extent, considering our crucial situation, but the words took me out of this perilous fjord and back to the palm-beach coast of Malaya where our staging post had been, and I heard again Peter Dawson's voice booming from a loudspeaker nailed halfway up a tree, singing 'The Road to Mandalay'. And now we were mocking it blind with tears in our eyes, but singing all the same as if it were a hymn.

'On the road to Mandalay,
Where the flying fishes play . . .'

and we were one of those fishes, about to lift off for longer than any flier of the deep sea could, which no one in the history of the world would be able to gainsay, our great flying boat ascending, its twin along the surface of the blue water accompanying as if to see us safe into the air, when we would say goodbye because we'd no longer be either visible or necessary to each other, and so slide apart. We sang as if China really was across the bay, and Bennett would get us there and beyond to a safety of his own devising.

The test-bed roar of four engines increased the distance between the port float and the water. A white bird spun from the windscreen. 'Per ardua ad astra,' Nash muttered, and the intercom almost went u/s with laughter.

The hull banged, destroying hope for a second, but the float lifted and the cliffs changed aspect, turned brown, then green, then opened out into sloping rocky hills, till underneath was a peace which meant contact with water had been lost. Ahead was a spur of black mountain, avoided by a quarter turn to port.

Bennett's voice came: 'Log the time for QAD, Sparks.'

'Roger-dodger.'

Heading into daylight, we were safe. On land was danger, but with four engines bearing us through the air, though overloaded with fuel and gold, the worst was over.

'They wanted us to surrender,' I said.

'Cheeky devils,' Appleyard laughed. 'I hope you told 'em what to do.'

'Radio silence. And no bad language.'

'Pity,' Nash put in.

'Keep it that way.'

Gaining height by inches. Kelp patched the narrowest point of the straits. An expanding funnel of land showed

265

our route to the open sea. We were flying, all weight fallen from us, and waiting for it to go from the boat.

'We'll be so high the earth'll be a tennis ball,' Appleyard said.

'But who'll have the bat?'

'Crawl down into your apple-pie bed and die,' said Nash.

'063 magnetic,' said Bennett. 'Until we're in the clear at 48 south 70 east. Log that as well, Sparks. Wind westerly, ten to fifteen. Bring the computer. When we're on automatic I'll work things out.'

I tore a sheet from Rose's log, noting the time and initial course. The island that divided us from the pursuing ship was two thousand feet high, so we were not visible. Nor when they turned the headland would they see any sign. They might search all indentations before realizing we had taken off, and then what could they do?

'They're not as daft as you think,' said Nash. 'But then, neither are we.'

17

∽∿∾

We would reach base with fuel to spare, Bennett claimed, and our cargo intact. Rational and hopeful, he had worked his doubts out of existence. But logic said that while each mile lessened the weight of fuel to be carried, every gallon spent increased the possibility of not getting where we wanted to go. Rose had been right. We might as well be heading into space. The situation was that of a man humping food on his back through an area where no supplies were available. He would eat much and frequently in order to generate the energy to carry such heavy cargo. The more he ate the lighter his load would become, and he would need to eat less in order to transport what remained. But when all food had gone and he had not yet reached terrain where more was at hand, he would die of starvation. So the flying boat on running out of fuel would crash into the sea. Even if we had a little in reserve, a few failures of navigation would still cause a shortfall.

The track of the *Aldebaran* clipped the eastern dagger-point of Howe Island at a height of little more than a thousand feet, our gentle climb due as much to conserving fuel as to the weight being hauled. We go for the Equator, Bennett said, and keep travelling, and if we can't reach Ceylon because of fickle winds we'll beg, borrow or steal petrol – or even buy if the price is right! – from Diego Garcia, only 350 miles off our track.

He had studied the matter well, but Diego Garcia, the first outpost of civilization, was a dot on the ocean, and even if he worked the stars as competently as Rose (Nash insisted he could do it better), it would be a feat to locate the place, whether occupied at the controls or not. Instead of a thermal back-up at the tail, side winds would nudge us here and there, and difficulties in making the required track would adversely affect our fuel supply. If we weren't forced to ditch a hundred miles short of our objective, 3270 miles away, we'd be lucky to alight with a pint in each engine. Shipping routes lessened the danger of drowning, but the sea was unlikely to develop woolly arms into which we could safely alight.

Radio would help little if star sights were impossible, bearings only useful when confirmed from other sources. It was the same old tale, I said. The first wireless beacon was on Mauritius, 1200 miles off our track. Then Diego Garcia would give bearings either to home in on or provide lateral fixes till I contacted HF DF at Negombo in Ceylon on 6500 kilocycles. The latter part of the trip would be safer in this respect, though how we would feel after twenty-eight hours on our Flying Dutchman was hard to imagine.

Blood had a smell, and that was a fact. The gun under my table was still tacky. With five rounds in the chamber I could persuade Bennett to make for Freemantle. The distance was a thousand miles less, and we would have the wind pushing from behind. But I couldn't hold the gun at his temple for ten hours, beyond which he would have no option but to carry on. Nash and Appleyard, what's more, had absolute faith in his ability to get us non-stop to Timbuctoo if he said he could – grumble as they might at his eccentricities. Against all three I was helpless. And then my duty was braced by a call from our pursuers, loud signals proving that we were not yet out of their reach.

'PZX DE WXYZ = RETURN TO TAKE OFF POSITION = +'

I passed the chit, and Bennett decided there would be no acknowledgement. I thought it would be best to ask for terms, having done well enough to secure peace with honour. I preferred to live rather than perish in trying to save the gold for Bennett's own use. And to fly on meant that, either way, destruction was certain. But to make clandestine contact would have been my last act. I was as chained to my position as a machinegunner in the Great War, for though my loyalty was not to Bennett and his gold, nor even to us as a crew, I felt much affection for this aircraft flying over the sea, with its engines, ailerons, guiding rudder, and all other parts. I viewed it as from outside, ascending slowly with sunlight occasionally flooding the canopy and shining on Bennett as if he had been fixed in his position during the plane's construction and launched at the controls. Whether it would have been possible to see him as an ordinary person like the rest of us I do not know, for perhaps I thought that if I succeeded in doing so I would not be able to defend any of us against him should the time ever come.

The same view of the *Aldebaran* that I envisaged was in reality obtained by a seaplane on the starboard quarter. Nash regretted that there were no dark nimbus-cupboards immediately available in which to play hide-and-seek. 'Watch that Dornier before he gets under our belly.'

'I'll have him, Skipper,' Appleyard said as it veered away.

The plane came back and flew level, fixed at our speed, and kept its distance so cleverly that we seemed to have spawned a satellite. Another hung onto our tail, but at a greater distance. The crew of two in tandem, canopies back, were clearly seen. The rear man flashed a lamp.

'Read it, Sparks.'

'Will do.'

Nash got the message over the intercom. 'We're out of range.'

'Hold them till we hit cloud.'

The message was repeated. 'TURN OR WE DESTROY YOU.'

'What kind of English is that? said Nash.

'Sounds like Fu Manchu,' said Appleyard. 'Tell 'em to go to hell.'

Bennett surprised me. 'Ask what's the matter.'

'"Going to a dance, send three-and-fourpence,"' said Nash. 'I don't mind a fighter plane. All's fair in love and war. But it's the flak I can't stand. Getting too old for it.'

My morse could not have been easy to read. The lamp was almost too heavy to hold. The second seaplane to starboard also winked its light across the blue, a message impossible to misread. At 2000 feet we were climbing, but like a flying barn compared to their nimble craft.

'Watch 'em, Nash. They'll try and nudge us in the opposite direction.'

'You take the bastard to port,' Appleyard said. And I'll sic the other.'

'Can't throw the old flying boat around like a Spitfire this time, Skipper.'

269

'Straight and level does it. Press on regardless.

Nash laughed. 'Did we ever do anything else?'

The message was always the same. I wanted to send 'Per ardua ad astra' in morse, something I'd never thought of doing while wearing the uniform. We could no more turn than if we were in a railway train. The refuge of cloud got no closer. They lacked the range to follow us far, but we were only a hundred miles north of the island, its black humps still close.

At getting no sense the seaplanes broke station, zoomed up steeply and ahead. What did the sky look like to them? They saw a victim, prime and squat, a lumbering tortoise sent for their enjoyment, with all the heavens a playpen. The scene gave me the horrors, until an order came from Nash. 'Sit in the mid-upper, Sparks, and see what you can do.'

Hindsight mellows, time distorts, so how can the reality be grasped as it was in the act? Only first impressions count. Sickness in the guts fled when I moved. I saw little. Nash waited till the plane was a few hundred yards away, then opened up. The attack came from astern. They thought we had put coloured sticks in the turrets instead of Brownings. 'Otherwise how could they be so daft?' Appleyard called. We spoke to ourselves. The plane lifted, smoke like shite-hawk feathers rippling the sky. A pale belly sheered up the side of our tailplane, a full view of two floats before slipping to starboard and down to the sea.

'One gone,' said Nash. 'But there's the other, so don't put your finger back in yet.' Was it bagatelle or skittles? Don't ask, said Bennett. The sky was empty, and not my turn to have a go, and a sense of solitude made me sweat. My hands shook, eyes wanting to close. There was something in my eye, but was it fear? The plane came at speed. Time slowed so that he was in my sights as he weaved side on in an attempt to unstitch us from stem to stern. My heart crashed into him as I fired the two guns.

270

'Cut the bad language.'

Appleyard tried, and the plane slid out of his sights. I sent another burst. He fell away early, not mad enough to die.

'Hold your fire,' said Nash. 'I'll get the gold-lover.'

He came from the north, a quarter turn to put his gunner in line. 'I see him,' said Appleyard. 'And would you believe it? He's blue-eyed, blond and wearing a yellow scarf.'

'Don't care if he's in his underpants,' said Nash. Bullets ripped the fuselage. They were throwing pebbles. I didn't know where they struck, but hoped the radio wasn't hit. I tasted ashy rage at the thought. Blowing bubbles, said Nash. Spite will get you nowhere. As the plane wheeled the length of the flying boat he fired from side-on. The plane continued south.

'Going home with a cat up his arse,' Nash mumbled.

Bennett kept his unflinching course. 'Call the roll.'

'OK, Skipper. You all right?'

'Nose shipped a few.'

'Sparks?'

'Sir!'

'Salute when you speak to me!'

'Hi-di-hi!'

'Ho-di-ho!'

There was a pause while levity sank away.

'Appleyard?'

Nash sounded weary: 'After action I'm knackered. Like an orgy – done in, for ever and ever, though it's nothing a good kip or a fried egg won't cure. Have a dekko, Sparks, there's a good lad.'

I knocked on all protuberances. The plane roared steadily, gaining height, but only by the mile. Take ten years before we need oxygen, but I felt light-headed at the thought that we had seen the last of the *Nemesis* and its bluebottle-seaplanes. Well, don't be so sure. Life's full of nasty surprises. They must have been discouraged, anyhow, by one down and the other damaged. I wanted to return to my wireless in case I learned something new.

Appleyard's turret was spattered with holes, and a mess of blood poured from his stomach. I was fixed by a paralysis that would enable me to remember, and then tell about it. He began screaming that he didn't want to die, and because I couldn't save him, I willed him to.

Nash opened a field dressing. To staunch the flow, he said, would be like trying to patch a burst dam with a postage stamp. Which might be something you can do in Holland, he added, his face flour-white, the lines deeply accentuated, but not here.

18

The reek of petrol and oil seemed to put up the temperature. Haggard from turning the nose-gunner's body into the sea, Nash said that one of the tanks might have sprung a leak. That last raking did damage. It was certain, however, that Bennett's high octane optimism hadn't yet started to spill out. Perhaps it was better so, because in the end only his press-on-regardless spirit might save us.

I clung to the refuge of my wireless station. The magic-eye would be the last glowing item before we went into the dark. Unless I could contract to homunculus proportions, assume salamander-like properties, take on the role of a phoenix and get between the valves of the transmitter, it would be a dark I would never come out of. As long as I didn't think of it I was not afraid, yet I resented being unable to dwell on matters for that reason.

Everything seemed so certain that I felt as if I were on a conveyor belt, but such thoughts insisted on being cold shouldered by my fingers flicking the various switches in spite of myself and to no real purpose, though my ears were listening for any tinkle of hope. The seaplanes must have radioed their base ship, for the wireless operator on board sent a message which he knew I must receive. 'TELL CAPTAIN PROCEEDS SHARED BETWEEN YOUR FORCE AND WE STOP SAFE CONDUCT GUARANTEED TO YOUR GALLANT CREW STOP TERMS HONOURABLY KEPT IF YOU RETURN.'

'Gee,' said Nash, 'let's throw the oboe out of the window and contact the consul!'

I passed the half-full bottle of whisky. 'Calm down. Have a drink.'

He imitated Tommy Handley's side-kick to perfection. 'Don't mind if I do!'

'Sing a song of sixpence,' Bennett chimed in, 'and let's live forever.' Knowing our kite to be damaged, the *Nemesis* was steaming north in the hope of being close when we came down. Our lives in danger, we would send an SOS with the ditching position conveniently attached. If the *Aldebaran* sank and the gold with it, and we were picked up by them from our dinghy, we would be killed. That much was implicit in their telegram. Bennett read the signal and said nothing, his mood like a yo-yo.

On my way to the set I looked at the port inner. There was a haze around the exhaust which is sometimes seen in hot weather. The shimmer attracted me when I hadn't expected to see anything at all. I was wary of pointing it out to Bennett. To tell him he should stop hoping was not worth the risk of a bullet. His face showed no threat, but his fixed pose daunted me. By his stillness he seemed to be in touch with more than either I or Nash could imagine. It was a mistake to think so. He wasn't. If he didn't wish for information he would have to be force-fed. But I was wrong.

273

As a pilot he had more senses than a cat in a snake pit. 'Sparks, get down to the panel and read me the oil temperature gauges, and the oil pressure gauges. Also the fuel contents gauges while you're about it. Routine stuff.'

We were near the woolly corrugations at five thousand feet, but no longer climbing. Because none of us should lack information on our plight, I copied the readings for Nash as well.

Bennett waved me away. 'Read them again in ten minutes.'

The same gunmetal glaze from the starboard inner tallied with the figures. Oil pressure was low in both engines. The angle between our longitudinal heading and the ceiling of cloud increased. Divergence was subtle, but we were going down. Nash sat on the bunk, and when I showed him the signal from the ship, and the engine data, he said: 'The old man won't turn back. He'll ditch first.'

'Isn't that the last thing we want?' I leaned against the bulkhead. The plane was no safer than a packing case. 'We'll keep half the loot if we turn. Otherwise we get nothing.'

'Don't believe that signal. They'd kill us on sight. We've given 'em too much stick.'

He gave a bitter smile of resignation, the sort of expression that must have been on his lips when he heard his prison sentence. Under Bennett's rule he had become mortally pliable. Then I saw a flicker of his former self. 'The only way to maintain height is to lighten the load. If we get as far as the shipping lanes and then come down we might be rescued.'

I felt the blow of defeat. The cardboard world was coming to an end. 'Tell that to Bennett.' There was bitterness in my smile too. 'He'll chuck us off, rather than the gold.'

'He's in no condition to do any such thing. There's nothing to throw out that weighs so much.'

'What about the guns?'

'They'll go last of all. And it would take too long.'

The blockage in the oil feed pipe had righted itself. We were flying level. Renewed hope was the measure of our desperation. We drew another tot of whisky. When I got back to the radio, the operator from the ship was repeating his message. To maintain silence seemed senseless, so I tapped sufficient to indicate that I had received and understood his text, and added that they could go to hell, because we were taking the gold to Shottermill as pre-arranged. Let them chew on that, and Shottermill bite the bullet if ever they got to him. In the meantime I told them to wait, wait, wait – till the crack of doom – as we must surely wait to find out whether we had any chance of getting beyond their range. That their signals were diminishing was due as much to the passing of time as to increase of distance. But at more than a hundred knots we had no difficulty leaving their orbit behind. To use a flying boat had been a fine ploy, though whether it had been good enough we didn't know.

Checking the gauges, there was a vibration underfoot, as if the fuselage was trying to explain its sickness. Too much cargo had been put on, and a substance was not getting freely through to the engines. The life force was failing. Endurance was one thing, but the weight of dreams was another. Perhaps Bennett, in his central position, was not aware of our tonnage grinding against the sky. Calmness in the midst of adversity had become a serenity which he did not want to lose even to save himself. After getting the aircraft off the water he had settled into a brittle senility of purpose. He threw the ship's message down, and smiled because the figures from the engineer's panel had not altered in ten minutes. His expression said that he would prove us wrong.

275

19

The sea was roughened by a breeze from the west. Airborne for two hours, we were out of the influence of the island. In the good conditions just after dawn there seemed more life on short wave. Even on low there was traffic between ships, though most was faint and indecipherable.

It was impossible to ignore the flow from the inner engines, or not to take note of the fact that the third reading of the fuel gauges showed a fall in pressure. Nash in the galley had seen the fumes. 'If the Skipper doesn't feather those props the engines will either catch fire or disintegrate.' The circular spirit-cap of the primus was about to burn itself dry. 'Or the whole caboodle will go up in smoke. I wouldn't forget where your parachute is if I was you.'

He pumped a flame under the kettle. 'I never thought there was much future in such things. But don't worry. It may not come to it. Bennett once brought a Lanc back from Germany on one engine and half a wing. Or near enough. We're still in the *Queen Mary* compared to that.'

He heaped six dessert spoons into the large pot as if we still had a full crew. The aroma of brewing tea came even through the smell of fuel and, connected to some comfortable past, seemed to promise a future. Who cared about danger anymore? Reality slotted to a lower level of my mind.

Nash swore but did not flinch when the vibration of the plane threw drops of scalding water across his hand. 'I wouldn't worry, Sparks. Bennett'll get us back to base.

I was angry at his assumption that I was afraid, and slopped a third of the tea out of my mug ascending the ladder to the wireless. Nash followed with two mugs hooked on one hand and spilled none. He sat in the co-pilot's seat and, with the controls on automatic, he and Bennett looked at the sea, and at the clouds they could not reach, as if they had only to stare long enough for land to appear a few miles to starboard.

I stayed tuned to the distress and general calling frequency, both for what I might hear, and to send our lifesaving message should the emergency come. Nash appeared uninterested in our common peril. Anxiety made it hard to devise a policy of salvation. He and Bennett were paralysed by optimism, or an ancient friendship difficult to break. I saw no alternative but to wait until that instant when we had to decide how to save ourselves.

Daytime atmospherics were in full sway, but an SOS had a habit of getting through. The Cape Town to Australia shipping route began 300 miles north of Kerguelen, and we had done almost that distance. There was no need yet to send an SOS, but I stayed alert for the sign of another ship. Every hour they would listen for fifteen minutes in case any vessel was in distress. I might try 8280 or 6040 for more long distance rescue, not in the hope of being reached in time, but so that there would be a record of our final plunge. The necessity of an SOS seemed a long way off. To send it not only admitted defeat, but would pull us into defeat even sooner – when it might not otherwise come at all. It was easy to be infected by the optimism of Nash and the skipper.

I put a hand towards my transmitter, fearing it would work loose from the mounting and fall forward. Thus the juddering of the airframe pulled me from my only refuge. Tea drops straddled the logbook like a stick of bomb-bursts. I steadied it and, gripping my morse key, managed to drink. With earphones around my neck I looked out, and saw the propeller of the inner port engine come to a stop, the distorted metal like a wave of greeting that had gone wrong.

Bennett emerged from his torpor. A hand went to the throttles, and he switched off the starboard inner for fear it

277

would explode and scatter bits into the sea. This righted our slide-and-bump across the sky, and the two engines seemed tinnier and further away. He pushed the two outers onto full throttle so as to maintain speed, and prevent us skimming like a stone into the sea.

Nash noted all readings on the panel, the most significant being those from the air speed indicator and the altimeter. Bennett had set the barometric pressure at take-off, which made our height fairly accurate, but such a load on low power meant that the only solution was to shed some weight.

I stood behind, phone-lead trailing. Neither spoke. Each minute was another victory. Nash glanced at the altimeter like a fox at the horizon with the hounds behind. The hand spoke an inevitable descent, the arm of a failing clock coming back to the zero of the ground.

I could hear the sky, ions shifting in millions and making their own peculiar noise. The subtle river formed and unformed, a world to which I belonged. One morse signal would shaft a path through, man-made like a sword. They had no option but to give way for such rocket-pulses. None came. I searched and waited. The sensible course was to send a CQ call and contact whoever heard. If Bennett knew that a ship was close perhaps he would ditch within its radius.

The sea was a sheet of steel taken from a fire after the last heat had gone, ragged and corrugated, with pieces of blue clinker still attached. At three thousand feet, Bennett fought for every inch of height. 'I can call a ship, in case we go down.'

Nash waved me angrily away. Bennett was cool. 'Radio silence, Adcock. We've got to hang on to those boxes. You're too young to know what they mean. A life without worries means freedom. Now I've got it. You lack the imagination to know what it signifies. As for you, Nash, I'll buy you a fish-and-chip shop! You deserve no less.'

278

Bennett–Nash between them made a star, Rose once said. And Bennett spoke as if much humour lay behind his words. We knew how right he was. Nash and I laughed. So did the skipper. As the *Aldebaran* whined and rattled on its northward way we laughed till the tears splashed at our faces. Bennett didn't believe it. There was more to it than that, his sombre face said. Beyond the gleam of riches was the challenge of getting our cargo – any cargo – to a destination. But that wasn't entirely the case, either, and Nash was to prove it. I was making up stories which had no truth, a sign of moral depravity in the face of death.

His amiability came as a surprise, and I felt guilty of having doubted that we would reach dry land. Confidence came back. We weren't losing height. Our airspeed increased. The outer engines, on full boost, seemed fit to run forever. 'Believe you me,' said Bennett when we stopped laughing, 'as soon as I've disposed of what's in those boxes, you'll have a fair packet coming to you. I don't forget good service.'

Nash said: 'I realize that, Skipper, but those boxes will have to go overboard, all the same.'

The altimeter showed below three thousand feet. Nash was right, Bennett wrong. The simple values came uppermost at last. A ton in weight would keep us longer in the air, but a minute at a time was all we had a right to. Bennett pulled a whitened cigar from his jacket pocket and put it between his teeth. In his agitation he moved it from left to right like a piece of stick.

Nash glanced at me. I put my hand to where the revolver lay, unashamed of the value we had put on our lives. Bennett sweated with the effort of flying the plane. When he reached for his lighter, the hand on my gun tightened. He smoked for a minute or so. 'All right, Mr Nash, open the hatch. Prepare to jettison cargo.'

I stood aside to let him by, a feeling of relief mixed with irritation. An operator on some ship not far off bounced his signals to all stations, whiling away his hours of boredom. Never so glad to hear that beautiful sparking rhythm, I tapped my call sign and the wireless operators' laugh, and he replied with 'Best bent wire', and we played on the ether as joyfully as two dolphins sporting on the surface of a warm sea. I requested his QTH. He asked for mine. To respond was illegal, for no signal should go from ship or plane without the captain's permission, but I looked at Rose's chart and decided that our position was close to 42 00 South 71 30 East.

The controls were on automatic pilot and, suddenly remembering, I rattled down the steps, though for no reason – or so I thought – except that a feeling of dread swamped me as one rung after another resounded under my feet.

20
∽∾

The hatch had gone into the sea. Nash stood in the patch of sky, ready to slide the first box out. We seemed to be gliding, without engines. My ears played tricks. A sunbeam like a scalpel – I almost felt its warmth – lay as if to cut my sleeve.

I pushed Bennett, half turned from me, doing what I did as if not yet born. The gap between each action was timeless because there were too many factors to measure. But not everyone has the opportunity of looking back, and so they go blind into action and never recover their sight.

The same with Bennett. His revolver fired during the lapse between the hand going forward and making contact with the cloth of his coat. I hardly saw the gun, perhaps not at all. Certain details will never become clear. I didn't need to. My life passed in that moment from one authority to another, as if the ultimate word came back and told me what to do, taking thought out of responsibility and leaving me only with action.

Nash's face, normally placid, showing a man to be relied on, with plenty of practical knowledge, a good share of courage, a temper lost only in the presence of fools, but flawed by being loyal at the wrong time and to unsuitable people, was a portrait of horror as the death-mist closed in. A hand went to his jacket where the bullet had left a zone of ragged flesh. Crimson liquid spurted from between his spread fingers. He swayed before I could reach him, and fell through.

I clutched the ladder so that my turn would not come, determined to prevent it as my finger eased down on the trigger. The rush of engine noise came back to clothe the senses – though there was little enough of what might have been there in the first place. He knelt, as if waiting for the sword of knighthood to tap him on both shoulders. I felt as if I had shot into myself, and almost wished I had, wanting to separate every minute of my life to find out what had led to it.

His hands searched the floor, felt the shape of each box like a blind man. He pulled the one nearest the door to safety, though with such steady flight it was in no danger of falling out. The universal clock never stopped ticking. He put on his cap, and when he stood I fired again. He brushed a hand across his face as if a bee had stung, and gave a grimace, almost a smile, of agony and surprise. I could not meet his eyes as he pushed by, but looked at the sea passing far below.

My foot caught the box that Nash failed to heave into the blue. I scraped my fingernails in sliding it over, fearful of being pulled out. The lid opened, and a stream of gold like a bird's wing swung towards the water, lighting its grey track. I wanted to leap after it, but the action would not come. Boxes that broke went down in an arc of sunlight, darkening as they disappeared. Those that stayed intact spun like a depth charge, but made no visible splash as they hit the curving waves. I forgot where I was. My soul was in contact with happiness. I was in danger of being caught in the slipstream but, agile and confident, knew I could not go. At the end of such labour, reality rushed back, and I moaned so loud that I heard myself even above the noise of the engines – the reverse of waking from a bad dream.

The work wasted my spirit to the marrow. I expected to be engulfed as the flying boat touched water, but the loss of weight reduced our rate of descent. How Bennett climbed to the flight deck I'll never know. I felt no surprise. He sat at the control column, staring towards the horizon. The altimeter read five hundred feet when I looked over his shoulder. He spoke.

'What did you say, Skipper?'

'We're going in.' The face below his cap-peak was carved in white marble, lips showing dissatisfaction at the state of affairs for which, his expression said, he blamed himself. His hand came to me, and I felt pressure from the ice-cold palm. The exhaustion from sending the boxes to oblivion made me afraid of the dark. His smile wrenched out of me a spirit that I never got back.

His voice was weak but clear when he said something about the fire-tender pinnace standing by. 'Take care, Sparks. Emergency landing.'

I put on my safety belt. Determined to make the best touch-down of his life, he controlled the plane so as to meet gently the swell of an empty sea. My mind registered dreams rather than impressions. I could be dead immediately, but couldn't have cared less. While holding their fearful chaos at bay, I knew that fate would have me in its power forever.

'We tried,' Bennett said.

There was one enormous bang after another, as if a giant hammered the hull with his fist, demanding to be let in. A rush of water streamed by. I thought we were already underneath, the *Aldebaran* like a hand fitting into a glove of water. The starboard engine cut, and when the floor came up my head struck against the clickstops of the transmitter. The port engine stopped, and we spun around. I thought the blood which poured was water as I rolled towards the ladder, an electrical shock pulsing through my arm.

One acts, or is acted upon. The will takes over when life is in danger. The threat from natural forces releases a natural force for combat. If the odds are too great, you succumb. If not, you have the chance to survive. No time to question who decides, and afterwards there does not seem to have been anyone else there but you.

I pulled myself to the bridge. Bennett had struck the windscreen and smashed it. I dragged his body over the controls, cold salt water giving back energy. I laid him between the navigation table and my wireless position, the sound of gurgling sea beyond the canopy and down by the hatch. The flying boat was a hulk, and I let myself down the ladder to the last box of coins. The boat lifted and slid in the swell, and I vomited from the rhythm and the intense reek of petrol until my stomach seemed about to detach from its moorings. I drank water, and spewed that too. When I was empty I felt glad that at least part of me would go down with the boat.

Strength came back, and in my madness (hard to think of it as anything else) I hauled the box along the deck, step by step to Bennett's body. I opened the box with a fire-axe, and scattered coins till his uniform was speckled. Then I closed his eyes, so that he would go down like a hero.

A strut of the port float buckled. The galley was flooding when I went for a canister of water, and diligently foraged for tins of food. My work was without thought. I laughed at such feeble precautions while throwing food in. In an untended ocean life could not go on. Being alone, there would be no casting lots to decide who would be eaten in order that others could survive. But I wanted to get as far from the flying boat as I could, a great weariness leaving me only enough energy to follow those who had preceded me.

Wing tip uncovered, bones of structure visible, float lopsided, the flying boat settled into its bed of water, and I got into the dinghy.

21

The tailplane passed overhead. Pushing away from the carcase I felt like the last man on earth, with no prospect of meeting anyone, and obsessed by the fact that there was nothing to live for.

The same grey ceiling covered the sky. Wind numbed me, in spite of hard work on a heavy sea. But I was not rowing as strenuously as I imagined. The *Aldebaran* subsided, seen as the swell took me high to show a white tangle and the upstanding blade of its tail. When the dinghy next lifted onto a crest there was only watery space. The wind never stopped, so I huddled under tarpaulin. Being cold, the dark comforted me. I had left my watch, and didn't know the time. The covering let in light, so I felt the difference between night and day.

I ate when hungry, and having eaten threw off the tarpaulin to look about. The heave of water and the wind that talked in a foreign language became normal life. I didn't care when food and water were finished.

The survival kit contained materials for a spinnaker sail. When hoisted, the tone of the wind changed. It would take three months to reach Australia. If I drifted from shipping lanes I would fall in with the icy seas of Antarctica.

With a length of rope I threaded the tarpaulin through rings that circled the dinghy, making a cover as far as the mast. I looked out from under during the day. A single-engined fighter came from above the cloud-base and made so fast towards me that if I had not retreated to the furthest side of the dinghy the space between my eyes would have been blasted by the propeller. The noise stretched my eardrums to bursting. When the plane left off shooting up my boat the sound of the sea became an amiable melody until, shipping so much water, I baled out for fear of becoming swamped.

My clothes were never dry. I fed on hard biscuit and what was in the tins. When the food was finished there would be nothing to worry about except the torment of dying. Lack of fibre was preceded by lack of moral fibre. I drank the water. There was no use delaying death.

A solitary black Pathfinder at five hundred feet was followed by so many four-engined bombers that the sky was full. Where did they come from? I counted more than four thousand. They went over the horizon. The noise deafened, then faded. Where had they gone? I wept without shame.

I went into and out of sleep, into hope and then despair, became raving, and then calm. I measured time by the minute, then willingly slept through appalling dreams to avoid the desolation, so that a whole day would go by.

Sometimes my sleep had no dreams. I drifted, and did not know where I went. Dreams waited to torment me in daylight. The sun was so menacing I imagined it, instead of rising, as if about to crawl along the surface of the sea towards me. At dawn I saw the *Aldebaran*. How could it have taken off when I had seen it sink? All parts intact, its beautiful form flew just above the sea, belly glistening in the

285

sun. I waved, and shouted for help. Those on board could hardly miss me. I prayed that the captain would alight to pick me up. Its portholes were black spots. Propellors were feathered, each set of triple blades stark in the air. But it moved as if the engines worked on full power. There was a rush and whistle as the aero-boat gained height, banked onto a reverse course, then came by again, Bennett's skeleton at the controls.

I leapt into the water. An icy blast wiped the flying boat from my eyes. The dinghy was a hundred yards away. I swam happily. The sky was empty. When I decided to stop swimming my arms would not obey. I shouted an order, but from the crest of a wave was thrown against the dinghy. I clung to the side, then pushed myself away.

I lay exhausted under the tarpaulin. Hands pressed my ears to keep out the roar of engines, the crackle of atmospherics, the insistent signals of morse which I'd hoped never to hear again, and speech in no language that I could understand, and bird-cries, and the barking of dogs. Even the grave-like hiss of the sea was held at bay, every sound muted as I stayed under cover and closed my eyes knowing that communication – the purpose of my life – had got me nowhere.

Light filtered in. Drinking water had gone, the last container finished. Dreams killed thirst, but when no dreams came I chewed biscuit, and held back my vomit for fear of entrails roaring out of my mouth. Read the omens. I slept in a black cone, drifted to the narrowest end. Engine noise increased, though I would not look. Kerosene smelled above the drumming. The dream was endless.

A broad, bearded man, wearing a duffelcoat, a woollen hat and fur-lined boots, and holding a boathook took over my vision. 'We nearly ran you down. Don't you have any lights? Good job we didn't pass you in the dark, mate.'

The black cliff had a ladder up the side. The journey was over, though I went on living. How I did so would not make a story. God drives a hard bargain. You live a dream, then have to pay for it, though with death in the offing no one loses.

They said I was talking funny as they hauled me on deck. But I laughed, knowing that nothing else would happen in my life worth recording. Even though I was alive, I had gone down with the flying boat.

JERUSALEM (MISHKENOT SHA'ANANIM)

LONDON

WITTERSHAM

DECEMBER 1981 – APRIL 1983

287